Dear Teacher by Wanda E. Brunstetter
Judith King enjoys her teaching position at the one-room schoolhouse along the Lehigh Canal. Until she meets Ernie Snyder, a widower with two children, she has had no hope of marriage. When Judith is asked to choose between teaching and romance, which way will her heart direct?

Prairie Schoolmarm by JoAnn A. Grote
Marin Nilsson, a Swedish immigrant schoolmarm, becomes a student of life and love when Swedish farmer Talif Siverson insists on joining her classes in the sod-hut schoolhouse to improve his English skills. Will he be able to break through the teacher's long-held reserve?

Reluctant Schoolmarm by Yvonne Lehman
When Christa Walsh steps off a train in the backwoods of North Carolina's Blue Ridge Mountains and reluctantly into the role of teacher, she finds the job more rewarding than she expected, winning the hearts of the children—and along the way, warming the heart of the man whose deception landed her the position.

School Bells and Wedding Bells by Colleen L. Reece
Freshly jilted and ready to take on the world, Meredith Rose Macrae enters an isolated Idaho hamlet with the force of a tornado. Neither she nor Last Chance will ever be the same. And Brit Farley, rugged head of the local school board, faces the challenge of exchanging the new teacher's school bells for wedding bells.

Schoolhouse Brides

TEACHERS OF YESTERYEAR
FULFILL DREAMS OF LOVE IN
FOUR NOVELLAS

WANDA E. BRUNSTETTER / JOANN A. GROTE
YVONNE LEHMAN / COLLEEN L. REECE

BARBOUR
PUBLISHING

©2005 *Dear Teacher* by Wanda E. Brunstetter
©2005 *Prairie Schoolmarm* by JoAnn A. Grote
©2005 *Reluctant Schoolmarm* by Yvonne Lehman
©2005 *School Bells and Wedding Bells* by Colleen L. Reece

ISBN 978-1-59310-837-3

Cover image © Getty Images

Interior art by Mari Goering

All scripture quotations are taken from the King James Version of the Bible.

This book is a work of fiction. Names, characters, places, and incidents are either products of the author's imagination or used fictitiously. Any similarity to actual people, organizations, and/or events is purely coincidental.

Published by Barbour Publishing, Inc., P.O. Box 719, Uhrichsville, Ohio 44683, www.barbourbooks.com

Our mission is to publish and distribute inspirational products offering exceptional value and biblical encouragement to the masses.

 Member of the
Evangelical Christian
Publishers Association

Printed in the United States of America.

Dear Teacher

by Wanda E. Brunstetter

Dedication

To Mrs. Rueger, my favorite schoolteacher,
who encouraged me to believe in myself.

Trust in the LORD with all thine heart;
and lean not unto thine own understanding.
In all thy ways acknowledge him,
and he shall direct thy paths.
PROVERBS 3:5–6

Dear Reader,

I have always appreciated teachers, but when I began doing research for this book, my admiration for those who taught in one-room schoolhouses increased a hundredfold.

Teachers who taught in one-room schoolhouses during the 1800s and early 1900s served not only as instructors but also as janitors and disciplinarians. They averaged working as many as ten hours a day and were expected to see that the building was clean and orderly at all times.

Education has changed a lot from the years of the one-room schoolhouse. The buildings are bigger, the classes are larger, and discipline is no longer of a physical nature. However, some things haven't changed—the basic curriculum of reading, writing, and arithmetic, and the need for qualified teachers.

During the days when the canals and other waterways were actively being used to transport coal and other items, the children who traveled and worked with their parents always had some time for fun. They played games such as marbles, dominoes, and checkers. Many had homemade toys, such as a spool with four nails used to weave a rope. Some little girls played with corn-husk or apple-headed dolls. Most of these children never had much more than a fourth-grade education, yet those who went to Sunday school or learned about God through their parents received a religious education that carried into their adult lives and gave them hope for the future.

—Wanda

Chapter 1

Parryville, Pennsylvania—1890

Judith King pushed her trunk to the foot of the four-poster bed and closed the lid. She would sleep in this cozy room tonight and every night for as long as she remained in Parryville as schoolteacher at the one-room schoolhouse near the Lehigh Navigation System.

Judith walked around the side of the bed and placed both hands on the thick mattress. Giving it a couple of firm pushes, she soon discovered it was soft and bouncy.

"Nothing like the thin straw mattress I used to sleep on as a child," she murmured. Nor did it compare to the hard bed she had shared with young Ellie Miller, the storekeeper's daughter, when she'd taken her first teaching position in northern New York.

Judith took a seat on the bed. She was pleased that during her stay here in Parryville she would room with the Rev. and Mrs. Jacobs and their twin daughters, Melissa and Melody, who were ten years old. The girls' bedroom was on the same floor as Judith's, and she could hear their laughter floating across the hall.

Starting Monday morning, I'll be Melissa and Melody's new teacher, she mused. *I pray things will go well.*

With a feeling of contentment, Judith gazed around the small, cozy room, noticing the blue and beige braided throw rug in the center of the floor, the oak dressing table and looking glass positioned along the far wall, and the colorful patchwork quilt spread across the bed. Then she stood and moved to the window, pushing the curtain aside so she could view the street below.

A little boy with shaggy brown hair and tattered overalls ran up and down the walkway in front of the parsonage. It was a blustery day, yet he wore no coat or hat. Judith noticed the slingshot hanging from his back pocket, and a scruffy-looking dog nipping at his heels.

Will that child be in my classroom on Monday morning? Will he and the other children be agreeable and easy to teach, or will many be full of mischief, the way my brother Seth used to be?

She let the curtain fall into place and meandered across the room to check her appearance in the mirror. A lock of curly blond hair had come loose from the bun she wore at the back of her head, and she reached up to tuck it in place. Her cheeks looked pale, probably because she was tired from her train trip that morning, so she pinched them until they turned pink.

Judith tipped her head to one side as she studied her reflection. *Sorry to say, but there is nothing I can do to make my eyes look any better.*

From the time she was a little girl, Judith had been teased about having one brown eye and one blue. That and the fact that she was taller than most girls her age had made Judith believe she was unattractive, and nothing had happened during her twenty-six years to change her opinion of herself.

"Judith the odd one. Judith with the creepy eyes." She'd been called so many names when she was growing up.

Children can be cruel, she thought ruefully. *And that is one thing I won't tolerate in my classroom. No teasing or making fun of someone because they're different or don't have as many nice things as someone else.*

She returned to her seat on the bed. There was no point thinking negative thoughts or expecting trouble. No point feeling sorry for herself because she was an old maid who in all likelihood would never fall in love or get married.

"Who would want a tall woman with eyes that don't match?" she muttered. "No one ever has before." Besides, as a child of God who had confessed her sins and accepted Christ as her Savior, she knew that her heavenly Father cared for her just as she was—no matter what she or others might think of her appearance.

A knock on the bedroom door startled Judith. "Yes?"

"Supper's ready, Miss King," one of the twins announced.

"Mama said we should let you know," the other twin said.

Judith stood and smoothed the wrinkles in her long gray traveling dress. She had planned to change into something more presentable before joining the family for the evening meal, but there wasn't time now. "Tell your mother I'll be right there."

Judith heard the shuffle of the girls' feet as they headed down the hall, then the louder *clomp, clomp, clomp* as they descended the steps.

She drew in a deep breath and sent up a quick prayer. *Help me to fit in here, Lord, and bless the Jacobs family for offering me such a fine room.*

❦

Ernie Snyder cupped his hands around his mouth and leaned over the bow of his boat. "Keep them mules movin' at a steady pace," he called to his ten-year-old son, Andy.

The boy seemed determined to dawdle, as he clomped along the muddy towpath like they had all the time in the world. "The mules don't like the mud puddles, and I can't make 'em go any faster," he hollered back.

"We'll never get to Mauch Chunk at the rate we're goin'," Ernie shouted into the wind. "Give Barney a thump on the rump if he won't move along."

Andy did as he was told, and soon Barney, the lead mule, picked up speed. Clyde, the other mule, followed suit, and Ernie breathed a sigh of relief. Maybe they wouldn't be late to pick up their load of coal after all.

"Keep us movin' without too many interruptions, Lord," Ernie prayed, glancing at the overcast sky. They'd had several days of rain, which had not only caused some flooding of the canal waters but had made the towpath almost impassable in several places. Even though it wasn't raining today and the waters had receded enough to travel, the towpath was a muddy mess, full of large puddles the mules refused to walk through. This took more time, as Andy and other mule drivers had to lead the stubborn critters around the standing water.

Soon winter would be here, and then much of the canal would be drained. Ernie planned to return with his two children to their small home outside of Parryville. He would spend the next few months cutting ice from the frozen sections of canal that had not been emptied.

"Papa, Sarah's lonely and needs a friend. Can we buy another dolly when we stop at the next store?"

Ernie glanced over his shoulder. His seven-year-old daughter, Grace, sat at the wooden table in the middle of the boat, which was where they ate most of their meals. The corn-husk doll she played with had been a gift from Ernie for her last birthday. Grace's long brown hair was unbraided today and lay across her slender shoulders in a mass of curls.

Ernie knew his daughter would need to go to school when they quit boating for the winter. It would be her first year at the one-room schoolhouse in Parryville, and he hoped she would do okay. Andy would go, too, even though the boy thought he didn't need any more schooling.

"Papa, are ya listenin' to me?" Grace asked in a whiny voice.

"I'm afraid you'll hafta be your doll's friend," Ernie replied. "Papa don't have enough money to buy another doll just now."

Grace's lower lip protruded, but Ernie knew he couldn't let her sway him. Money was tight, and unless he did well on his next couple of loads, he might have to let his helper go.

" 'Course that would mean I'd be stuck with all the cookin' and cleanin', not to mention havin' to steer the boat," he grumbled. No, he would scrimp by without luxuries in order to keep Jeb Walker as his helper, even if the elderly man was a complainer, who sometimes fell asleep when he should be working. After Ernie's wife died of pneumonia, it hadn't been easy to find someone willing to watch Grace and do the cooking. Ernie was relieved when Jeb came to work for him shortly after Anna's death.

It's either keep Jeb on or get married again, Ernie told himself. *And who would want to marry an uneducated canal boat captain like me?*

Chapter 2

As Judith stood behind her scarred wooden desk, she was surprised to see how few students were in class on this first day of school. Pastor Jacobs had said there would be more once the canal was closed for the winter, but in the meantime, there were only ten children in attendance.

Melissa and Melody, both in the third grade, shared a desk. Carl, the boy with the tattered overalls she'd seen from her bedroom window the other day, was in the second grade and sat beside Eric, another second grader. The other two boys, Garth and Roger, were fourth graders but looked much older. Judith wondered how many times they might have repeated the same grade. The four other girls in class were Beth, Sarah, Karen, and Ruby. Beth, the oldest was in sixth grade; Karen and Sarah were fifth graders; and Ruby, the youngest, was in the first grade.

Besides the lack of students, Judith noted a deficiency of school supplies. Only a few pieces of chalk sat near the blackboard, and she didn't have nearly enough reading books to go around. Each child had been required to bring his or her own pencil and tablet. One map with several tears hung on the back wall. No art supplies were available, and the school's only bell was the small handheld one that sat on Judith's desk.

I'll need to make a trip to the general store after school lets out today, Judith mentally noted. *Maybe they'll have some of the things I need. If not, I'll speak to the school board and see if they would be willing to order a few items.*

Not that she wasn't used to going without. Her parents had never been well-off, and after Mama died giving birth to Judith's youngest brother, Papa became despondent and had a hard time holding on to a job. Just a few months after Mama's passing, he'd married Helen Smithers. Even though Papa's attitude had improved, Helen was stern, and she and Judith often clashed. At the age of eighteen, Judith had been offered a teaching position at a one-room schoolhouse several towns away, and she had eagerly accepted.

Judith turned her attention to the children, who sat at their desks, looking at her with expectant expressions. "The first thing I'd like you to do is write a one-page theme about yourself." She smiled. "That way I can get to know each of you better."

Melody's hand shot up.

"Yes?"

"What kinds of things do you want to know?"

"Yeah, this is gonna be hard," Eric put in. "Our old teacher never asked us to write anything about ourselves."

"Each teacher has her own way of doing things," Judith said patiently.

"How come you get to know us and we don't get to know you?" Carl spoke up.

"That's a fair question, so I'll tell you a few things about myself." Judith went to the blackboard and picked up a piece of chalk. She quickly wrote the following list:

My name is Miss Judith King.
I like to teach school.
My favorite time of the year is fall, when the air is
crisp and clean.
The color I like best is blue.
My favorite food is apple pie.

She turned to face the class. "Does that help?"

Carl wrinkled his nose. "Not really. We only know what you like."

"That's right," Sarah put in. "Tell us about yourself."

"What would you like to know?"

"Do you have any sisters or brothers?" Ruby asked.

Judith nodded. "I have two older brothers, one younger brother, and two half sisters."

"What's a half sister?" Melissa wanted to know.

"We both have the same father but different mothers."

"How can that be?" This question came from Garth.

None of the children raised their hands or waited to be called on, but Judith figured since this was the first day of school and everyone probably felt nervous, it would be all right to dispense with the usual rule.

She explained how her mother had died and her father remarried, then later, his new wife had given birth to the two girls.

Carl leaned forward, his elbows on the desk and his chin cupped in his hands. "Have you always had those strange lookin' eyes?"

Judith squinted and rubbed the bridge of her nose, feeling like a headache might be forthcoming. How could the first assignment of the day have turned into questions and answers about her personal life? The last thing she wanted to discuss was the one physical feature she disliked the most about herself.

"One's blue and one's brown," Melody announced. "I've never known anyone with two different-colored eyes before."

Judith knew her cheeks must be red, for they felt like they were on fire. "My eyes have been like this since I was born."

"Do you see different colors out of each eye?" Carl questioned.

"No. I see everything the same as you do. Now would you please write something on your tablets about yourself?"

She sank onto the wooden chair behind her desk. This was going to be a lengthy first day of school!

※

"Hey, boss, can we stop at Henson's General Store!" Jeb called to Ernie from the stern of the boat.

"What are ya needin'?" Ernie hollered back.

"Just a couple of kitchen supplies."

"Can't it wait? I'm tryin' to keep on schedule."

"Shouldn't take that long to get a few things."

Ernie released an exasperated groan and signaled Andy to slow the mules. "We're stoppin' at the store," he shouted.

Andy waved, and soon he had the towrope tied to a tree near the edge of the canal, not far from the general store.

Ernie lowered the gangplank, and Jeb ambled off like he had all the time in the world.

"Can we get some candy, Papa?" Grace asked, leaning over the railing and swishing her long braids from side to side. Apparently Jeb had taken the time to do her hair up properly this morning. Ernie noticed she was even dressed in a pair of clean overalls.

He gave one of her braids a gentle tug. "You think I have money to spend on candy, little one?"

"Just one hunk of licorice will do."

He chuckled and hoisted her onto his shoulders. "Well, okay. We'll go inside the store and see what's in the candy counter."

Ernie was pleased to see that Andy had already tied up the mules, and he patted the boy on top of his head. "Why don't ya run into the store and see if you can find somethin' to satisfy your sweet tooth?"

When Andy looked up, his dark eyes gleamed and his lips curved into a smile. "Ya mean it, Papa?"

"Said so, didn't I?"

The boy didn't have to be asked twice. He galloped off toward the store, and by the time Ernie and Grace entered the building, Andy already had an all-day sucker in his hand.

Ernie set Grace on the floor in front of the candy counter and went to join Jeb and Lon Henson at the back of the building.

"Got any chewin' tobacco?" Jeb asked the store owner.

Before Lon could reply, Ernie stepped between the two men. "Jeb don't need none of that awful stuff. It stains your teeth, makes your breath smell foul, and it's bad for your health."

Jeb ran a hand along the bald spot on top of his head. "Where'd ya hear that, boss?"

Ernie wasn't sure where he'd heard it, but he wasn't about to let on. Instead, he merely shrugged and said, "Take my word for it, Jeb."

"Yeah, well, I like chewin' tobacco," his helper argued. "Gives me somethin' to do with my mouth." He squinted at Ernie. "But then, I don't know nothin'; just ask anybody."

Lon shook his graying head and pounded Jeb on the back. "Ya know plenty 'bout flappin' your gums!"

Jeb looked like he was ready to offer another comeback,

but the front door opened, and a blast of chilly air whipped into the store.

"Whew! Sure is gettin' cold out," Lon said, rubbing his shirtsleeves and turning toward the front of the building.

"Yep. Won't be long now, and the canal will be shut down 'til spring," Ernie agreed. He glanced in the direction Lon was heading and froze. A young woman stood near the front counter talking to Grace. She was tall, with blond hair pulled back into a bun, and curly bangs spreading across her forehead. She wore a solid navy blue dress that reached the top of her black leather shoes, and a white knitted shawl was draped around her shoulders.

"Now there's a looker for ya," Jeb said with a crooked grin. "Don't recollect seein' that beauty 'round here before, have you, boss?"

Ernie shook his head, unable to form the right words. He stared at the woman a few seconds, then pulled his gaze away. This wasn't right. She could be married, and if she was, he had no call to be gawking at her.

Don't have no reason to be starin' even if she ain't married, he berated himself. *The only thing I should be thinkin' about is gettin' my load of coal hauled up to Easton.*

"Ain't ya gonna go up front and see why that woman's talkin' to Grace?" Jeb's bony elbow connected with Ernie's ribs, and he jumped.

"Hey, cut that out!"

"I was only tryin' to get your attention. You've been standin' there like you was struck dumb or somethin'."

Ernie ran a hand through his thick, wavy hair and grimaced. "You're right. I should find out who she is and why she's talkin' to my daughter."

Before Jeb had a chance to comment, Ernie tromped across

the wooden floor and stopped beside the blond-haired woman. He cleared his throat. *"Eh-hem."*

She turned and offered him a tentative smile, then glanced down at his daughter. "Is this your papa, Grace?"

The child nodded and pointed to the woman. "This here's Miss Judith King, Papa. She's the new schoolteacher in Parryville. She says she ain't married and don't got no kids."

"But I do like children, and that's why I teach." Judith extended her hand. "It's nice to meet you, Mr.—"

"Snyder. Ernie Snyder." He shook the woman's hand and then released it, feeling like an awkward schoolboy who didn't know up from down.

"Your daughter tells me she's never been to school before."

"That's right, but as soon as the canal's drained, she'll be goin' with her brother." Ernie motioned to Andy, who stood near the potbellied stove warming his hands as he held the sucker between his lips.

"That's good to know, but don't you think your children should be in school all year?" Judith questioned.

Ernie's defenses rose, and he clenched his fingers while holding his hands at his sides. "I own my own boat, and my kids need to be with me when the canal's up and runnin'."

"What about your wife? Can't she bring the children to school?"

His forehead wrinkled. "Anna's dead. Died a few years ago from pneumonia."

Judith blinked a couple of times, and he noticed that one of her eyes was blue and the other was brown. He'd never seen anyone with two different-colored eyes before, and it was hard not to stare.

"I'm sorry about your wife, Mr. Snyder," she said in a

sincere tone. "I'm sure you're doing the best you can by your children."

"Yep, he sure is. That's why he hired me to cook, clean, and watch out for Grace," Jeb declared. He stepped up beside Ernie and offered Judith a toothless grin.

"My kids don't get the kind of learnin' that some do," Ernie said, "but I've taught 'em a few Bible verses, and they can recite several by heart."

"That's right," Grace chimed in. " 'God has made everything beautiful in his time.' Ecclesiastes 3:11."

Judith touched the child on the shoulder. "Well done."

"I know more. Want to hear 'em?"

Before the schoolteacher had a chance to reply, Ernie tapped Grace on the shoulder and said, "Not now, Daughter. We need to pay for our things and get back to the boat."

Judith leaned over so she was eye-level with Grace. "I'd be happy to hear some other verses when you come to school." She straightened again and looked directly at Ernie. "I'll look forward to having your children in class. . .sometime next month?"

"Right. The weather's gettin' colder now, so most of the canal will probably be drained by then." *She's tall. Really tall.* Ernie chewed on that thought a few seconds. *Never met a woman who could look me right in the eye.*

He shook his head, hoping the action would get him thinking straight. Then, with a sudden need for some fresh air, he slapped some money on the counter in front of the store-keeper. "Give Jeb the change when he finishes his business."

"Will do," Lon said with a nod.

Ernie grabbed his daughter's hand. "Me and Grace will be waitin' on the boat, Jeb."

"Okay, boss. Andy and me will be along just as soon as we gather up the supplies."

Remembering what his mama used to say about good manners, Ernie called over his shoulder, "Nice meetin' ya, Miss King." Then he and Grace went out the door.

Chapter 3

As Judith stood on the front porch of the schoolhouse, ringing her bell, she was pleased to see the Snyder children tromping up the path with their father. School had been in session a little over a month, and now that freezing weather was upon them, many of the canalers' children would be coming to the new schoolteacher for some book learning.

"Good morning, Mr. Snyder," she said as Ernie and his children stepped onto the porch.

He gave his navy blue stocking cap a quick tug and offered her a crooked grin. "Aw, just call me Ernie. Mr. Snyder sounds too formal-like."

Judith smiled in return. "Ernie it is, then." She glanced at his daughter, noting several places where her jacket was torn. "Hello, Grace. I've been looking forward to having you in my class."

Grace stared at her rubber boots. " 'Mornin', Miss King."

Ernie gave his daughter's arm a pat. "She's feelin' kind of nervous, what with this bein' her first day of school and all."

Judith's heart went out to the child. When she was a girl, she had been shy and self-conscious, rarely speaking unless she was spoken to and always worried about her appearance.

"You'll be fine once you get to know everyone," Judith assured the child. She bent down, so she was eye-level with Ernie's son. "And what's your name?"

"Andy," the boy mumbled. "Papa said I have to come to school, but I'd rather be helpin' him cut ice all winter."

Judith glanced back at Ernie. "You're an ice cutter?"

He nodded. "Just durin' the winter months. Gotta make a livin' somehow when I can't run the boat."

"Do you live on the boat all year?" she asked.

"Naw. We have a little house on the far side of town. Like to hunker down there durin' the colder months."

Judith was about to comment, but she heard a ruckus going on in the schoolhouse, and her attention was drawn inside. "Please come in and take off your coats," she said, motioning to the door. "Apparently I've got some rowdy students who must be anxious for their day to begin."

As they stepped inside the schoolhouse, a wadded-up piece of paper sailed across the room, just missing Judith's head. She hadn't seen who had thrown it, but from the guilty look on Roger's face, she suspected it was him.

She bent to pick up the paper. "Everyone, please take your seats. We have two new students today—Andy and Grace Snyder."

Ernie shuffled his feet a few times. "I reckon I should be headin' back to work. I'll be by after school to pick up my kids." He looked first at Andy, then at Grace. "You two behave yourselves, ya hear?"

"Yes, Papa," Grace said meekly.

Andy only gave a brief nod.

Judith motioned to an empty desk near the front of the room. "Why don't the two of you sit there today?"

24

As the Snyder children took their seats, she escorted Ernie to the door. "I'm sure they'll be fine, Mr. Snyder—I mean, Ernie."

He grunted and reached up to rub his chin, which appeared to have recently been shaved. Judging from the spot of dried blood, Judith figured he'd probably nicked himself.

With a quick "See ya later," Ernie tromped out the door.

That man needs a warmer coat, Judith thought when she noticed Ernie pull the collar of his threadbare jacket around his neck. *And what a nice father for escorting his children to school.*

❧

As Ernie headed for the icehouse on the other side of town, all he could think about was Judith King, with her haunting multicolored eyes and dimpled smile. It was dumb, just plain stupid, to think a woman as beautiful and smart as she would ever give anyone like him a second glance.

I only went through the fourth grade. If she knew that, she'd probably think I was a poor canaler who's dumber than dirt. Ernie kicked a hefty stone with the toe of his boot, hoping the action would get him thinking about something else.

"Sure hope my boy don't give the teacher no sass," he mumbled, shoving his hands into his jacket pockets. Andy had been a handful since Anna died, often playing tricks on his sister and not always minding the mules the way he should. Ernie knew if he didn't stay firm with the child, he might grow up to be lazy.

Ernie had begun walking the mules when he was eight years old. Later, when his pa was sure he could handle the boat, he'd become the spotter and sometimes got to steer. From the beginning Ernie had known he would own a canal boat someday. He loved being on the water, moving up and down the canal hauling anthracite coal, and he hoped Andy would want to follow in his footsteps—although with the growing competition from trains, the family business might come to an end before then.

Ernie picked up his pace. His primary goal in life was to see that his kids were properly cared for. He also knew it was important for them to memorize some Bible verses and learn to do an honest day's work.

Guess they might need a bit more book learnin' than I had, too.

Judith stood at the window overlooking the schoolyard, watching the children during their afternoon recess. Even though it was cold outside, it was good for them to run and play. When the students came back inside, they would be ready to settle down. She might have a spelling bee for the older ones and get the younger children involved in an art project. Soon Christmas would be here, and some colorful decorations for the schoolhouse would be a nice addition.

Judith turned to study the room. *I'll need to think about a Christmas program soon and who will get what parts. The children would probably enjoy singing some Christmas carols, too.*

A commotion outside drew Judith's attention back to the window. Several children stood in a circle, chanting, "Hit him! Hit him! Hit him!"

Judith rushed out the door, not bothering to fetch her shawl. "What's going on?" she shouted above the noise.

The chanting stopped, but no one spoke. Then she spotted Grace crouched next to the teeter-totter.

When Judith pushed through the circle, she realized that Andy stood in the center, toe-to-toe with Garth. Both boys held up their fists as though ready to take a swing.

She ducked between them. "What is the problem?"

Garth squinted his eyes, and Andy stared at the ground.

Judith rubbed her hands briskly over her arms as the stinging cold penetrated her skin. "If someone doesn't tell me what happened, the whole class will be punished."

Sarah stepped forward. "Garth was makin' fun of Andy's sister, calling her 'sissy-face' and 'runt.' So Andy challenged him to a fight, but you got here before either could land the first punch."

"Is it true that you were calling Grace names?" Judith asked, taking Garth by the shoulders and turning him to face her.

He shrugged. "Maybe."

Judith's patience was growing thin, and she prayed for wisdom. "Either you did or you didn't. Which is it?"

Garth lifted his chin and glared at her. "Okay, I did, but the little baby deserved it."

"No one deserves to be called names," Judith said sternly. She remembered some of the names she had been called as a child. *Giraffe with the long neck. Judith the freak. The girl with the spooky eyes.*

"Garth, you will stay after school today, and we'll talk about your punishment then." She tapped him on the shoulder. "In the meantime, I want you to tell Andy and Grace you're sorry for being rude."

The boy folded his arms in an unyielding pose. "Why should I apologize? He's the one who said he was gonna clean my clock for teasin' his baby sister."

Garth had a point. Andy shouldn't have started the fight. However, Judith figured he was only defending his sister. "Andy, apologize to Garth, and Garth you do the same. Then you must tell Grace you're sorry."

With an exaggerated huff, Andy wrinkled his nose and mumbled, "Sorry."

Garth followed suit.

Judith shooed the others inside, then took Garth's arm and led him across the schoolyard to the teeter-totters where Grace was still squatted.

"Sorry for callin' ya sissy face and runt," the boy said, his jaw tight.

"Let's get back to class." Judith reached for Grace's hand, but the little girl stayed firmly in place. Garth had already sprinted toward the schoolhouse.

"Come on, sweetheart," Judith pleaded. "You can't stay out here; it's too cold."

"I want my papa."

"He said he would return after school."

"I wanna go home."

"You can't go home until school is over for the day."

The child gave no response, and Judith, though shivering from the cold, knelt beside her. "I remember when I saw you at the general store last month," she said. "You had licorice candy."

Grace nodded.

"Would you come inside if I promise to give you a piece of licorice when school lets out?"

"You got some?"

"Yes, in my desk. I keep it there for children who've done well on their assignments or have been extra good."

"I didn't do nothin' good," Grace said, her chin quivering.

"Obeying the teacher is a good thing. So if you come with me now, your reward will be the licorice."

The child clambered to her feet. "Okay."

Judith breathed a sigh of relief. The role of a schoolteacher brought lots of challenges, and there were days like today when she wondered if she was up to them.

Chapter 4

The days sped by quickly as Judith settled in with her larger class. Five more children from the canal had started coming to school, so now there were seventeen. Grace wasn't quite as shy as she had been at first, and Andy and Garth had calmed down, too.

Even though all the children behaved better in class and during recess, Judith felt some concern because of their lack of interaction. She had tried a question-and-answer time following their lessons, but most of the children just sat there, staring at their desk or out the window.

Today Judith decided to try something new—something she hoped everyone would take part in.

"Children," she said, clapping her hands together. "I've come up with an idea I shall call the letter box."

She reached under her desk and retrieved the small cardboard box she'd put there before class, placing it in the middle of her desk. "During our art lesson today we'll decorate this and put a hole in the lid. Then each of you may write down any questions, ideas, or concerns you have and put it in the box. If your letter is signed, you will receive a letter back. If it's not, I will respond to it orally in front of the class."

Ruby's hand shot up.

"Yes?"

The freckle-faced little girl grinned. "I'd like to get a letter from you, Teacher."

"Thank you, Ruby."

"Me, too," several of the girls chorused.

Noisy snickers from the back of the room drew Judith's attention to the boys who sat in the last row of desks. "Would one of you care to tell me what you think is so funny?"

"Nothin', Miss King." Roger folded his hands in front of him and sat straight as a ruler.

"What about you, Eric?" Judith questioned. "Why were you laughing?"

The boy slunk down in his seat, and Carl, who sat beside Eric, jabbed him in the ribs.

"Hey, cut that out! Want me to slug you?"

Maybe this wasn't such a good idea, Judith thought with dismay. *If the children don't take this project seriously, nothing will be gained by doing it.*

"I like the idea of a letter box," Andy spoke up.

"Why is that?" Judith asked.

The boy pulled his fingers through the shaggy brown hair curling around his ears. "Seems like a fun way to learn about others, that's all."

Judith nodded, feeling more hopeful.

"Can we decorate the box now?" Karen asked.

"I suppose we could."

"Yes!" the children shouted.

"After I hand out some glue, scissors, and paper, you can all get busy," Judith said. "If you each make a small decoration, we'll take turns gluing them to the box."

The room became quiet, as every child began work on their decorations. A short time later, the plain cardboard box had been transformed into a collage of brightly colored squares, circles, and triangles. Judith printed the words LETTER BOX on a piece of white paper and glued it to the center of the box. She allowed Beth, the oldest girl, to cut a hole in the top, and the box was placed on Judith's desk.

"For the next half hour you may each write your questions or comments on a slip of paper. When I ring the bell for recess, you can deposit them in the box," Judith announced. "A few minutes before it's time to go home, I'll read some of the letters that are unsigned and hand out my reply to those who have included their name."

"I hope Teacher reads mine," she overheard Ruby whisper to Grace.

Grace only nodded in reply, as she seemed to be concentrating on the paper before her.

Judith drew in a deep breath and returned to her desk. *This project might be the very thing that will make my class successful.*

❦

Ernie shivered as he clomped through the fresh-fallen snow, on his way to the small building where the ice he'd been cutting would be stored. It was early December, and the weather had turned bitterly cold. He hated to think what the rest of winter might be like.

"Probably need to get me a heavier coat and a new pair of gloves," he muttered, glancing at the gaping hole in the thumb of his left glove. "Sure hate to spend money on clothes for me, though. Not when there are so many other needs."

Ernie's children came first, and they always had. That's why he worked such long hours hauling coal during the warmer months, and it was why he also planned to work hard this winter, cutting ice. If anyone needed a new coat, it was Grace, and he hoped to get her one for Christmas. Andy needed a new pair of boots, too. The ones he wore now were pinching his toes.

Ernie thought about his helper and wondered if Jeb had been able to find work in Easton. Jeb had a daughter who lived there, and he would stay with her, even if he didn't secure a job for the winter.

The thought had crossed Ernie's mind to look for work in the city, but his home was in Parryville, and he hated to uproot Andy and Grace. They were happy here. Happy with their new schoolteacher, too.

A vision of Judith King flashed into Ernie's mind. Several times he'd gone to pick up his kids after school, yet he'd never said more than, "Howdy, how are you?" or "Hope my kids are doin' okay," to the schoolmarm. He'd wanted to say more. Truth was Ernie would have liked to invite Judith to join him and the kids for supper at Baker's Café, but he couldn't work up the nerve.

"Not that she'd give me a second look," he mumbled. "She's probably had all kinds of offers from men a lot smarter and handsomer than me."

Ernie was glad when the icehouse came into view. He was supposed to meet Abe McGinnis there, and the two of them would spend most of the day cutting ice on a section of canal nearby that hadn't been drained. Ernie figured hard work was good. It kept him too busy to do much thinking, and when he worked up a sweat, he didn't mind the cold so much.

"Yep. That's what I need all right," Ernie mumbled, opening the door of the icehouse. "Need to get busy and quit thinkin' about that purty schoolteacher."

While the children romped in the snow during recess, Judith sat at her desk, reading the letters that had been deposited in the letter box a short time ago. The first one was from Bobby Collins, and it read:

Dear Teacher:
How come you have two different-colored eyes?

The boy was new to class and was one of those who led the mules along the canal. Judith knew he hadn't been at school the day she'd explained to the students about her unusual eyes. Therefore, he deserved an answer to his question.

Dear Bobby:
God makes each person different, and He chose to give me one brown eye and one blue.
Miss King

She unfolded the next piece of paper.

Dear Teacher:
How do I get to be a teacher like you?
Ruby Miller

Judith's reply was:

Dear Ruby:
Study hard, get good grades, and someday you might be offered the job of teaching school, too.
Miss King

The next letter caused Judith to do some serious thinking.

Dear Teacher:
  Why can't we have a longer recess?

                                              Carl Higgins

Judith tapped her pencil along the edge of her desk. Carl's question was one she had asked herself when she was a girl. Maybe she could extend their recess a bit, perhaps on Friday afternoons.

The next letter was a surprise.

Dear Teacher:
  I wish you was my mama. I think Papa might like that, too.

The letter was unsigned.

Judith felt a trickle of perspiration roll down her forehead. If one of the children thought this way, could there be more with the same idea? And who had written this note?

She studied the handwriting, noting that the letters were uneven and some were barely more than a scribble. It had to be written by one of the younger children.

Could it be Carl? she wondered. He seemed to like Judith, and often gave her a hug when no one was looking.

Judith heard the children's footsteps clomping across the porch. "How can I possibly answer this letter out loud?" she moaned.

Chapter 5

As Judith left the pastor's home and headed toward the church on Sunday morning, she noticed several of her students coming up the walkway. Grace and Andy were not among them, however, and neither was their father.

When Ernie mentioned that he had taught his children some memory verses, Judith assumed he was a churchgoing man. Apparently she'd been wrong, for in the month she'd been living in Parryville, she had not seen him at church even once.

" 'Mornin', Miss King," Beth called with a cheery wave.

Judith nodded at her student and smiled. Already she had a fondness for those she taught, and she truly liked living and working in this small town near the canal. Rev. and Mrs. James had made her feel right at home, although their identical twin daughters could be a little trying at times. On more than one occasion Melody and Melissa had attempted to fool their teacher by taking on the other sister's identity, but Judith had finally figured out who was who.

She continued walking toward the church, as she thought about the past week and how the atmosphere in the classroom had changed since they had begun using the letter box. The children seemed more attentive, and they were getting to know one another better.

Judith reflected on the way she had handled the unsigned letter from the child who wished Teacher could be his or her mama. She'd waited until the end of the day to respond to the letters that weren't signed. Since there was only enough time left to read a couple, the personal one about her was left unread.

The following day, Judith had made a new rule. "Starting today, I will answer all letters addressed to me, even if they aren't signed. My replies will be written and put inside another box, and I'll set both boxes on a shelf inside the coatroom. If you write an unsigned letter and want an answer, you may look for it in the reply box."

In response to the letter about her being someone's mama, Judith had written:

Dear Student:
   It's nice to know you would like me to be your mother. Even though that's not possible, I care about you and every-one in my class.

                                              Miss King

Judith pulled her thoughts aside, as she climbed the steps and entered the church. Pastor Jacobs was inside the foyer, and he greeted her with a smile. "May I speak with you a moment, Judith?"

"Of course." She followed the pastor to the other side of the room, where they could talk in private.

"I've just learned that Margaret Jones fell on the ice and broke her leg last night," he said.

Judith frowned. "I'm sorry to hear that."

"Margaret has been teaching our girls' Sunday school class for the past year, but she'll have to give up teaching for a while." He tugged on the end of his dark mustache. "I was wondering if you might consider taking over for her."

Judith didn't hesitate. "I'd be happy to, although I'm not prepared with anything today."

"Could you read them a story from the Bible and have them draw a picture of what they've learned?"

Judith didn't want to leave any little girl without a Sunday school teacher, so she agreeably nodded.

"Thank you. I appreciate that." Rev. Jacobs pointed down the hall. "The girls meet in the last room on the left."

Judith was prepared to head in that direction when she noticed Ernie and his children enter the building. Her heart pounded as their gazes met. What was there about the man that fascinated her so? They were as different as her unmatched eyes. She was a schoolteacher who carefully chose her words; Ernie worked the canal and often spoke in broken sentences. She was tall and unattractive; he was ruggedly handsome and strong. Yet Ernie's apparent love for his children and his friendly smile had touched Judith's heart from the moment they had first met.

"Good morning. How are you, Ernie?" Judith asked when he and his children came alongside her.

"Fair to middlin'." He stared down at his boots. "Are my kids doin' okay in school?"

She glanced at his children and smiled. "I believe they are."

"I like the letter box, Teacher," Grace said.

"I'm glad." Judith tapped Andy on the shoulder. "How about you? Do you still think our letter box is a good idea?"

He shrugged. "Did at first, but some of the kids write sissy stuff."

"Letter box?" Ernie tipped his head and gave Judith a curious look.

She quickly explained what the box was and how it worked.

Ernie rubbed his chin, which Judith noticed had again been recently shaved. Only this time there were no nicks or bloody scabs.

"Hmm. . .might be a good idea," he mumbled.

She nodded. "I believe some of the children have been able to say things they might not have had the courage to say in person."

"I wrote a letter once, but I didn't sign—" Grace's cheeks turned bright red, and she covered her mouth with the back of her hand.

Judith didn't wish to cause the child further embarrassment, so she reached for Grace's hand. "Starting today, I'll be teaching the girls' Sunday school class, so if you'd like to come along, we can go there now."

"How 'bout me and the boy?" Ernie motioned to Andy, who stood off to one side fidgeting with the stocking cap he held in his hands.

"I believe Deacon Miller teaches the class for the boys, which is somewhere down the hall. I can help Andy find it when Grace and I go to our class." She nodded toward the sanctuary. "Rev. James meets with the men in there, while Mrs. James teaches the women in another classroom."

Ernie opened his mouth, like he might want to say something more, but he shrugged and headed for the sanctuary instead.

Judith led the way down the hall, with Andy and Grace at her side.

Ernie took a seat on a pew in the back row, feeling self-conscious and as out of place as a snowball in summer. He hadn't been in Sunday school for many years, but he had brought his children to church several times, although it was mostly during the winter months when they lived in town. He knew it was time for the kids to get regular Bible learning, and he figured they would receive a lot more in Sunday school than what he could teach them at home.

Ernie glanced at his faded blue trousers. They were the only pair he had that didn't have holes or a noticeable stain. The white shirt he wore had fit him at one time, but after many washings in too hot of water, it had shrunk. The cuffs were now several inches above his wrist.

"It's good to see you this morning," Rev. James said, tapping him on the shoulder. "Wouldn't you like to move up closer so you can hear the lesson better?"

Ernie noticed that all the other men had taken seats on the first two rows. Reluctantly, he stood and followed the pastor up front, easing himself onto a third row pew and trying not to look conspicuous.

Sure hope the preacher don't ask me no questions, he thought with a frown. *I read a few Bible verses every day and have memorized some, but when it comes to speakin' out loud, I'd sound like a dimwit.*

"Our lesson today will be from Proverbs," the pastor announced. "So if you will open your Bibles to chapter 16, we'll take turns reading."

A trickle of sweat rolled down Ernie's forehead, as he heard the rustle of pages. *Maybe he won't call on me. And if he does, I'll just say I left my Bible at home, which won't be a lie.*

"In this passage of Scripture, one verse I'd like to bring out has to do with the way we talk," Rev. James said. "Henry Bonner, would you read verse 24?"

Henry, a tall, heavyset bank teller, stood and cleared his throat real loud.

" 'Pleasant words are as an honeycomb, sweet to the soul, and health to the bones.' "

"Now if the kind words we speak are pleasant enough to be health to our bones, what might our unkind words be compared to?" The preacher's gaze traveled from one man to the other.

Ernie knew the answer to that, but he wasn't about to raise his hand.

"Let's turn back to chapter 15." Rev. James nodded at Frank Gookins, who Ernie knew was also a canaler. "Would you read verse 1?"

Ernie held his breath, waiting to see what Frank would do. The man was as uneducated as Ernie; surely he would refuse to read out loud.

Frank stood, and in a faltering voice he said, " 'A soft. . .uh. . . answer turn-eth a-way wrath: but grieve. . .uh. . .grieve. . .' "

"Grievous," the pastor said patiently.

" 'But griev-ous words—stir up—anger.' " Frank closed the Bible and flopped onto the pew with a look of relief.

Rev. James smiled. "Thank you, Frank."

Ernie groaned inwardly. He felt sorry for poor Frank but was relieved it hadn't been him the pastor called on.

"This is what we've learned," Rev. James continued. "If our words are pleasant they will be like honeycomb, bringing health to the bones. If our words are grievous, they will stir up anger."

Ernie thought about his helper. Jeb could cut a body down with only a few words. It was a good thing the man wasn't in charge of the canal boat because there were times when more than one boat arrived at the lock gates. Ernie could only imagine how Jeb would handle things if he were the boss. He'd probably shake his fist at the other captain and holler, "Get your boat outta my way, or I'll box your ears!"

Ernie stared at his calloused hands. *I may not know lots of big words, but them that do come from my mouth oughta be kind. I'll need to keep prayin' for Jeb and try to set a good example.*

☙

On Monday morning, Judith was surprised to see Ernie walk up to the schoolhouse with his children. She knew he'd been busy cutting ice, and lately Grace and Andy had come to school by themselves.

"Good morning, Ernie. Good morning, children," she said with a smile.

"Mornin'," they responded in unison.

The children scampered into the classroom, but their father lingered a few moments on the porch. "Is there something you want to say, Ernie?" Judith asked.

He jammed his hands into his jacket pocket and rocked back and forth on the heels of his boots. "Well, I. . .uh. . .was wonderin' if—"

Carl and Eric raced past just then, bumping into Ernie and knocking him against Judith.

"Oh!" she exclaimed, trying to regain her balance.

Ernie grabbed her around the waist. "Are. . .are you okay?"

The man's face was red like an apple, and Judith figured hers was, too. "I–I'm fine," she said breathlessly.

Ernie released his hold on her, and she took a step back. "Guess I'd best be goin'," he mumbled.

"But I thought you wanted to ask me something."

"It weren't nothin' important." He shook his head and hurried away.

Judith shivered, realizing how cold she'd become standing on the porch with no wrap. "I wish I knew what Ernie had planned to say," she murmured. "He certainly is a man of few words."

Chapter 6

While the children were outside during afternoon recess, Judith sat at her desk, reading the letters she had found in the letter box earlier. Two were unsigned, both asking questions about whom the teacher thought was her best student.

"Strange," Judith murmured. "Either the same person wrote both letters, or two students are competing for my attention."

She figured it was probably Melody and Melissa. The twins were competitive, and Judith had noticed several times that at home the girls often argued and tried to get one of their parents to take a side.

Judith turned the notes over and wrote the same response on each one:

Dear Student:
    I care about all the children in my class, and it wouldn't be right to have one favorite. Keep doing your best and you will learn much.

                                                              Miss King

Loud voices in the schoolyard captured Judith's attention, and she set her pencil and paper aside. Opening the front door, she stepped onto the porch. Several of the boys raced around the yard shaking their fists and hollering at one another.

"He did it!"

"No, it was your fault."

"He started it."

"No way; it was you!"

A few of the girls leaned over the porch and pointed, like there might be someone or something beneath them.

"What happened?" Judith asked, easing her body between Melody and Karen.

"It's Andy Snyder," Melody replied. "Roger shoved him off the porch, and now the bully's bein' chased by some of the other boys who know what he did to Andy was wrong."

Judith's heart lurched when she saw Andy lying on the ground, whimpering and holding his right arm. She hurried down the steps and knelt to examine the boy. His arm was red and starting to swell, but it didn't look like it was out of place. "Andy, is it true that Roger pushed you?"

The child nodded, as tears rolled down his cheeks.

"Why did he do that?"

"Roger was shoutin' names at Andy and some of the other boys from the canal," Karen spoke up. "He said they were a bunch of dirty canalers who don't have no more brains than a dumb mule."

"That's right," Melody agreed. "I think Andy got sick of it, 'cause he told Roger what he thought. That's when the mean fellow pushed him off the porch."

Judith clenched her fingers. She hated name-calling and thought she had made it clear that it would not be tolerated. Glancing at Andy's arm again, she knew the first order of business was to take him to the doctor in case it was broken. She would deal with the troublemakers tomorrow morning.

"Clem, please get my horse hitched to the buggy," she called to one of the older boys. "When that's done, could you find Andy's father and let him know what's happened? Be sure to tell him that I'm taking his son to see the doctor."

"Sure, Miss King. I know right where Ernie's cuttin' ice today, 'cause my pa's workin' there, too." Clem sprinted toward the corral where Judith kept her horse during school hours.

"Beth, would you please take over for me until school is out?" Judith asked the older girl.

Beth's dark eyes became huge. "You—you want me to teach the students?"

Judith shook her head. "Just have them finish their reading assignment and then dismiss the class."

Beth nodded and called to the other children, while Judith helped Andy to his feet and over to her waiting buggy.

"Can I go along?" Grace asked, running beside them.

"Of course. Hurry and climb into the back of the buggy."

A short time later, Judith and Grace sat in the waiting area at the doctor's office, while Andy was being examined in the next room.

"What if my brother's arm is broken?" Grace questioned. "How's he gonna do his schoolwork?"

Judith patted Grace's hand, and in so doing, noticed a tear in the sleeve of the child's faded green dress. "Would you like me to fix this for you?"

Grace nodded. "Jeb and Papa don't know how to sew. Mama used to fix the rips in my clothes, but now she's in heaven with Jesus; Papa said so." The child stared at her hands, clasped tightly in her lap.

Judith reached into her satchel and retrieved a needle and thread. As she stitched the tear, she told Grace about losing her own mother when she was ten years old.

"Guess maybe our mamas are visitin' each other up there with God." Grace's tone was so sincere, and her expression of such conviction, it caused tears to spring into Judith's eyes.

She sniffed and tried to keep her focus on the needle going back and forth through the hole in Grace's dress. "I'm wondering why you don't join the other girls at school whenever they play on the swings during recess," she asked, feeling the need to change the subject.

The child stared up at Judith with huge brown eyes and shrugged her slim shoulders.

"Don't they make you feel welcome?"

"They say mean things to me, 'cause Papa's a dirty old canaler. Some even sing that awful song we don't like."

"What song is that?"

" 'You rusty ole canaler, you'll never get rich.' " Grace's eyebrows drew together. "That's all the words I can say, 'cause Papa says some of 'em are bad." Her chin came up and quivered slightly. "He said if he ever catches me or Andy sayin' bad words, he'll wash our mouths out with soap."

Judith nodded and broke off the piece of thread, then tied a knot. "There, it's almost as good as new."

"Thank you, Teacher."

"You're welcome."

The front door opened then, and Ernie rushed into the room. Grace jumped up and hurried to his side. "Papa!"

He patted the top of his daughter's head, but Judith could tell he was barely aware of the young girl's presence. "What happened? Where's my boy? Is he gonna be okay?" Ernie's eyes were wide, and his face was a mask of concern.

Judith stood and moved to stand beside him. She quickly explained how one of the boys had been calling names and then told what had followed.

Ernie's eyes flashed angrily. "I knew it was a mistake to put my kids in school with a bunch of younguns who think they're better'n us." He leveled Judith with a look that made her toes curl inside her high-top shoes. "I can't believe you'd let somethin' like this happen."

She reached out and touched the man's arm, hoping to calm him down, but it seemed to have the opposite effect. Ernie pulled away like he'd been stung by a hornet. Strangely enough, Judith felt as if some stinging insect had attacked her, too. Could it have been the contact of her fingers touching Ernie's skin?

She took a step back. "All children tend to argue and fuss at times. But you can be sure the boy who pushed Andy will be punished."

"Glad to hear it." Ernie looked around the room. "Where is my boy? Is he gonna be okay?"

"He's with Dr. Smith, and we should know something soon." Judith nodded toward the wooden chairs. "In the meantime, why don't we have a seat?"

With an exaggerated shrug, Ernie marched across the room and flopped into a chair. Grace took the seat beside him, and Judith sat on the other side.

"Teacher fixed the hole in my dress," Grace said, lifting her elbow and leaning toward her father.

His face softened, and he gave Judith a half smile. "That was right nice." Then he glanced back at his daughter. "Did ya tell your teacher thanks?"

"I did."

Just then the adjoining door opened, and Dr. Smith stepped out. Andy followed, his right arm in a sling.

Ernie jumped to his feet, as did Judith. They both took a step forward, and in so doing, collided. Judith's face heated with embarrassment, as Ernie's hand went around her waist. This was the second time today he'd kept her from falling over. "You all right?" he croaked.

Not trusting her voice, she only nodded.

Ernie turned to face the doctor. "How's my boy? Is his arm broke?"

Dr. Smith shook his head. "It's just a bad sprain, but he'll need to wear the sling until the swelling goes down."

"Glad you're not hurt real bad," Ernie said, patting Andy's shoulder.

Andy grimaced. "Me, too, but it still smarts somethin' awful."

"It'll feel better in a day or so." Ernie nodded toward the chairs, where Grace sat. "Have a seat by your sister while I settle up with the doc."

Judith joined Grace and Andy, while Ernie and Dr. Smith tended to business.

"I'm sorry about your accident," she said to Andy. "You can be sure that Roger will be punished."

Andy hung his head. "He thinks I'm dumb and dirty 'cause I lead my papa's mules."

"You're not dumb, Andy. You're a quick learner, and—"

"It's time to go," Ernie announced, sauntering toward them. "Should we stop at the café for somethin' to eat before we go home?"

"Can Teacher come, too?" The question came from Grace as she grabbed hold of Judith's hand.

"I should probably get home," Judith was quick to say. She didn't want Ernie to feel obligated to include her in their supper plans.

Ernie shuffled his feet. "Would ya. . .uh. . .like to join us at the café? You're more'n welcome."

Her heartbeat quickened, and she moistened her lips with the tip of her tongue. "That would be very nice, thank you."

Chapter 7

For the last ten minutes, Judith had been sitting inside Baker's Café with Ernie and his children, and so far the only words Ernie had spoken were to the waitress, when she took their order.

If he wasn't going to talk to me, then why did he invite me to join them for supper? Of course, I'm not doing such a good job of making conversation, either.

Judith hated to admit it, but she was attracted to Ernie. There was only one problem—she was sure Ernie didn't feel the same way about her. For that matter, no man had ever shown an interest in her, and she knew why.

She lifted her glass and took a sip of water, hoping the action might help her think about something other than how handsome Ernie was and how homely she must seem to him. *He probably thinks I'm a lonely old-maid schoolteacher and only included me in this meal because it was Grace's idea.*

The tantalizing aroma of sizzling steaks caused Judith's stomach to rumble, and she drank more water to tide her over until the food arrived. *Where is that waitress? I'm hungry and so nervous I feel like I might faint.*

Judith glanced over at Grace. The girl's elbows were on the table, and her chin rested in the palm of her hands. Judith fought the urge to mention that it wasn't polite to lean on the table. *She's Ernie's daughter, not mine. He probably wouldn't appreciate me correcting the girl when he's sitting right here.*

The child offered her a wide smile. "It's sure nice havin' ya eat with us, Teacher. Wish we could do this every night."

Judith's cheeks warmed. "It's nice for me, too." She looked at Ernie, wondering if he would say something, but he merely smiled, then looked away.

She sighed. *I wish I'd had the good sense to go home after we left the doctor's office.*

Ernie toyed with his fork as he stared across the table at Judith. Grace sat beside her, and Andy was seated next to Ernie. The children had been chatting with one another, but Ernie felt too nervous and tongue-tied to say anything sensible to Judith. He didn't know what had come over him when he'd invited her to join them for supper. Being around the pretty schoolteacher made him feel so scruffy and dim-witted.

He thought about his late wife and how she used to make him feel. Anna had been quiet, meek, and pretty, but in a plain sort of way. She'd been the daughter of a lock tender and hadn't received any more education than Ernie. He'd loved her, though, and would never regret the years they'd had together.

Ernie wondered if his attraction to Judith King went deeper than her physical beauty. *Maybe I'm interested in her because I know I can't have her. Sort of like the fish in the canal that can never live on land.*

He chanced another peek at Judith, and she offered him a brief smile but then looked quickly away. Did she feel as

51

nervous as he did this evening?

Sure wish our food would come. At least then we'd have somethin' to do besides sit here and stare at each other.

Ernie was relieved when Grace leaned over and said something to her teacher. That left Andy free to talk to him. "How's that arm feelin', Son?" he asked. "Does it still hurt real bad?"

"Naw, it'll be okay." Andy shook his head, but his pained expression told Ernie he wasn't quite as brave as he pretended to be.

"You gonna be able to do your schoolwork with your left hand?"

Andy frowned. "I don't write so well even with my right hand, so I'll probably make a mess of things when I try to use the other one."

"We could spend time in the evenings practicin'," Ernie suggested.

"Yeah, maybe so." The boy leaned closer to his father and whispered, "I'm wantin' to write somethin' to put in Miss King's letter box."

Ernie smiled. "I'm sure you'll do fine. Just take your time as you print each letter." He reached for his glass of water and took a drink. *If I was one of Judith's pupils, I know what I'd say.*

<hr/>

The following day, Judith waited until school was dismissed to check the letter box. Roger, the boy who had pushed Andy off the porch, had been sent outside to chop wood as his punishment. She'd kept two other boys, Garth and Eric, after school to write essays because they had talked out of turn today. While the boys worked, Judith planned to answer the recent letters she'd received, putting those that were unsigned in the second box inside the coatroom and saving the others to hand out to the students who had signed their names.

Judith pulled the first one out and read it silently.

Dear Teacher:
*   How come Beth gets to play the part of Mary in the Christmas program?*

*   Ruby*

She turned the paper over and wrote on the back:

Dear Ruby:
*   Beth is older, and there are more lines for her to speak. I think you will make a sweet little angel.*

*   Miss King*

The next letter brought a smile to Judith's lips.

Dear Teacher:
*   Is it true that a giraffe sleeps standing up? Can I sleep that way, too?*

*   Andy*

Judith noticed the boy's disjointed letters. It must have been difficult for him to print with his left hand. She flipped the paper over and wrote the following reply:

Dear Andy:
*   The book I have about giraffes says they do sleep standing up. Horses and mules do that sometimes, too. If we tried to sleep while still on our feet, we would lose our balance and fall over.*

*   Miss King*

There was one more letter in the box, and this one was not signed. It read:

Dear Teacher:
I think you're smart and very purty.

Judith heard some snickering and glanced at the back of the room. Eric and Garth had their heads together, and she wondered if they knew something about the unsigned letter. Perhaps one of them had written it as a practical joke. It had to be a prank, because she was sure none of her students thought she was pretty.

She rose from her chair and marched over to the boys. "What's so funny, and why are you out of your seats?"

"Nothin's funny. We was just talkin'." Garth wrinkled his nose, and Eric looked kind of sheepish, but they both scampered back to their desks.

"Are you finished with your essays?" she questioned.

"Not yet," Eric replied.

"Almost," said Garth.

Judith glanced at the clock on the far wall. "Please get them done, or you'll be late getting home for supper." She moved back to her desk, and the unsigned letter caught her attention again. Should she respond to it, and if so, what should she say?

Pursing her lips, she picked up her pencil.

Dear Student:
It's nice to know that you think I'm smart and pretty.
No one has ever told me that before.

Miss King

She held the end of the pencil between her teeth. *Should I have said that? If this letter was written by one of the troublemakers, anything I say could be used in their next joke.*

Quickly, she erased what she had written and started over.

Dear Student:
It's nice to know that you think I'm smart and pretty.
                                        Thank you,
                                        Miss King

Ernie stepped into the small clapboard house he shared with his children during the winter months. It had been a long day, and he was tired and chilled clear to the bones.

"How's your arm?" he asked Andy, who sat on the living-room floor in front of the woodstove, reading a book.

"Gettin' better, Papa."

Ernie bent over and ruffled the boy's hair. "Glad to hear it." He glanced around the room. "Where's your sister?"

"When we got home from school, Grace said she was tired, so she went to her room to take a nap."

"Okay." Ernie squatted down beside his son. "How was school today? Did everything go okay?"

Andy shrugged. "Same as always."

"That's good."

"Think we can eat supper with Miss King again?"

Ernie stiffened. He wanted that, too. Fact was he'd give most anything to spend more time with Judith.

"Papa? Did ya hear what I said?" Andy persisted.

"Yeah, I heard."

"Can we ask her then?"

Ernie blew out his breath. "We'll have to wait and see."

Chapter 8

C hristmas was only a few days away, and an air of excitement had filled the school for the past week. Judith had dismissed her class nearly an hour ago and had almost finished cleaning the schoolhouse when she heard a *thump, thump* on the porch. Had one of the children forgotten the gift he'd made for his parents?

She rushed to the door, and when she opened it, a gust of chilly air blew in, sending shivers up her spine. To her surprise, no student waited on the porch. It was Ernie Snyder, and he stood beside a perfectly shaped pine tree that was nearly as tall as him. "I was on my way home from work and saw this growin' along one section of the canal. Thought you'd like it for the Christmas program," he mumbled, looking down at his snow-covered boots.

"Oh, Ernie, this is so nice. I wasn't sure if we would even have a tree, and it will certainly make the room look more festive."

He only nodded in reply.

"Are Grace and Andy with you?" Judith glanced into the schoolyard, thinking the children might be playing in the snow.

He shook his head. "Naw, they're at home."

She opened the door wider. "Please, bring it inside and come warm yourself by the woodstove."

Ernie brushed the snow off his jacket—the same threadbare one he'd been wearing since the canal closed for the winter. "I ain't so cold." He bounced the tree up and down and gave it a good shake before stepping inside. "Didn't wanna track too much snow into the schoolhouse."

Judith laughed and shut the door behind him. "This floor has gotten snow, mud, and all sorts of other things on it; I don't think a little bit more will hurt."

"Where do ya want the tree?" Ernie questioned.

"How about there?" Judith pointed to the far corner of the room. "We don't want it too close to the stove."

"No, that wouldn't be good." Ernie lifted the tree like it weighed no more than a baby and hauled it across the room. "Have ya got a bucket?"

"A bucket?" Judith placed both hands against her flushed cheeks. She didn't know why she felt so flustered whenever she was around Ernie, but being alone with him made her insides feel all quivery.

"Got to have somethin' to hold the tree upright," Ernie said. "It'll need some water so's it don't dry out."

"I–I suppose we could use the mop bucket I keep in the back room. I think it's big enough to do the job." Judith headed in that direction and returned a few minutes later. She handed Ernie the large metal bucket.

He set the tree inside, but when he let go, it teetered and almost fell over. He grabbed it before it hit the floor. "Guess I'm not thinkin' straight. We're gonna need some rocks in the bucket to hold the tree in place."

"There are plenty of rocks in the schoolyard, but they're

buried under the snow," Judith said with a frown.

"That's no problem." Ernie leaned the tree against the wall. Then he grabbed the bucket and headed out the door. Several minutes later, he returned. His face and hands were bright red, and Judith realized he wasn't wearing any gloves.

Ernie dumped the rocks onto the floor, picked up the tree, and positioned it in the middle of the bucket. "Would ya mind holdin' onto the tree, while I put the rocks in place?"

"No. . .no, not at all." Judith held the tree steady as, one by one, he dropped the rocks into the bucket.

"There, that oughta do it. You can let go now."

Judith eased her fingers off the trunk and stepped slowly away. Ernie was right; the tree stayed in place. "It looks good." She moved to one side and appraised their efforts. "Tomorrow the students can decorate it with paper chains and strings of popcorn."

Ernie added water to the bucket, then pointed to the floor, where he'd dumped the rocks. "Sorry 'bout the mess. If you'll tell me where ya keep the mop, I'll clean it up."

"Oh, that's all right. I was in the process of cleaning anyhow."

He glanced around the room. "Looks like you're purty well done."

She reached up to push aside a wayward strand of hair that had escaped her bun and nodded. "Yes, I was almost done, but I'll just mop up the mess and be on my way home."

Ernie opened his mouth, like he might argue with her, but then he clamped it shut and moved toward the door. Instead of opening it, however, he dragged the toe of his boot across the floor, making a scraping sound.

"Will you be free to come to the school program tomorrow evening?" she asked.

He nodded. "I'm aimin' to."

"I'm sure your children will be glad. Andy is one of the shepherds, and Grace has the part of an angel."

"So I heard."

Judith was tempted to open the door and order the man out so she could finish cleaning and have a chance to calm down before heading to the Jameses', but she knew that would be rude. Instead, she stood off to one side with her arms folded, waiting to see what he would do or say next.

Ernie finally grabbed hold of the doorknob. "Guess I'd best be gettin' home. The kids will start to worry if I ain't there soon." After a long pause, he added, "I'll be makin' Andy's favorite meal—fried potatoes and ham. Don't make it nearly as well as my wife used to, but it fills the hole." With that, he stuffed his hands into his jacket pockets and ambled out the door.

"Thanks for the tree," Judith called to his retreating form.

His only response was a backward wave.

She closed the door and leaned against it with a sigh. "That man is so hard to figure out. One thing I do know is he cares about his children."

❧

"You need to calm yourselves down some," Ernie said to his kids as they headed to the schoolhouse the following night for the program. "You two have been jumpin' around like a couple of squirrels ever since we left home."

"I'm scared I'll mess up my part," Andy told his father.

"Well, there's nothin' to be nervous about," Ernie asserted. "You've been practicin' your lines for weeks, and not once have ya messed up."

"Didn't have no audience at home," the boy muttered.

"You'll do fine, just wait and see."

"I ain't nervous," Grace put in. "But I am excited 'bout the candy Miss King is gonna give everyone after the play."

Ernie smiled. Judith certainly liked her pupils, and from what he could tell, they liked her, too.

By the time they got to the schoolhouse, Andy and Grace had calmed down. The room was full of parents—some who'd crammed into their children's desks—others who stood at the back of the room, prepared to watch the play.

"Where's all the kids?" Ernie asked his son.

"Must be in the coatroom. That's where Miss King said we was supposed to put our costumes on over our clothes."

"Guess you'd better get in there." Ernie found a place at the back of the room, and his children disappeared into the coatroom.

A short time later, Judith appeared wearing a long red skirt and a white blouse with lace around the cuffs. Ernie thought she'd never looked more beautiful, and he couldn't help but stare.

Judith welcomed everyone and introduced each child who had a speaking part. Next came the pageant, complete with nativity scene.

Ernie felt a sense of pride when his kids said their parts without missing a word. They might not be as smart or be dressed as well as some of the other students, but at least they hadn't done or said anything to make them look stupid.

All the parents seemed to enjoy the program, and afterward, during a time of refreshments, Ernie poured a glass of punch and handed it to his son. "Give this to your teacher, would ya?"

Andy's forehead wrinkled. "Why don't ya take it to her yourself, Papa?"

Ernie shook his head. "Naw. It'd be better comin' from you."

Andy shrugged, took the glass, and started across the room.

Ernie stood beside the Christmas tree, now decorated from top to bottom, and watched as the boy handed his teacher the punch. Judith smiled, said something to Andy, and then looked Ernie's way. He felt the heat of a blush creep up his neck and sweep onto his cheeks, so he quickly averted her gaze. Had Andy told his teacher the punch was his dad's idea? *Naw. My boy knows better than to say somethin' like that.*

Chapter 9

As the weeks moved on, Judith was pleased that the letter box continued to work well and that the children asked more questions about things pertaining to their education. However, she was troubled by some of the unsigned letters she had received. She suspected that one of her students might have a crush on her. She'd taken it lightly at first, answering each of those letters with some comment about her being glad the student liked her. The letter she'd gotten this morning, however, was a bit harder to answer. It read:

> *Dear Teacher:*
> *My heart beats like a hammer and my hands get all sweaty whenever you're near. If it were possible, I'd ask ya to marry me some day.*

Judith squinted at the letters on the page. She hadn't been able to match the handwriting to any of her students, but she figured whoever wrote the letter was probably not using the hand he normally wrote with. She'd thought for a while it could be Andy, since his arm had been in a sling for a few days. But Andy was better now and had been using his right hand for several weeks.

She needed to call a halt to this before it went any further, so she picked up her pencil and wrote the following reply:

Dear Student:

I'm flattered that you think I'm beautiful and wish you could marry me. However, I'm too old for you, and I'm your teacher, not your girlfriend. I think it would be best if you only wrote letters with questions about things we are learning in class.

Miss King

The *splat* of a snowball hit the front window, and Judith knew it was time for the students to come in from their morning recess. She left her desk to open the front door, and a blast of frigid air hit her full in the face. How could the children stand to play in such cold weather?

Judith rang the bell, and her pupils filed into the room, talking, laughing, and shaking snow off their coats, hats, and mittens. After putting their wraps inside the coatroom, they took their seats.

Judith scrutinized the desks and realized one child was missing. Where was Grace Snyder? Had she gone to the outhouse or not heard the bell?

She opened the front door and peered into the schoolyard. Several feet from the porch Grace was sprawled in the snow, moving her arms and legs up and down.

"Recess is over and you need to come inside," Judith called to the child.

Grace hopped up and raced over to another untouched snowy area. "In a minute, Teacher. I'm makin' twin snow angels."

"You can do that at noon or during afternoon recess."

Grace folded her arms and pouted. "I wanna do it now."

The child had never carried on like this before, and Judith was taken by surprise. "I'm only going to say this once more. Come inside."

Grace shook her head. "Not 'til the snow angels are done."

Unmindful of her long skirt or the fact that she had no wrap on, Judith trudged through the snow and took hold of Grace's arm. "Since you disobeyed, you'll have to stay after school and clean the blackboard."

Grace burst into tears. "I don't wanna do that!"

"Then you should have come inside when I asked you to."

The child sniffled all the way to the schoolhouse and even after she had removed her coat, hat, and mittens.

Judith knew she couldn't allow any of her students to talk back or defy the rules. Hopefully by tomorrow, Grace would realize that her teacher was also her friend.

❧

"You've gotta go to the schoolhouse with me tomorrow mornin', Papa!" Grace shouted when Ernie arrived home from work and found his children huddled in front of the woodstove.

He bent over and scooped the little girl into his arms. "What's all this about me needin' to go to the schoolhouse?"

"I want ya to talk with Teacher. She's mean, and I don't like her no more."

Ernie lifted his brows. "What's the problem?"

"Aw, she's just mad 'cause Miss King made her stay after school and clean the blackboard," Andy said, stepping up to his father.

Ernie was puzzled. Grace had never been in trouble with the teacher before. In fact, ever since she'd received the sack of candy from Judith after the Christmas program, all Grace could talk about was how sweet her teacher was. "Tell me what happened, Daughter."

Tears pooled in the girl's blue eyes. "She said I couldn't make snow angels."

Ernie clenched his teeth. Why would anyone deny a child the right to make an angel in the snow? This didn't sound like something Judith would do, but he needed to find out.

He placed Grace on the floor. "I'll take you and your brother to school tomorrow, and we'll get to the bottom of this."

Judith was surprised when she saw Ernie walk up the snowy path toward the schoolhouse with Grace and Andy at his side. He hadn't accompanied them in quite a while, and she wondered if he'd come today because it was snowing hard again and he felt concern for their safety.

She lifted her hand in a friendly wave. "Good morning, Ernie. Good morning, children."

"'Mornin'," Ernie mumbled as Grace and Andy clomped up the steps and slipped past Judith. "Can I. . .uh. . .have a word with ya?"

"Certainly. Would you like to step inside where it's warmer?"

He shuffled his boots across the frozen snow, and it crunched beneath his weight. "Guess it wouldn't be good to keep ya out here in the cold, but what I got to say probably shouldn't be said in front of the kids."

"Why don't we talk inside the coatroom?" she suggested.

"That's fine."

Judith stepped into the schoolhouse and led the way to the coatroom, near the back of the building. "I need to ask one of the older students to keep an eye on the class," she told Ernie. "If you'd like to wait inside, I'll only be a minute."

Ernie shrugged and offered a quick nod.

Judith leaned over Beth's desk and asked the girl to read a story to the children.

"Sure, Miss King."

"Thank you, Beth." She smiled and hurried to the coatroom, where she found Ernie pacing between the coatrack and the shelves where the letter boxes sat.

"What did you wish to speak with me about?" she asked.

He twisted his stocking cap between his fingers and cleared his throat. "Grace told me ya kept her after school yesterday. Said it was 'cause she wanted to make snow angels."

"That's true."

"You got somethin' against snow angels, Miss King?"

Judith frowned. Miss King? Why had Ernie reverted to calling her Miss King?

"I have nothing against snow angels, Mr. Snyder," she said, emphasizing his last name. "However, your daughter wanted to make them after recess was over."

He stared at the floor. "She was wrong to disobey, but she's only a little girl. Don't ya think ya could have been a bit easier on her? I mean, forcin' her to stay after school to clean the blackboard made her think ya don't like her."

Judith folded her arms and released a sigh. "I care about all my students, but I can't make exceptions for anyone who disobeys the rules."

Ernie looked up again, and the intensity of his gaze sent chills down her back. "It's been hard for my kids to grow up without a mother, can't ya see that?"

She nodded, as tears filled her eyes and memories from the past flooded her mind. "I understand better than you know, for my own mother died when I was ten years old."

His forehead wrinkled, and he reached up to rub the bridge of his nose. "Sorry. I didn't know."

Judith took a few steps forward, bringing herself close enough to the man that she could feel the warmth of his breath. She shivered.

"Ya cold?"

"No, no. I'm fine." She rubbed her hands briskly over her arms. "Ernie, I'm sure you love your children."

"Ya got that right."

"But you can't baby them. They need to know there are consequences when they do something wrong."

"I discipline my kids when they do somethin' bad." He lifted his chin. "But I don't think playin' in the snow a few minutes longer'n you would've liked was such a terrible thing. You was wrong, Miss King!"

Judith's defenses rose higher. Was this man questioning her ability to teach the students right from wrong? He had said he was a Christian and had taught his children memory verses. He'd been going to church fairly regularly, too. So why was he talking to her this way? Maybe Ernie Snyder wasn't the man she'd thought him to be.

She blew out her breath. "I was hired to teach here, so until the school board says otherwise, it's up to me to decide when and how to discipline."

"We'll see 'bout that!" He slapped his hat on his head and stormed out of the coatroom. Judith heard the front door slam shut and knew he had gone.

What have I done? She placed both hands against her hot cheeks. *Ernie will probably never speak to me again, and he might even decide to pull his children from school before spring. I'd better spend some time praying about this matter.*

Chapter 10

Judith had looked for Ernie at church the following Sunday, hoping to apologize for their disagreement, but he wasn't there, and neither were his children. Grace and Andy showed up for school on Monday morning, and for that, she felt relief.

All weekend she'd been reading her Bible and praying about the situation. She had asked the Lord's forgiveness for snapping at Ernie, but now it was time to offer an apology to Grace's father.

While her students read to themselves, Judith decided to write Ernie a note. She opened her desk drawer, took out a piece of paper and a pencil, then wrote the following message:

Dear Ernie:

I've been thinking about the discussion we had last week concerning Grace and her refusal to come inside after recess. I'm sorry for our difference of opinion. I shouldn't have spoken to you in such a disagreeable tone.

I care about all of my students. When I kept Grace after school, I was only doing what I felt was best. But as her parent, you had the right to ask me about it.

Your children speak highly of you, and I'm glad you're teaching them God's ways, for His Word is our best teacher.

I realize it must be difficult for you to raise your children without a wife. From personal experience, I know it's hard for them to be without their mother. Grace and Andy are fortunate to have such a caring, loving father.

I hope you will accept my apology, and I look forward to hearing from you soon.

Sincerely,
Judith King

Judith folded the paper and set it aside. When school was dismissed, she would give the note to Andy and ask him to deliver it to his father. By tomorrow morning, she hoped to receive a reply from Ernie.

Long after his children went to bed, Ernie paced the living-room floor, thinking, praying, and worrying. He'd read and reread Judith's letter so many times he knew some of the phrases by heart.

He stopped in front of the stove and added two more chunks of wood—not because he was cold, but because he hoped the action would take his mind off Judith King. It wasn't bad enough he was an ignorant canaler who was at a loss for words whenever he was with the woman, but now he'd lost his temper in front of her. He should go to the school and apologize in person, but how could he face her after the things he'd said?

"I sure can't write the teacher no letter," Ernie mumbled as he shut the door on the stove. "She'd really think I'm a dunce if

I did somethin' like that."

He moved to the window and stared out at the night sky. Several inches of snow remained on the ground; he could see it glistening in the moonlight. Soon spring would be here, and then he could return to the canal. Things would be better once his kids were out of school. He'd have less chance of running into Judith and getting all tongue-tied and squirrelly.

Ernie hadn't known Judith very long, but during the time they had spent together, he'd seen her patience and kindness toward his children. Andy and Grace often came home from school with stories of the interesting things their teacher had said or done. It was evident that Judith cared about her students and enjoyed being a teacher. He knew that included disciplining when it became necessary.

Whenever Ernie had taken his children to church, he'd watched Judith from a distance. She listened intently to the preacher and always had her Bible open during the reading of the Scriptures. There was a look of peace on her face as she sat in the pew singing praises to God. It was a look he could get used to seeing on a daily basis.

Ernie groaned. "I need to apologize to her."

❦

"You got a letter for me to give the teacher?" Andy asked his father the following morning.

Ernie shook his head. "Nope."

"But she wrote you yesterday, and I thought—"

"This ain't none of your business." Ernie gave Andy a pat on the head. "I'll handle things with Miss King in my own way."

"I could sneak the note into the letter box, so the other kids wouldn't know, and then—"

"No."

"Okay." Andy grabbed his lunch pail and turned to face his sister. "Ready, Grace?"

"I'm comin'." Grace gave Ernie a hug and scampered out the door.

"Have a good day at school," Ernie called to his children.

A few minutes later, he donned his coat, hat, and gloves, then headed out the door. He still hadn't decided how to go about apologizing to Judith, but he'd worry about that later. Right now there was some ice waiting to be cut.

Judith stood at the front door as her students filed into the room. She smiled at Andy and waited expectantly to see if he would hand her a letter. When the boy headed for the coatroom without a word, she began to worry. Maybe Andy hadn't delivered her note to his father. Then again, maybe he had, but Ernie hadn't sent a reply.

Judith didn't wish to embarrass the boy in front of the others, so she waited until morning recess to broach the subject. Andy made it easy for her when he was the last one out the door.

"May I speak to you a moment?" she asked him.

He turned around. "What about? Have I done somethin' wrong?"

She shook her head and motioned him back inside. "I want to ask you a question."

Andy leaned against the nearest desk and stared up at her.

"I was wondering if you delivered my letter to your father yesterday?"

He nodded.

"Did he write me a note in return?"

Andy shook his head.

"Did he ask you to tell me anything this morning?"

"Nope. Just said to have a good day at school."

Judith sighed. If Ernie hadn't sent a note or given Andy a verbal message, he must still be angry with her. Was he planning to speak with the school board about the rules she'd made? Would he try to get her fired?

"Is that all, Teacher?" Andy asked. "I'd like to get outside and help with the snow fort some of the kids are makin'."

"Yes, that's all I had to say. Run along, and tell the others I said to be careful. The snow started to melt yesterday, but now that it's turned cold again, it will probably be slippery."

"I'm used to walkin' in slippery places. Once the ice thaws and the canals open again, there'll be mud and lots of puddles along the towpath."

Judith shuddered. Just thinking about the poor boy trudging up and down the towpath six days a week made her feel sad. He was too young to be put to work like that. And then there was Grace left to run around Ernie's boat with only the supervision of an elderly man.

"Do be careful, Andy," she said as he stepped onto the porch.

"I will."

She shut the door and moved over to the potbellied stove. The room had cooled some, and it was time to add more wood to the fire.

❧

On Friday morning, Ernie made a decision. "I'll be walkin' with you to school today," he announced to his children after breakfast.

Andy looked surprised. "How come, Papa?"

"Need to speak with your teacher."

Grace stared at him with questioning eyes. "Am I in trouble again?"

72

He reached across the table and took her hand. " 'Course not. I need to say a few things to Miss King."

"Okay." Grace picked up her spoon and delved into the bowl of cornmeal mush set before her.

A short time later, Ernie found himself on the steps of the schoolhouse one more time, asking the teacher if he could have a word with her. At first, Judith looked undecided, but then she gave him a nod. "Come inside."

"In the coatroom again?" he asked, looking in that direction.

"That's probably a good idea."

Ernie waited until Judith instructed the class on what they should do in her absence, then he followed her to the back room. Once inside, he had second thoughts about his mission. Being in such cramped quarters with her standing so close, he could smell the sweet scent of the soap she'd probably used this morning. His knees began to knock.

"What did you wish to speak with me about?" she asked.

He shuffled his feet a couple of times, then decided to plunge ahead. "I got your note."

Her only reply was a brief nod.

"I. . .uh. . .want ya to know that there's no hard feelin's."

She smiled. "I'm glad."

"And. . .I–I'm sorry for spoutin' off the last time we talked. I had no call to get so upset."

Judith opened her mouth as if to say something, but Ernie hurried on before he lost his nerve. "You were right about Grace. She shouldn't have disobeyed the rules. She deserved to be punished, too." There, that felt better.

She extended her hand. "I'm glad you understand."

When his fingers curled around hers, it felt like a bolt of lightning had shot up his arm. He pulled away quickly, and

Judith did the same. Then she lowered her hand and smoothed her long gingham dress as though there might be wrinkles. "Thank you for coming, Ernie. I know you have a job to do, so I mustn't keep you any longer."

"No, it's me who shouldn't be takin' your time. You've got a class waitin'." He moved toward the door but turned back around. "You're a good teacher, and I'm glad my kids have been in your class this winter. I'm sure they'll miss ya come spring."

"I wish they didn't have to drop out of school when the canal opens again," she said. "They'll miss so much and will probably have to repeat the same grade when they return next winter."

He shrugged. "I only made it through the fourth grade, and I'm managin' okay. Besides, Andy will be walkin' the mules for a few more years, and after that he'll work on the boat with me. Sooner or later, the boat will be his to captain. He don't need much schoolin' for that."

Judith's wrinkled forehead told him she didn't agree, but she never offered a word of argument.

"Have a nice day," Ernie said, turning toward the coatroom door.

"You, too."

Ernie grasped the knob and gave it a yank, but the door didn't open. He tried again. Nothing happened. "It seems to be locked," he mumbled.

Judith rushed forward and pulled on the doorknob, but it didn't budge for her, either. She pounded on the door. "Somebody, please open this!"

Not a sound could be heard, and the door remained firmly shut.

"I'll bet one of those troublemakers who sits near the back

of the room decided to lock us in," she said.

Ernie bent down and squinted, as he peered through the keyhole. "Can't see a thing. The key must be in there."

Judith clucked her tongue. "Whoever did this will be cleaning the blackboard until school lets out for the summer." She folded her arms and released a puff of air that lifted her curly bangs right off her forehead.

Ernie fought the temptation to touch one of those curls, wondering if Judith's shiny blond hair was as soft as it appeared. Her pinched expression and squinted eyes made him want to laugh. She looked awful cute when she was mad.

"I wish I knew what I'd done to make one of my students angry enough to lock us in," Judith said.

Ernie rubbed his forehead. He couldn't imagine anyone wanting to get even with her. Judith was a good teacher, and he'd come to realize that her firmness with Grace had been necessary. The child had gotten over her anger, so he was sure she wasn't responsible for this.

The key rattled in the hole, and Ernie and Judith bent toward it at the same time. Their heads collided.

"Ouch!" they said in unison.

"You okay?" he asked, reaching up to feel her forehead. The minute his fingers came in contact with Judith's skin, he wished he hadn't touched her. An unfamiliar jolt shot through him, and his face grew hot and sweaty.

Her eyes were wide as she slowly nodded. "I–I'm fine. How about you?"

"I've got a hard head. I'm sure there ain't no damage."

Suddenly, the door swung open, and Grace rushed into the room. "It was Andy who done it!"

Ernie stepped out of the coatroom and sought out his son.

Andy sat at his desk with his head down. "Sorry, Papa," he mumbled. "I just wanted to make sure you and Miss King stayed in there long enough to patch things up."

Ernie could hardly believe his own son had been the one to lock the door. "Everything's fine between me and the teacher," he muttered, "so the only thing you did is to get yourself in trouble. And now you're gonna have chalk dust on your clothes for a long time to come."

Chapter 11

As she stood on the schoolhouse porch, saying good-bye to her canal students on a Friday afternoon in late March, Judith felt as if her heart would break. She was going to miss them all, especially Grace and Andy, for whom she had formed an attachment that went beyond teacher to pupil.

Judith thought about Ernie and how she would miss seeing him at church and various community functions. Now that he was hauling coal up the canal again, it wasn't likely she would see him much at all. He was a good father, and she knew his children belonged with him. But the thought of Andy returning to the hard work of mule driving, Grace running around the boat with little supervision, and the two of them going without schooling for so many months made her sad.

If only there was a way they could receive their education during the spring and fall. Judith turned toward the door, knowing it was time to clean the blackboard and secure the schoolhouse for the weekend. She knew the logical thing was to commit Ernie and his children to the Lord.

As Ernie guided his boat past Parryville, his thoughts went to

Judith King. What was she doing right now, and did she ever think of him?

"Why would she?" he muttered. "Even if she knew how I felt, she'd never take an interest in someone like me."

"You talkin' to yourself, boss?" Jeb called from the center of the boat, where he stood in front of the small cookstove.

"Yeah, guess I was."

Jeb grunted and kept stirring the pot of stew he'd started some time ago.

Ernie glanced at the shoreline, and his breath caught in his throat. Judith sat under a tree not far from the towpath. Her long blond hair lay across her shoulders like a ray of golden sunlight. Andy approached her and halted the mules. Any other time Ernie would have hollered at the boy to keep moving, but he was as anxious to see his kid's schoolteacher as they were.

Judith joined Andy in the middle of the towpath, and a short time later, Ernie had the boat docked near the shore. He'd no more than set the gangplank in place, when Grace bounded off the boat and rushed over to Judith. "Teacher! Teacher! It's mighty nice to see ya!"

Judith bent over and gave Grace a hug. "I'm happy to see you and Andy, too." She smiled at Ernie, who now stood beside his children. "Hello, Ernie."

He swallowed around his Adam's apple and nodded. "How have ya been?"

She pushed a windblown strand of hair away from her face. "I'm fine. How are you and the children?"

He wiped his forehead with the back of his shirtsleeve, wondering if he looked as dirty and sweaty as he felt. "Fine. We're all fine. Keepin' busy, as usual."

"Papa's hopin' to make enough money so's me and Grace

can have new boots for school come winter," Andy interjected.

Judith smiled. "That's good. It's always nice to have something new."

"What are you doin' down here by the canal?" Grace asked, voicing the question that had been on the tip of Ernie's tongue.

"I thought it would be nice to enjoy a Saturday afternoon near the water. I brought along a picnic lunch and have been watching the boats go by." She motioned to the wicker basket sitting on the blanket where she had been sitting.

"Wish we could have a picnic," Grace said with a pout. "I get tired of stayin' on the boat all the time."

"Yeah," Andy agreed. "It'd be awful nice to eat somethin' besides Jeb's funny-tastin' soups and gritty stews."

"What do you do on the boat?" Judith asked, touching Grace's shoulder.

Grace wrinkled her nose. "Ain't much to do 'cept play with the corn-husk dolly Papa gave me. Sometimes I just watch the other boats go past."

"Isn't, not ain't," Judith corrected.

Ernie shifted from one leg to the other. *I say ain't all the time. She probably thinks I'm really a dunce.*

"You still usin' the letter box, Teacher?" Andy asked, changing the subject.

She nodded. "We are, but there aren't as many unsigned letters as there used to be."

Ernie wiped his sweaty palms on the sides of his trousers. "Well, guess we'd best be goin'. Won't get that load of coal hauled up to Easton if we keep on jawin'."

Judith's eyes were downcast, and there was a tiny crease between her brows. She was no doubt missing Andy and Grace and probably wished they could be in school all year.

"Aw, Papa, do we hafta go so soon?" Grace whined. "I'd like to visit with Teacher awhile."

"Same here," Andy agreed.

Judith placed both hands on top of the children's heads. "You'd best do as your father says. Maybe I'll see you sometime this summer." She turned to face Ernie. "Might you be coming to church in Parryville soon?"

He shrugged. "Don't rightly know. Guess it all depends on where we stop on a Saturday night."

"I understand."

Grace gave her teacher another hug, then trudged back to the boat.

"Be careful to stay away from the edge," Judith called to the child.

"I will."

"Between Jeb and me, we keep an eye on the girl."

"Yes, I'm sure you do, but—"

Ernie gave his son a pat on the back. "Get them mules movin', Son. They've had a long enough rest." He lifted his hand. "See ya, Judith."

When school was out for the summer, Judith often went for walks along the towpath, where she watched the boats and hoped to see Ernie and his children go by. Sometimes, on hot, muggy days like this one, she would take off her shoes and wade in the cool water. It was also a good time to read her Bible, pray, and contemplate the future.

Judith stopped walking long enough to watch a pair of ducks settle on the water.

" 'Male and female created he them,' " she quoted from Genesis. "Will I ever find a mate, or will I spend the rest of my days as an old maid?"

Judith moved on, wondering if God might have something else in mind for her besides teaching at the schoolhouse. *I'm in love with Ernie and care deeply for his children, but he's given me no indication that he feels the same way toward me.* She sniffed and forced her tears to remain in check. *Dear Lord, help me learn to be content.*

❦

"Simmer down and quit your runnin'," Ernie hollered at his daughter as she scampered from the bow of the boat to the stern and back again. He glanced around, hoping Jeb would find something for her to do, but the elderly man was nowhere in sight. "Must have gone below to get somethin'," he muttered. "He'd better not be sleepin' on the job again."

Ernie guided the boat through the locks, glad when it went well and the mules cooperated. It would have been easier if Jeb had been on deck to keep an eye out for other boats and be sure they weren't getting too close.

They'd only gone a short way past the locks when Ernie heard a splash. Thinking it must be some kid throwing a rock into the canal, he continued to steer the boat as it moved forward.

"Help! Papa, help me!"

Ernie froze.

"Get her, Papa; Grace is drownin'!" Andy shouted from the towpath.

Ernie rushed to the side of the boat and looked over. He saw nothing but the swirling waters and a tree branch bobbing up and down.

"She's over there!" Andy hollered, pointing to the water splashing against the bow of the boat.

Ernie made a beeline in that direction and dove into the

chilly canal. He spotted Grace a few feet away, her arms pawing the water, her legs kicking frantically. Down she went, then up again, gurgling, screaming, panting for air.

He reached her seconds before she went under again and wrapped his arm around her chest. Several minutes later they were on the shore, Grace gasping for breath, Ernie thanking God he'd gotten to his daughter in time.

Once they were on the boat again, Ernie made sure Grace changed into dry clothes and went to bed. Then he headed for Jeb's sleeping quarters and found the man sprawled on his bunk, fast asleep.

Ernie grimaced and shook Jeb's shoulders. "Wake up!"

His helper's eyes popped open, and he released a noisy yawn. "What's the matter, boss? How come you're all wet?"

Ernie quickly explained about Grace falling overboard, and Jeb's face blanched. "It's my fault. If I'd been up there watchin' her instead of takin' a nap, she never would have fallen off the boat."

Ernie couldn't argue with that, but yelling at his helper wouldn't change what had happened.

Jeb sat up and swung his legs over the edge of the bunk. "It's time for me to put myself out to pasture."

Ernie's eyebrows lifted. "What are you talkin' about?"

"I should have stayed in Easton with my daughter and not returned to the canal this spring. I'm gettin' too old to be watchin' out for a little one while I try to cook, clean, and keep an eye out for boats that might be comin' ahead." Jeb shook his head. "Ya need someone younger'n smarter'n me. What ya really need is a wife."

Ernie stood there a few seconds, letting Jeb's comments run through his befuddled brain. Finally, with a feeling of determination, he tapped the elderly man on the shoulder and said, "I think ya might be right 'bout some of that. And I believe it's time for me to take action."

🐝

"Teacher, there's somebody here to see you!"

Judith looked up from where she sat on the sofa, darning a pair of long black stockings. "Who is it, Melody?" she asked the preacher's daughter.

"It's that canal boatman."

"Who?"

"Andy and Grace's pa."

Judith's heart thudded in her chest, as she stood on trembling legs. Had Ernie come to pay her a call? *Of course not, don't be ridiculous.* She went to the door and found him standing on the porch with his arms crossed. "Hello, Ernie. I'm surprised to see you."

He rocked back and forth on the heels of his boots. "I. . . um. . .that is. . ."

"What is it?" she prompted.

"The other day Grace fell overboard and almost drowned."

Judith gasped and covered her mouth with the back of her hand. "Is she all right?"

Ernie nodded. "My helper fell asleep and wasn't watchin' her. Now he's plannin' to move to Easton to live with his daughter, and that leaves me with no one to mind Grace." He stared at the porch. "You were right about her needin' more supervision."

Judith didn't know how best to reply, so she just stood there.

"The thing is. . .I. . .uh. . .well, I think we should get married!"

"What?" Judith felt the blood drain from her face. Had she heard him right? Had Ernie just asked her to marry him?

"I said, I think. . .I mean, would ya marry me?" he stammered.

Judith grasped the doorknob, feeling as though she could topple over. She had wished so long that someone might propose to her, but she never thought it would happen, and certainly not like this! What about love? What about romance? Could she marry Ernie simply because he needed a mother for his children? He obviously didn't love her, or he would have said so. And what about her teaching job? If she were to marry, she would have to give that up. No, it was impossible, and she told him so.

He blanched. "I thought you cared about my kids."

"I do."

"Then what's the problem?"

Judith fought the desire to tell Ernie how much she loved him, but that would be the worst thing she could do. "I hope you're able to find a suitable replacement for Jeb—someone who will be able to watch out for Grace." She gathered the edge of her skirt, turned, and rushed inside.

Chapter 12

After a sleepless night, Judith wasn't sure she could go to church the following morning. As she stood in front of her bedroom mirror, she realized that her eyes were rimmed with red, her cheeks looked puffy, and her nose was sore from having blown it so much. When Ernie left yesterday, she'd gone to her room and cried until no more tears would come.

How could the man expect her to marry him when there was no love involved? She knew he needed someone to cook, clean, and watch out for Grace, but surely he could hire a young, able-bodied helper to do those things.

"Then why did he ask me to marry him?" she moaned.

Judith's gaze fell on her Bible lying on the dressing table. It was never good to begin the day without reading God's Word. She picked up the Bible, took a seat on her bed, and opened it to Proverbs. One particular verse seemed to jump right out at her. " 'Trust in the Lord with all thine heart; and lean not unto thine own understanding. In all thy ways acknowledge him, and he shall direct thy paths.' "

Judith drew in a deep breath. "I know I should trust You in all things, Lord," she prayed, "but sometimes it's hard to do. Could it be that You might have something else in mind for me other than teaching? Would it be better for Grace and Andy if I were to marry Ernie? Could it be Your will for me to be his wife?"

She moved back to the mirror. "I know I'm not beautiful, but perhaps in time Ernie could come to care for me the way I do him."

Judith remembered hearing Pastor James's wife tell her daughters that real beauty comes from the inside, not the outward appearance. Perhaps if she allowed God to work through her and set a good example to Ernie's children, he might learn to appreciate her inner beauty.

☙

Judith sat on the grassy banks of the canal, waiting, watching, hoping Ernie's boat would come around the bend. She had been coming here every day for the last week and hadn't spotted him. In the past he'd come by Parryville about the same time of day. Maybe he had been delayed. She knew there were often pileups at the locks, and sometimes breaks in the canal occurred.

"Or maybe he changed his schedule, and I've missed him." She lifted her face to the sun, leaned back on her elbows, and closed her eyes. "Heavenly Father, I'm trusting You to direct my paths. If it's Your will for me to speak with Ernie, then he will come by at the right time."

A sense of peace settled over Judith, and she knew what she must do. When summer was over and the children of Parryville returned to the one-room schoolhouse, would Judith still be their teacher? Her fate was in God's hands.

☙

For the last week, Ernie had been held up a few miles outside of Mauch Chunk, waiting for a break in the canal to be repaired. Normally he would have been upset about the time lost, but the days of waiting had given him time to think and pray—something he should have done before asking Judith to marry him.

When the boats were finally given the go-ahead and they rounded the bend near Parryville, Ernie's heart skipped a beat. Judith sat on the grassy banks, her face lifted to the sky. She looked like an angel.

Ernie maneuvered the boat toward land. "Halt the mules!" he shouted to Andy.

Judith must have heard him, for she stood and rushed toward the boat.

"Stay put. I'll be right back," Ernie said to Grace, who stood next to the rails, hollering and waving at her teacher.

Ernie leaped over the side and waded to shore, not caring that his trousers and boots were getting wet. Before Judith could open her mouth, he reached into his shirt pocket and pulled out the note he had written. He handed it to her and took a step back.

"What's this?" she asked, tipping her head, a curious expression on her face.

"I have trouble speakin' what's on my heart, so I thought I could say things better this way."

❦

With trembling fingers, Judith unfolded the piece of paper and read Ernie's note.

Dear Judith:
  I'm sorry for the dumb things I said the day I asked ya to marry me. I got all tongue-tied and couldn't say everything on my mind. I want us to get married but not just 'cause my kids need a mom. You're the sweetest, purtiest woman I know, and I love ya.
  I ain't much to look at, and I don't have much education,

but I'd sure be pleased if you was to become my wife.

Love,
Ernie

Judith stared at the letter, tears clouding her vision. Ernie loved her and thought she was pretty. It was more than she could fathom. She blinked the tears away and squinted. *I recognize this handwriting. I've seen it before.* Then a light dawned, and realization set in. "Ernie, have you written to me on other occasions?"

He nodded.

"Did you put some notes in the letter box at school?"

He shook his head.

"No?" Maybe she was wrong. Maybe the handwriting wasn't the same as the anonymous letters she'd received last winter from a secret admirer.

"Papa wrote the letters, but it was me who put 'em in the letter box," Andy spoke up.

Judith stared at the boy, too stunned to say a word.

Ernie stepped forward and took her hand. "I'm sorry for deceivin' ya, but I didn't have the nerve to say those things to your face. Thought ya might think I was dumber'n dirt, and that I was bein' too forward."

Judith smiled. "Oh, Ernie, do you know how I have longed to hear such words?" She waved the letter in front of his face. "You're not dumb, and I would be honored to be your wife."

He looked surprised. "Really?"

She nodded. "I've come to love you as well."

"Yippee!" Grace hollered as she scampered over the side of the boat and plodded through the water.

When the child reached Judith's side, Judith gave her a hug. "I love you and your brother, too."

Andy grinned from ear to ear, but then his expression sobered. "If ya marry Papa, will ya still be our teacher?"

Judith slowly shook her head. If she married Ernie it would mean giving up her teaching position, but she felt this was what God wanted her to do.

Ernie snapped his fingers. "Say, I've got an idea."

"What is it?" she asked.

"As we're goin' up and down the canal, whenever we stop for the night, maybe you could give Grace and Andy some lessons—and any other kids whose folks work the canals. That way they won't get behind in their schoolin'."

"I think that's a wonderful idea," she said with a smile.

Ernie cleared his throat. "Uh, Andy, why don't ya unhitch the mules and tie 'em to a tree? Then ya can take Grace back to the boat, so's your teacher and me can make some plans."

Andy grinned up at his father. "Okay."

Once the children were on the boat, Ernie led Judith to a clump of trees a short distance away. There, under a canopy of leafy maple branches, he drew her into his arms and kissed her so tenderly, she thought she might swoon.

Judith closed her eyes and leaned against Ernie's muscular chest. "I thank the Lord for bringing you and your children into my life. Through His Word, God showed me that I need to trust Him in all things."

"I love ya, dear Teacher," Ernie murmured.

"And I love you."

WANDA E. BRUNSTETTER

Wanda E. Brunstetter lives in Central Washington with her husband Richard who is a pastor. They have been married forty-two years and have two grown children and six grandchildren. Wanda is a professional ventriloquist and puppeteer, and she and her husband enjoy doing programs for children of all ages. Wanda's greatest joy as a Christian author is to hear from a reader that something she wrote has touched that person's heart or helped them in some special way.

Wanda has written eleven novels with Barbour Publishing's **Heartsong Presents** line, five novellas, and an Amish romance novel, *The Storekeeper's Daughter*—a bestseller! Wanda believes the Amish people's simple lifestyle and commitment to God can be a reminder of something we all need.

Visit her web page at: www.wandabrunstetter.com.

Prairie Schoolmarm

by JoAnn A. Grote

Dedication

For Vicci and Joey Danens,
two special children who are wonderful
teachers in my own life.
For my relatives who show their commitment to,
and love for, children through teaching:
Jody Kvanli Capehart, Fran Olsen Strommer,
and Heather Adamson Olsen.
And for Sophia (Sophie) Olsen Fletcher.
Welcome to the family, little one!

*I can do all things through Christ
which strengtheneth me.*
PHILIPPIANS 4:13 KJV

Dear Reader,

I grew up in a small town on the edge of the Minnesota prairie.

The history of Scandinavian settlers has always intrigued me, as I've Scandinavian ancestors who immigrated to Minnesota in the late 1800s. Recently I moved to a farmhouse built in the 1880s on the Minnesota prairie. I love it here! Just out of sight from our home is an old one-room schoolhouse that children trodded across the prairie to attend many years ago.

Painted blackboards such as the one in *Prairie Schoolmarm* were not uncommon in early prairie schoolhouses. A one-room schoolhouse not far from my present home used such a blackboard well into the 1930s.

One of my favorite true stories of nineteenth-century children on the Minnesota prairie took place in the 1870s in the county next to the one where I grew up. A group of farm boys desperately wanted an education, but there was no school close enough for them to attend. They reclaimed an abandoned homesteader's shack, rebuilding it themselves. Their determination was my inspiration behind Talif's plan in *Prairie Schoolmarm*. It also inspired a schoolhouse reclaimed by boys in my **Heartsong Presents** novel *Unfolding Heart*, which has been reissued in the collection titled *Minnesota*. I'm sure no teacher ever had more committed students than the teacher blessed to teach those boys.

Working with the other authors in the *Schoolhouse Brides* collection was a special blessing. Yvonne Lehman has been a friend for years. She gave me advice on the manuscript, which in 1993 became my first published book, *The Sure Promise*. Colleen Reece has been a friend and mentor for over ten years, though we've never met in person. I've also never met Wanda Brunstetter, though we've become friends through e-mail. I admire the work of all three women. They are a joy to work with, and I am honored to have a story included in this collection with them.

—*JoAnn*

Chapter 1

May 1871

Marin Nilsson leaned against the ship rail, turned her face into the May winds, and spoke in Swedish to her older sister, Elsbet. "There it is—the United States. I'd begun to think we'd never see it."

Elsbet's gaze rested on the nearing shore, but Marin could see no joy in her sister's blue eyes.

The lack of expression cut into Marin's heart. Would Elsbet's pain last the rest of her life? Two years had passed since her fiancé, Anton, left for America with the promise to send for her when he'd saved enough money for her passage. Two years since Elsbet had word from him. One year had passed since the news came through friends that he'd married a young woman he'd met in the new land. In the year between, Marin had watched Elsbet's joy and her faith in Anton's love slip slowly into fear—fear he'd been hurt or killed. She rejected speculation from friends and relatives that Anton had abandoned her, as so many men who emigrated had abandoned fiancées, wives, and families in Sweden.

At first, Marin was relieved when news came of Anton's marriage. Perhaps now, she thought, Elsbet would forget him and find someone new. Instead, Elsbet wrapped herself in her pain, in her longing for the love in which she'd believed so strongly. It seemed to Marin that rather than recover from the loss, her sister died a little more each day.

I'll never give a man my heart, Marin promised herself. *Not if I live to be one hundred. When Moder and Fader get old and die, Elsbet and I will take care of each other. Better two old maids than two women with broken hearts.*

Marin had made the same promise almost every day for the last year. Each day her resolve grew greater as the light in Elsbet's eyes failed to return.

"Maybe her heart will heal in America," their mother had said. "Plenty of young Swedish men are there looking for brides."

Marin wasn't so certain America held the remedy.

A young man's wide, smiling face slipped into Marin's view, pushing away her memories. The wind caught at his blond hair as he leaned against the rail on the other side of Elsbet. His gaze met Marin's. "Hello." He addressed the sisters in the lilting language of their homeland. "Exciting, isn't it? Soon we'll walk on American soil."

Elsbet ignored him.

Marin pulled back slightly, dropped an invisible veil over her eyes, and made her voice cool. "Yes, it is exciting." This wasn't the first time Talif Siverson had attempted to start a conversation with her during the crossing. She'd politely rebuffed each effort. It wasn't as though he was a family friend. He wasn't even from the same part of Sweden as the Nilsson family.

She'd noticed him before he approached her the first time, noticed him before they boarded. His handsome face beneath the wide-brimmed, brown felt hat and his gaze filled with excitement at the prospect before him had drawn her attention more than once. *It's natural that a good-looking man should catch a woman's attention,* she assured herself. *It doesn't mean I want to know him better.*

Talif made another attempt. "Maybe we'll see each other in the new land. Where is your family planning to settle?"

"Minnesota," Marin replied, though she was certain Talif already knew the answer. She'd seen him talking with her father and brothers.

"That's where I'll be homesteading. Where in Minnesota is your family headed?"

"Mankato. Our family will stay another family while Fader looks for land."

Talif's eyes brightened. "That's my plan. My friend, Afton Thomton, says he knows of good land about one hundred miles to the north and west of Mankato, near the Minnesota and Chippewa rivers. We're going to look at it as soon I arrive."

"I hope you find what you want." Marin turned her back to the man and her gaze back to the water. Against all wisdom, her heart insisted on quickening in this man's presence. It was all she could do to keep the welcome from her eyes.

A long pause met her action. She was sorely tempted to shoot a glance back at where he'd stood, but she refrained herself with discipline. Was he still there?

A clearing of his throat finally broke the silence. She heard the pain of her rebuff in his voice. "I'd best be getting my things together. I want everything ready so my time is free to stand up here and watch as we near shore. Good day to you, ladies. I hope to see you in America."

Marin heard his boots smack softly against the deck as he walked away. Her throat burned from holding back her response. She didn't want to see him in America. She didn't want to see any men in America who might threaten her heart.

Chapter 2

Chippewa County, Minnesota—January 1873

Marin heaved a sigh of frustration. "Einer, pay attention," she demanded in Swedish. She glared at her fifteen-year-old brother, who sat across from her at the homemade wooden table in the one-room sod house. Light from the kerosene lantern played across his hair, which was pale brown like their father, Hjalmar's. "I've asked you three times to read the verse from Philippians in English. How do you expect to improve your English if you don't try?"

"What does it matter? We've been in America for a year and a half, and never leave the farm or see anyone but other Swedes."

August, twelve and the youngest of the Nilsson family, leaned forward on the barrel he used as a chair. "That's not true. Sometimes you go to town with Fader. You see people who aren't Swedes there."

Einer grunted. "I've gone to town with Fader exactly twice since we moved here last spring."

"More than me," August insisted. "And all our neighbors

aren't Swedes. The Andersons are Norwegian. And there's the bachelor on the homestead to the south who came from New York."

"We won't stay so isolated forever," Moder broke in. "New people keep moving into the area."

Marin nodded. "Yes. Besides, we all agreed it's important to learn the language of our new land."

Anger smoldered in Einer's eyes. "None of my friends study English every night." He pushed the family's only copy of the precious Swedish-English translation of the New Testament from in front of him, narrowly missing the kerosene lantern.

"Watch out!" Moder grabbed for the lamp's clear glass base.

"I didn't hit it." Impatience filled Einer's defensive words.

"Einer." Fader's deep voice, low but stern, tumbled through the one-room soddy.

Silence filled the air in the wake of Fader's gentle reproof. Fader never allowed the children to speak with disrespect to Moder.

Einer crossed his arms over his chest and glared at the table.

Marin shifted her weight, uncomfortably aware that everyone was staring at Einer: Moder, who sat beside Marin on the crude log bench; Elsbet, on Marin's other side; August, who sat beside Einer; and Fader, who stood talking in quiet tones with their neighbor, Talif Siverson, beside the large, Dala-painted trunk at the end of Moder and Fader's bed. Normally Fader would be at the table with the rest of the family during the English-learning hour, but he'd excused himself when Talif arrived a quarter-hour ago.

Only with difficulty had Marin kept her gaze from Talif

and her attention on the lesson. As their nearest neighbor, it wasn't uncommon for Talif to visit with Fader after the day's work was done.

Moder touched Marin's hand. "Marin, let's begin again."

Marin hesitated. No doubt Einer thought he should be visiting with the men instead of sitting with the women and youngest child. Was he embarrassed that Fader reprimanded him in front of Talif?

As the family member who knew English best, Marin led the family's daily English-learning hour. She knew Einer wouldn't dare chance Fader's disapproval by leaving the table, but perhaps she shouldn't insist he read the verse. She cleared her throat and repeated the verse in Swedish from memory before asking, "August, would you read the verse in English?"

The tow-headed boy pulled the New Testament near. "Which verse was it again?"

"Philippians, chapter 4, verse 13."

August frowned at the pages before him and read haltingly, " 'I can do all things through Christ which strengtheneth me.' "

The class continued only a few minutes longer. As the four gathered about the table stood up, Moder asked Talif, "Would you care for some bread and coffee before leaving, Mr. Siverson? There's quite a chill in the air tonight."

Marin smiled. A guest never left the Nilsson home without such an offer, regardless of the time of day or the amount of food available or even whether the Nilssons liked the visitor. Hospitality was as much a part of Fader and Moder as their faith.

"*Tack*, Mrs. Nilsson. A little warmth in my belly would be welcome against the cold. Besides, your coffee is always better than mine." He grinned at her and sat down on the barrel

Einer had vacated.

As Moder put water in a huge graniteware kettle to heat on the stove, Fader headed to the sod barn to check on the cow and oxen. Einer and August, always glad to leave the dark little house which they considered the womenfolk's place, followed.

Talif reached for the New Testament. "I received one of these from a representative of a Lutheran church in New York when I arrived in America."

"That's where we got this one," Marin told him.

"Your fader tells me your family studies English for an hour each day."

"Yes, it's true, except for *Söndag*. We take turns reading in both Swedish and English. Then we choose a verse to memorize in English."

"That's a good plan. Does your family also speak in English around the house and while they work together each day?"

"We say we will, but it's easy to fall back into Swedish, as you heard tonight."

"Still, it is important to learn English. Those Swedes who know the language best will be able to get along best with Americans in business. Einer knows that. He's just tired."

Marin nodded. "I think he's right about other parents not requiring their children to learn English or even to read and write Swedish, as is required in the homeland."

"It's understandable. Everyone is so busy establishing their fields and homes. It takes all the time and energy available for parents and children alike."

Marin rested her forearms on the table and leaned forward. "But everyone will pay in the end if the children don't learn. How will the parents feel when the children are grown and still unable to communicate easily with the merchants, for instance?"

"I agree with you, but there isn't a school near enough for the children to attend. Chippewa City is the nearest village, and it's too far for the children to walk. The county doesn't have money to build a school here or pay another teacher."

"I know." Deflated, Marin sat back, her shoulders slumping. "For months I've been asking our heavenly Father to provide a school for the children in the area."

"Perhaps you should start one."

"I. . ." Marin stared at him, stunned. "But I'm not a teacher."

Talif shrugged. A smile lit his wide face. "You certainly sounded like one tonight."

"That was only with my family. I've no training to *truly* teach others."

"You've the knowledge that others need, and from your father's comments, I've no doubt you've the ability to share that knowledge with others. What else is required to teach?"

Marin spread her hands. "I don't know, but surely some test must be passed or permission received from the county school superintendent." Still, prickles ran along her skin at the possibility.

"You have a dream, a dream for a school for the Swedish children, and you've asked the Lord to grant this dream. It seems to me the best way for Him to do that is for you to do what you can toward building that dream. If it's to be, He will show you the next step and the next."

"What steps?" As soon as she asked the question, ideas popped into her mind. "Maybe I can talk with Miss Allen, the school teacher at Chippewa City. I can ask her what I need to do to become a teacher in this county—whether I need more training or to take a test."

"Yes, that would be a perfect place to start."

"But it won't be possible for me to get more training if I need it."

"Now you're trying to cross a bridge you don't even know needs to be crossed."

"You're right." Another problem loomed. "There's nowhere to hold lessons."

"You teach just fine right here."

"But this is our home. There isn't room for students."

"We hold church services here sometimes, and in other homes, too, some smaller than this."

She couldn't argue the truth of that. Excitement started to build, even as other problems came to mind. "We've no supplies."

"If the Lord can provide the teacher, students, and building, He can certainly provide whatever else is required."

Marin sat quietly for a minute, her mind racing. "Do you truly think it's possible?"

Moder set a cup of coffee on the table in front of Talif. "Didn't we just read tonight that 'All things are possible through Christ'?"

All things. Even a school, with herself as teacher? A thrill of hope ran along Marin's spine.

A minute later, Fader and the boys returned. Moder poured a cup of coffee for Fader and explained Talif's idea. Marin watched her father's face closely, knowing he was good at hiding his true feelings, good at using tact to give a gentle refusal.

"Sounds like a fine idea, Marin. Would you be agreeable to it?"

At Marin's surprised, cautious nod, he continued. "You couldn't give all of your time to it. Moder and Elsbet need your help, too."

Marin nodded again.

Fader glanced up at Moder and smiled. "What do you think, Tekla? Could we share our humble home with the neighbor children a few hours each day?"

"I think we could." Moder's smile lit up Marin's heart.

Marin's gaze darted to Talif, and caught him grinning back at her like a coconspirator.

"We'll need to rise early tomorrow, Marin," Fader advised, glancing at her over the rim of his pottery cup, "if we're to make it to Chippewa City so you can talk with Miss Allen."

"Yes, Fader." Joy bubbled within Marin's chest. A trip to town, a visit with the teacher, Moder and Fader agreeing to let her use their home as a school, and above all, her parents and Talif's belief in her ability to teach. It seemed too good to be true.

❦

Excitement, ideas, possibilities, and fears churned in Marin's mind, keeping sleep at bay for two hours after the rest of the family fell asleep. Pushing aside the bed curtain, Marin slipped out from under the heavy quilts, careful not to disturb Elsbet, who shared the bed. One of their brothers grunted and rolled over in the bed above Marin and Elsbet's, and Marin held her breath until all was again still.

She trod in stocking feet across the cold dirt floor to the window between the end of her parents' bed and the door, the window by which Fader and Talif had conversed earlier. A cotton curtain hid the bed from view, just like the curtain around the children's bed.

Marin picked up a quilt from the top of the trunk and climbed onto the wide window seat formed by the three-foot-wide blocks of sod. A woven rug of red and blue brightened the sill, and warmed the dirt a bit. She pulled her knees up, glad to have her feet off the cold floor, and wrapped the quilt around herself.

The sky was bright with starshine, clear of clouds. *The way the path of my dream appears tonight,* she thought, *bright, guided by starlight, clear.*

Her gaze drifted over the snow-covered prairie. There wasn't much to see, not even one tree. The sod barn, which sheltered the oxen, horse, and cow, stood silhouetted against the night sky. If the hour were earlier, a small point of light would be shining from Talif's window. No light there now. He'd be sleeping, of course. Without the light, his sod house was too far away to see even in the starlit, snow-bright night.

Even so, Marin's gaze searched the prairie where she knew his home stood. Gratitude filled her chest, warming her heart. In all the months they'd lived as neighbors, she'd treated him with a cool politeness. In return, he'd shown her how to reach for her heart's dream: to establish a school for the Swedish children. "Forgive me, Lord," she whispered. "Forgive me, Talif, and *tack.*"

Chapter 3

Marin studied her image in the silver hand mirror Moder had brought from Sweden and patted the blond braids wrapped in a coronet from ear to ear on top of her head. "Do I look proper, Elsbet?"

Elsbet's usually sober face sparkled with laughter. "Like a proper school teacher, yes, and beautiful besides. It's time to quit admiring yourself and get ready to greet your students."

"*My* students." Marin handed Elsbet the mirror. Wonder and dismay battled for supremacy. "Do you truly believe I can do this?"

"Of course. You'll be a blessing to your students."

Marin pressed the palms of her hands down the skirt of her best plaid dress, straightened the prim black ribbon bow at the neck, and took a deep, shaky breath. "I hope so."

She pushed back the curtain that divided the beds from the main room, walked to the table, and looked down at her few supplies: the Swedish-English New Testament; the small slate she'd bought at the general store last week when she visited Miss Allen; an old, well-read Mankato newspaper; the few letters they'd received from relatives and friends in Sweden and other parts of America; and the faithful kerosene lamp. The lamp would be needed, for even during the day there wasn't enough light in the sod house by which to read. Marin sighed. "Not much to begin a school with, I'm afraid."

Moder patted Marin's shoulder. "Beginnings are often small."

"Another Swedish proverb, Moder?"

She gave a sweet chuckle. "No, my own."

Marin glanced about the room. Who had ever heard of a schoolroom with the only desk a table on which the family had eaten breakfast an hour before school was scheduled to begin? The odor of corn cakes, ham, and coffee lingered in the air. The stove lent welcome warmth to the room.

August sat on the trunk, his eyes wide with anticipation. Einer leaned against the wall beside the window, trying to look uninterested, but Marin could see his excitement.

Fader entered the room, letting in a blast of chill January wind before he shut the heavy door. His cheeks shone red beneath his fur cap. "Here, Marin. It's time to announce that school will begin in a few minutes." He held out a cowbell. "Every schoolmarm needs a bell to ring."

Marin accepted the cold bell with a laugh and hugged him. "*Tack*, Fader."

"English, daughter." He shook a finger at her playfully.

Moder placed a thick, gray wool shawl about Marin's shoulders. Marin took a deep breath and opened the front door, bell in hand. A sign Elsbet had tatted hung on the outside of the door: SCHOOL. Marin smiled, feeling wrapped in her family's love. Each member of the Nilsson family had contributed something to the new school.

The clear sky above the horizon was still bathed in dawn's

pale lavender and rose above the snow-swept prairie. At the sight before her, Marin's heart missed a beat. Children waded through the foot-high snow toward the Nilsson house, their jackets, scarves, and hats dark or colorful splashes against the white background. Some of the students were almost to the Nilsson yard. Others were still distant enough that Marin couldn't make out their faces.

With a grin, she closed the door behind her and began to ring the bell. At first, in her excitement, she barely felt the chill. The family's black-and-white dog jumped up on her, barking the news that he saw people coming. "Shush, Sven," she scolded, pushing him down. "It's the school children. You must be nice to them when they arrive. No jumping on them."

Soon the cold from the air and the metal bell handle seeped into her bones, but she continued ringing the bell until the first group of children arrived at the door. Sven ran circles about them, barking in joyful greeting. Marin recognized the students as the Skarstedt children who lived over two miles to the east.

"*God morgan*, Eva, Anders, Sture. *Stig in*, come in."

"*God morgan*, Marin," ten-year-old Anders and eight-year-old Sture mumbled as they stepped over the threshold. "*God morgan*, Miss Nilsson," Eva greeted in her quiet, shy manner.

Marin was torn between the desire to stay outside until all the children arrived or to go in where it was warm. Warmth won. It wouldn't do for the teacher to come down ill on the first day of school. Besides, the other students were on the way and not likely to loiter in the winter morning. She could greet them beside the door inside as well as out.

Ten minutes later, she stood at one end of the table and stared in amazement. Children filled the sod house to bursting.

Students, she reminded herself, a thrill warming her chest, *not just children, but students. Nineteen of them.*

Marin was glad her plaid skirt hid her knocking knees. She'd longed for this day, and now that it was here, she was terrified. *Don't think about the fear,* she ordered herself. *Just do what you planned. The Lord will take care of the rest.*

"*Velkommen.* Let us begin our first day of school with a prayer of thanksgiving." She clasped her hands and bowed her head. "Our heavenly Father, we thank Thee for granting us a place to gather and learn. Help us to use this opportunity to grow in knowledge and wisdom. Amen."

A murmur of *amen*s echoed in the little room.

Marin looked up and smiled brightly. "Now, then, we're ready to begin." She immediately faltered once more at the sight of nineteen pairs of eyes concentrated upon her.

The youngest children sat on the beds, their legs dangling over the sides, boots and shoes on the floor. Students' coats and scarves were piled on the quilts behind the children. Elsbet sat on the sod window seat between the bedsteads, keeping watch for the moment over the little ones for Marin. The older boys, including Einer, stood along the wall. Orpha Stenvall and Viola Linder, the oldest girls at thirteen and ten, claimed the top of the Dala-painted immigrant trunk. The in-between-aged children sat at the table. Every child watched her intently.

She swallowed hard, keeping the smile in place. *Just follow your plan,* she reminded herself again. *They're only the children from the church. You know them all. Your family and Talif and the children's parents all believe you can do this.* "We'll begin with the school rules. Each day will begin with a prayer or hymn. In the beginning, we'll speak mostly Swedish, but you'll be required to speak English more as you learn that language. Often I'll say something in Swedish, then repeat it in English. That way you'll become accustomed to hearing both languages and perhaps learn English more quickly. There will be no whispering. You will raise your hand and wait for me to call upon you to speak. When I do call upon you, or when you are to recite a lesson, you'll stand. You will address me as Miss Nilsson. Do you understand?"

Most of the students nodded. Jems Stenvall and Knute Linder, two of the older boys, shifted their feet and stared at her without nodding, but they didn't challenge her, either. Marin noticed that the youngest children frowned or looked confused. Was it too much for such little ones to remember at one time? She smiled at Sophia Linder, the tiniest of the students. "Don't worry. If you forget the rules, I'll remind you."

A relieved smile spread across the round face between thick blond braids. "What if I need to go the necessary?"

Snickers filled the air.

Marin bit back a grin. "You raise your hand and ask permission."

Sophia shook her head, her eyes wide. "I don't like to go alone." She grasped the hand of the seven-year-old girl beside her. "Can my sister, Stina, come with me?"

"Yes."

"Does she have to raise her hand, too, or just me?"

"Just you, Sophia."

Sophia frowned. "I'm thirsty."

"The water pail and dipper are by the wall beside the barrels." Marin pointed to the place. "Students must also raise their hands when they need a drink."

Sophia raised her right hand high.

"Yes, Sophia?"

"I need a drink."

"May I have a drink, Miss Nilsson?"

Sophia shook her head. "I'm not Miss Nilsson. You are."

The other students burst into laughter. Marin swallowed a chuckle. "I meant, the proper way to ask for a drink is, 'May I have a drink, Miss Nilsson?' "

"Oh." Sophia didn't repeat the question. She only looked more confused.

"You may get a drink if you wish, Sophia."

All smiles, Sophia slipped off the bed and headed across the room.

Marin began to relax and turned to the other students. "Your parents were asked to send along with you any books or supplies they had available. Let's see what everyone's brought. Everyone please stand." She looked over at the older boys. "We'll start with you, Jems. Then Knute. Everyone follow in an orderly manner and set your items on the table."

When all the students had passed the table and returned to their seats, Marin's heart sank. The supplies were meager: Marin's small slate, five Swedish-English New Testaments, one well-read and torn Swedish newspaper, and one book of Swedish poetry. She'd known supplies would be limited, but how could she teach so many students with so little?

It wouldn't do to let the students know how discouraged she found their offerings. She forced another smile. "Wonderful. I'm glad to see that each family has a Swedish-English New Testament. That means every student can study reading both languages at home, not only here at school. Now I'm going to talk to the oldest student from each family to find out what education each of you had in Sweden and America. While I do that, my sister, Elsbet, will lead the rest of you in an exercise, memorizing a Bible verse in Swedish and then in English."

The school day went by faster than Marin anticipated. It seemed the day had barely started before the students were filing out the door toward home. Marin stood just inside the door, smiling at the departing children in spite of her exhaustion. "*Vi ses i morgon,*" she repeated again and again. "I'll see you tomorrow."

She leaned down to tighten the ties on little Sophia's red crocheted headband beneath the girl's pointed chin. Sophia smiled her thanks with a charming grin made of little teeth with big spaces in between. "*Tack*, Teacher."

Marin's heart took a little leap. *Teacher.* "*Ingen orsak*, Sophia. You're welcome."

When the last student had left, Marin leaned back against the door, closed her eyes, and heaved a sigh of relief. The first day was over, and she'd lived through it. She'd been called "Teacher" for the first time. She was living the role she'd asked the Lord to give her. She'd expected it to bring joy, and it did. It also terrified her.

❧

Marin was helping Moder and Elsbet clear the dinner dishes from the table when Talif arrived that evening. As usual, he visited with Fader, Einer, and August at the table where light from the kerosene lamp chased away the darkness of the winter evening. All four enjoyed cups of Moder's coffee.

Marin felt her gaze drawn to Talif continually while she worked. Each time she looked in his direction, she saw him watching her, a smiling curiosity in his eyes though he continued chatting about farm topics with Fader. She longed to share with Talif the experiences of her day. After all, he'd helped make the school possible.

"Elsbet and I will do the dishes, Marin," Moder said as she took a large wooden bowl from Marin, "while you prepare tomorrow's lessons."

"*Tack*, Moder." Marin smiled her gratitude and walked to the immigrant trunk to pick up the New Testament and her slate.

Talif stood, looking contrite. "I should be going. I'm intruding on your English hour again."

Fader pushed himself up from the barrel on which he'd been seated. "No. We've agreed to pass on the family English hour while Marin is teaching. Moder, Elsbet, and I will take time when possible to join Marin's class for our English lessons. Marin doesn't need an extra hour of teaching us each evening in addition to her responsibilities to her students." He reached for his coat hanging on a nail on the wide wooden door frame. "I'd best check on the beasts. Einer, August, come along."

While the brothers put on their coats, Fader lit a lantern. Moder handed him a plate of scraps for the dog. A swirl of cold air entered the warm house when the men left, chasing away a bit of the chicken stew and dumpling odors, and the warm smell of heat from the stove. Marin shivered as she sat down across the table from Talif.

Talif smiled at her. "One good thing about sod houses, they keep the cold out."

"*Ja*, that is true when the door isn't open."

"How did your first day of school go?"

"Wonderful!" Marin leaned her forearms against the table's edge, her hands clasped. "And awful." She laughed at the dichotomy.

Talif's grin answered her mirth. "Like most things in life, part good, part not-so-good, huh? Tell me about it."

"I'm afraid I didn't think my plan through well. Including

Einer and August, I've nineteen students. Nineteen!"

"That's a roomful, I'd say."

"They're all ages. Sophia Linder is the youngest. She's five. Knute Linder and Einer are the oldest at fifteen. Most of the older students know some math and geography, and how to read and write in Swedish. The youngest students need to learn everything. Some of the students can speak a bit of English, but none of them can read it except my brothers." Marin spread her hands, palms up. "How can I teach so many children who start with such different abilities?"

"With patience," he replied promptly, "and wisdom and ingenuity. The Lord wouldn't have put you in this position if you weren't able to do it."

"I hope you're right." She leaned forward. "We've barely any supplies beyond the Swedish-English New Testaments."

"What supplies do you most need?"

"A blackboard would be wonderful. Slates for each of the children." Marin began ticking items off on her fingertips. "A globe for geography. Math books and readers." She sighed. "Not that it does any good to wish. There's no money for these things."

"Doesn't hurt to make a prayer list for them, does it?"

Marin opened her mouth to protest. It seemed impossible that God could furnish the supplies. The families needed all their money for their homes and fields, yet Scripture assured that nothing was impossible with God. "You're right; it won't hurt to ask. After all, the Lord answered my prayer for a school even though it's not what I expected."

Talif laughed. "Things seldom are what we expect. Tell me more about your first day."

She told him of the mixture of excitement and fear with

which she'd started the day, of her fear she wouldn't know how to handle the older boys if they chose not to respect her authority, and of Sophia's funny comments. "The best part of the day was when the students left."

"You don't mean it!" Talif raised his blond eyebrows in astonishment.

"Not the way you think," she hastened to assure him. Marin touched the fingertips of her right hand to her throat and swallowed. "When Sophia Linder left, she called me 'Teacher.' " Marin almost whispered the word. "It's the first time anyone's called me that."

Talif met her gaze and smiled into her eyes, a sweet smile that wrapped around her heart.

Marin dropped her gaze to the table, feeling suddenly vulnerable and a bit foolish. "It probably doesn't seem like much, but it is to me. I've always thought teachers such special people, and now. . ."

"Now you are one."

She bit back the words on the tip of her tongue: *If I'm capable of meeting the challenge.* Talif would only repeat that God wouldn't have put her in the position if she wasn't able to meet the duties. Talif was right, of course, but it was going to be more work than she'd ever imagined. Well, she wasn't afraid of hard work. She squared her shoulders and met his gaze. "Yes, now I am one."

Warmth, contentment, and faith spread through her chest as she and Talif shared smiles across the flickering flame from the kerosene lamp.

The joy that shone from Marin's eyes when she proclaimed herself a teacher shone again in Talif's memory an hour and a half later. He stared out the wavy glass in his window, looking across the prairie to where the lights from the Nilsson home gleamed. Marin's happiness stirred his soul.

What an extraordinary woman she was, to take on such a challenge! He'd been attracted to her from the first moment he saw her, but he hadn't known then what a strong, giving person lay hidden by her outer beauty. She'd made it plain from the beginning by her cool attitude that she didn't want him to court her. He'd bided his time, offering only friendship. During that year and a half, his attraction had grown into love. At least lately she acted more friendly toward him. Was he a fool to hope she'd one day return his affection?

He'd encouraged her to believe that with God all things are possible, to believe the Lord would make her dream a reality. Yet Talif didn't quite trust that his own dream of making a home and building a family with Marin would come true. What if the Lord had other plans for her? Even if it was best for them to be together, the Lord allowed people free will. Talif remembered many times seeing people make choices he felt weren't in their best interests.

With a sigh, Talif turned from the window and crawled beneath the heavy quilts on his cornhusk mattress. He slipped his hands beneath his head and stared at the once-white cloth covering the ceiling. Moonlight rested gently on his face, but he didn't notice. His thoughts remained with Marin: *Miss Marin Nilsson, teacher*. A twinge caught at his heart. He envied Miss Nilsson's students, the time spent in her presence.

Chapter 4

Talif laughed at the sight before him as he approached the Nilsson's soddy. Driving his runner-mounted wagon from his place to theirs across the snow-bound prairie, he'd wondered what all the people were doing in the yard. Now he knew. Letters and words were carved into the snow. Marin had found an ingenious solution to the lack of a blackboard and slates.

Sunlight bounced off the snow-covered yard and off the young students' red cheeks as they looked up from their work to greet him. Marin glanced up, too, from where she knelt beside Sophia and shot him a quick, small smile before turning her attention back to Sophia's attempts at spelling. *En. Två. Tre.* The little girl was obviously learning to write her Swedish numbers.

His chest constricted in a warm, pleasant way at the sight of Marin so involved with the child. He welcomed the feeling but didn't dwell on it as he directed the horse toward the sod barn.

Talif barely reached the barn when Mrs. Nilsson came out of the house, carrying the cowbell. Within minutes, laughter drifted through the cold air as children of all ages headed toward home. Boys teased and chased girls and tossed snowballs at each other. Swinging metal lunch pails glinted in the sunshine. Marin stood in the doorway, still in her coat and scarf, watching the students depart.

"Get along there." Talif urged the horse toward the house, stopping only feet from the door. He nodded at Marin. "I apologize for interrupting your class."

"Classes were almost over anyway, as you can see. Are you looking for Fader? He's in the barn."

"*Nej*. I've come bearing gifts." He climbed over the wagon seat and into the wagon bed.

"Gifts? For us?" Curiosity filled Marin's eyes as she walked toward the wagon.

"For your school. For you and your students." Talif's heart picked up speed. Would she like his gifts? All the while he'd worked on them, he'd imagined the pleasure he'd see reflected in her face. Now he doubted the worthiness of his gifts.

He lifted the largest of them and held it up above the side of the wagon for her to see. "Do you know what this is?"

She frowned slightly, studying the gift, and disappointment began to seep into his hope. Then the frown cleared, and her eyes gleamed with excitement. "It's a blackboard. You made us a blackboard."

"*Ja*. Not a fancy one. It's just boards painted black."

"But it will work, don't you think?"

"*Ja*. It will work just fine. It won't be as smooth as a real one to write on, of course, though I sanded it down as best I could." He refrained from mentioning the hours and hours he'd spent smoothing the wood with a piece of broken glass.

"Oh, it's a wonderful gift, Talif. The students will be so excited tomorrow when they see it. No more need to write in the snow."

119

He chuckled as he lowered the blackboard over the side of the wagon bed. "They may not appreciate that part so well. Seemed to me they were enjoying themselves out here."

"It's nice for them to get out of the house. I've tried having them write in the dirt floor, but it's too dark to see well, and Moder doesn't appreciate the way it loosens the dirt. Wherever did you find extra boards for this? Surely you didn't go to the expense of buying them for us?"

"There's an abandoned homesteader's shack, barely larger than a necessary, a couple miles to the west. I took the wood from there. The homesteader headed to the Black Hills after the grasshoppers left. Said he's never coming back. Rather take his chances on finding gold dust than farming. He won't be needing the wood."

Marin's smile blazed. "I never thought I'd be thanking God for the grasshoppers. Imagine the Lord using them to help the school I didn't know last summer would exist now."

"That's our Lord, not one but many steps ahead of us. If we remembered that, we'd trust Him a lot more." Talif leaned down and picked up a small pile of wood from the wagon bed. "Here's some more supplies for your school." He handed them over the side, and Marin took them from him.

Surprise and wonder swept over her face, and a laugh erupted. "You made slates for the students."

"More like tiny blackboards."

"The students will love them. So do I. I'm so grateful for your kindness and the way you've supported this school from the beginning."

Talif shrugged, unexpectedly self-conscious about his offering. "It's little enough compared to the hours you give to the students." He climbed down from the wagon and lifted the large blackboard. "I'll help you get these inside."

Once inside the sod house, he glanced around at the crowded floors and wall space. He hadn't considered the limited space when making the blackboard.

Marin didn't seem to have any misgivings about the cramped conditions. "Set it in front of that curtain at the end of the double bedstead." She flashed a smile at Moder and Elsbet. "Look what Talif brought; a blackboard and slates for the children. He made them himself."

Talif tried to discount the joy and pride that flooded him at her words, but he wasn't successful. He set the board down where she'd said and removed his hat.

Mrs. Nilsson and Elsbet came over to "Ooh" and "Aah" over his work, making him feel foolish but happy. Soon they moved back to the kitchen area to continue preparing the dinner of pork roast and potatoes that was filling the house with mouthwatering odors.

Marin turned her shining blue-eyed gaze on him. "How can I ever thank you for all you've done?"

Talif pushed the hand not holding his hat into his jean's pocket. He'd been waiting for an opportunity to tell her what he wanted. He knew this was the right moment, but it was still hard to say. "There's one thing you can do for me. I'm not a child like your students, but I need to learn how to speak and write English better. If you want to thank me, you can tutor me."

"No!" Shock widened Marin's eyes, and she stepped back, clutching her tan shawl.

Disappointment twisted through Talif. He struggled to keep it from showing.

Marin's gaze darted in one direction and then another. Her

refusal to meet his gaze told him she was embarrassed about her sharp and instant refusal. "I–I can't tutor you," she started to explain. "Teaching the students takes all my time." Her words rushed over each other. "I spend every evening planning the lessons for the next day. And I need to help Moder with duties around the house, too."

"Of course." Now it was Talif who looked away. "It was thoughtless of me to think you'd have time. Your obligation is to your students and your family. I understand." He put on his hat and stepped around her toward the door. "I'd best be going. Evening, Mrs. Nilsson, Elsbet."

"I–I'm sorry."

"Don't give it a thought," he reassured Marin, not looking back.

Disappointment cut through him, keen and sharp, as he climbed into the wagon and headed the horse toward home. Marin's excuse was true; he knew that. How she found time to prepare lessons for nineteen students with such a vast difference in needs was beyond his comprehension. He should take her words at face value.

But it wasn't the words that hurt. It was the expression on her face, her first reaction to his request. The horror that spoke of more than a mere lack of time. The repulsion in her eyes and the explosive "No!" said she couldn't bear the thought of spending time that close to him.

"And I can't bear the thought she feels that way," he whispered into the early evening dusk, his gaze on his lonely little sod house on the rise ahead of him, pain tugging at his heart.

❧

Moder stared across the room from her place beside the hot

stove, a wooden spoon in one hand. "Marin, how could you be so unkind?"

Marin glanced at her mother, then away. The fingers of one hand twisted her gray woolen skirt while guilt skittered through her. "I wasn't unkind. I haven't time to tutor him. You know better than anyone how much time the teaching takes me."

"You could have been gentler in your refusal. Talif has given so much support to your school, to say nothing of the many ways he's helped your father out of friendship."

The truth in Moder's words deepened Marin's guilt and caused a strange discomfort. She usually got along so well with her mother. They shared ideals and interests, and seldom had sharp words for each other. Marin wasn't accustomed to Moder's disapproval. "I didn't mean to speak unkindly. His request seemed so impossible to grant, and—"

"I'm going for a walk." Elsbet stepped toward the door, slipping her coat on. "I won't be long. Don't worry, Moder, I won't go far." She was out the door before Moder or Marin could say good-bye.

Elsbet's actions didn't surprise Marin. Her sister often went for walks in the dusk, before night settled too darkly on the prairie and covered potential dangers such as wolves and coyotes. Marin knew Elsbet liked to spend time away from everyone else in the quiet with her own thoughts. She hated disagreements, also, and that was probably the true reason she'd left now. The knowledge didn't add to Marin's comfort.

Moder's gaze rested on the door. "You don't want to become like Elsbet." Her voice was quiet, filled with sadness.

Marin studied Moder's face. The sadness in her voice shone in her eyes. "Elsbet is a good person. She has such a kind heart. I'd be glad to be more like her." *Elsbet wouldn't have spoken so roughly to Talif. She'd probably have made time to tutor him if she wasn't attracted to him.*

"Elsbet is a lovely person, yes." Moder reached for Marin's hands. "But her heart is closed to love. You don't want to end up like that."

Marin tugged her hands away. "Talif didn't ask me to love him; he asked me to tutor him."

"You said no to him as a man as well as to his request," Moder admonished. "I'm not only a mother but a woman. It is unfortunate that the man Elsbet loved treated her so harshly. My mother's heart aches for her every day. I hate that she was hurt by him, but I hate just as much that she continues to hurt herself."

"How does she do that?"

"By keeping a wall around her heart and refusing to believe that any other man might truly love her. A heart blocked off from love grows cold, Marin. Remember the proverb, 'A life without love is like a year without summer'? I don't want both my daughters to live their lives without love's warmth."

"But I'm not—"

"Talif Siverson cares for you, that's easy to see. He's a good man. Perhaps you truly don't care for him in the way I hope you will one day care for a man, in the way I care for your father, with a love that makes your life larger and better and more beautiful. Yet you could choose to treat Talif more kindly and to entertain the possibility of falling in love with some young man. You've turned down every man who's expressed an interest in courting you."

Marin slipped off her shawl and gave her attention to carefully folding it. "I haven't time for courting. I'm teaching. My first responsibility is to the students."

Moder sighed. "Perhaps it would be best for them to have a

teacher who is not only good at English, Swedish, arithmetic, geography, and history, but courageous enough to keep her heart open to love."

"Moder, I—"

Her mother pulled her close in a hug. "I love you just as you are. I only want you to be happy."

"I am happy."

"Then I'll keep my thoughts to myself." Moder loosened her hug and patted Marin on the shoulder. "Why don't you ring that school bell and call the family in to dinner? By the time they get inside and we finish setting the table, the meal will be ready."

The clang of the bell didn't overcome the words whispering in Marin's heart. She'd had no idea Moder knew so clearly how she felt about men and marriage. Her mother's perceptions made Marin feel vulnerable.

Moder was right about Talif, of course. Marin knew the true reason she'd refused to tutor him wasn't lack of time, though her time was filled to overflowing. The true reason she'd refused was that she liked him too much. If she allowed herself to spend as much time with him as tutoring required, she might do exactly as Moder wished and allow her heart to open to him.

"That I will never do," she promised herself, glancing at Talif's house in the distance. Determination hardened like rock inside her chest. "Never."

Chapter 5

Marin looked up from the opening prayer and glanced around at the students stuffed into every corner of the house. Wind and snow whistled around the corners of the sod house and down the stovepipe, though even a winter storm had no power to penetrate the three-foot-thick sod walls.

It always encouraged her to see the students show up in inclement weather. Their dedication to learning gave her strength to work long into the night to plan lessons.

She smiled at the children. "Since you all walked through the stormy weather this morning to get here, I think for our first lesson we'll work together to learn the English expressions regarding weather. I'll say the expression first in Swedish, then repeat it in English. After I say it in English, you will all repeat it in English together. Understood?"

The children responded with nods

"Good. We'll start with a description of today's weather. *Det är kallt.* It is cold."

"It is cold," the class repeated.

"*Det blåser.* It is windy."

"It is windy."

"*Det snöar*. It is snowing."

"It is snowing."

"Good, class. We'll repeat—"

The door opened, and surprise stopped Marin's speech as Talif entered, a windy gust of cold and snow following him inside.

Talif removed his snow-covered, wide-brimmed hat and nodded at her, a polite, challenging smile on his wind-burned face. "*God morgon*, Miss Nilsson. I'm sorry to be late." He walked to where Einer leaned against one wall. "I'll just take a place here and join the class, if you please."

Marin bit back the response that leaped to her tongue. *If I please? I don't please at all, and he knows it.* Anger roiled through her at his presumptuous action, yet she refused to make a scene over it in front of the students. Likely Talif was counting on that. Well, she'd act like she'd expected him today, and tell him after school that under no circumstances was he to return.

The other students stared at Talif and at her, clearly as surprised as she at the presence of a grown man in the classroom. She ignored the fury in her chest and forced a smile. "Of course you may join us, Mr. Siverson. We're learning English terms for weather today." She turned her gaze deliberately away from him. "We'll repeat the phrases all together once more. Then I will write them on the blackboard, and we will break into small groups to memorize the spelling. Tomorrow we will have a quiz on the terms."

A groan erupted from the older boys.

Marin ignored it. "Repeat after me, *Det är stormar*. It is storming." *Storming inside and out,* she raged silently while the students chanted the phrase.

Talif's deep voice made its way through all the others to her ears no matter how many students spoke at the same time. Even when the students broke into groups and she helped the youngest girls with the weather phrases, the sound of Talif studying aloud with the older boys distracted her.

Once Marin caught Elsbet watching her with sympathy in her eyes. The knowledge that Elsbet saw through Marin's defenses only added fuel to her anger. Her mother's comment flashed through her mind: "A heart blocked off from love grows cold." *Better cold than fiery with pain like Elsbet's.*

Little Sophie tugged at Marin's sleeve.

Marin pushed away her uncomfortable thoughts and smiled down at the girl with the blond braids. *"Ja?"*

"Did I say it right, Teacher?"

Warmth spread over Marin's cheeks. How could she let Talif fill her thoughts to the point she didn't hear her student? "I'm sorry, Sophie. Would you repeat it for me?"

It took a few times for Sophie to learn to drop the *t* that ended the Swedish *kallt* when she said *cold*, but in the end, she said it properly and beamed when Marin praised her.

The day seemed long to Marin and more difficult than usual with her constant awareness of Talif's presence. By the end of the school day, the anger she nursed created an unfamiliar fatigue within her. Still, she stopped Talif as he prepared to leave with the other students. "Mr. Siverson, I'd like to speak with you."

For a moment he hesitated, and she thought he'd refuse, but then he nodded. "Certainly, Miss Nilsson."

As they'd grown to know each other better, they'd fallen into the practice of calling each other by their first names. It sounded strange to hear him address her formally, though she grudgingly appreciated it in front of the students.

She waited uncomfortably while the other students left before turning to him beside the closed door, with a glance at Moder and Elsbet standing by the stove talking while they started dinner. "What do you think you are doing?" Marin kept her voice low and stood closer to him than she'd like, hoping to avoid her mother and sister overhearing the conversation, an almost impossible task. She hated the way her voice shook with the anger she'd held inside for hours.

"Two weeks ago I asked you to tutor me." His spoke quietly, evidently as eager as Marin to keep the conversation between the two of them. "You said—"

"I said I hadn't the time, and I don't."

"I realize that. It was inconsiderate of me to ask you when you're so busy with the school."

"If you believe that, why did you barge into my classroom today?"

His gaze met hers evenly. "I came because I want to improve my English, and I don't know how to do that on my own. I figured if I'm just another student in your school, my learning won't make any extra demands on your time."

The guilt she'd originally felt at refusing to tutor him began to creep back. He'd helped her start the school, he wanted to learn, and she'd turned her back on his request for her assistance. Still, that didn't change the fact that she didn't want him around constantly, and she wasn't ready to let go of her anger at him for shoving his way into her class.

She glared at him, tapping one high-top booted toe against the hard-packed dirt floor. "The school is for children, not men."

Something akin to anger flashed in his blue eyes, and his

lips pressed together firmly before he spoke. "I thought the purpose of the school was to help people learn. I may be a man, but I'm a student when it comes to learning the language of my new country, and I need help. I plan to attend class and study hard, like any of the other students." He placed his black hat on his head and nodded grimly. "See you tomorrow morning, Miss Nilsson."

She stepped back quickly to get out of his way as he opened the door.

Then he was gone, leaving Marin frustrated. Her head throbbed. She'd meant to insist he not return to her classroom. Wasn't that what she'd done? It had been the intent behind her words, and certainly Talif Siverson knew that. Through the weeks of teaching, she'd grown accustomed to students acquiescing to her demands. It hadn't occurred to her he'd attend class if she made it clear he wasn't welcome.

She looked toward Moder and Elsbet. Elsbet turned quickly back to the stove and dumped the onions she'd just chopped into a hot, cast-iron frying pan, but Moder returned Marin's gaze. Obviously the women knew what Talif and Marin had discussed in spite of their attempts at privacy.

Marin lifted her arms, feeling helpless. "What can I do, Moder?"

"Teach him."

"But he's a man. He doesn't belong in the school."

"Then tutor him."

"You know I haven't time!"

Moder wiped her hands on her apron. "Would you refuse to allow him in class if he were any other man?"

"Of course." In spite of her instant response, the question caught Marin off guard. Would she truly mind if, for instance,

Sophie's father wanted to join the class? Honesty made her admit to herself that, rather than be angry, she'd likely be flattered. But then, there was no man whose presence affected her like Talif's.

Moder still watched her intently. Did she again know what Marin was thinking? Marin blushed. "It doesn't matter whether I 'allow' him in class or not. I can hardly force him out if he shows up, and he says he intends to continue attending."

Moder shrugged. "Then there's nothing to do but accept the fact and teach him, is there?" She put a coat over her shoulders. "I'm going to see whether Einer has the cow milked yet. We need some milk for the cooking."

When Moder had left, Marin walked about the room, picking up the small board slates students had used during the day. Another sign of Talif's help with the school. Another reason to feel guilty for not wanting to teach him.

With a sigh, she set the boards on the floor beside the large blackboard, then walked over to Elsbet and reached for a paring knife. "Let me help you slice those potatoes."

"*Tack.*"

For a couple minutes, they worked together in silence, the only sounds the sizzle of the sharp-smelling onions in the frying pan and the crack of burning wood in the cookstove. Marin's thoughts swirled about Talif, his declaration of intent, and her powerlessness to stop him.

"What do you think, Elsbet? I mean about Talif. Do you agree with Moder?"

Elsbet's gaze stayed on the potatoes as she pared. "Do I agree with what? That you should accept the fact that he is going to attend school, and teach him as you do the other students? Or that you would not be upset if it were any man other than Talif?"

If anyone but Elsbet had asked the question, which so directly struck at the heart of the matter, Marin's anger and embarrassment would have increased. But Elsbet's gentle voice and manner made it easier for Marin to accept the probing questions. "You believe, like Moder, that I care for Talif?"

Elsbet shrugged one shoulder, her attention still on her work. "As more than a friend, perhaps. Are you in love with him? Perhaps not. At least, not yet." She lifted her gaze to Marin. A little frown cut between her brows. "Why don't you allow anyone to court you, Marin? Don't you want to be loved, to be married, to have your own family one day?"

Marin looked away. "Because a man wants to court a woman doesn't mean he loves her. All husbands don't love their wives." She refrained from saying that Elsbet, of all people, should know those things. "Some men only want a woman to take care of things like cooking, cleaning, and sewing."

"I think Talif likes you very much. I think he'd court you if you let him and not just to get a housekeeper."

"I don't want to be courted by him, or marry him, or be his housekeeper. I don't need a husband. I'm a teacher. I don't make enough to live on now, but maybe when I have experience and more settlers come here, I can get a teaching job for the county. Then you and I can live together. We'll be just fine, the two of us, without any men."

Elsbet added the sliced potatoes to the onions in the skillet. "You've never been in love. You don't know what it feels like to love someone."

"I don't want to know what love can be like if it can hurt someone as much as it did you."

"Is that why you don't let anyone court you?"

"Maybe." Marin hadn't meant to let Elsbet know how she

felt. She took plates out of the cupboard and began setting the table.

"I still think about Anton," Elsbet said quietly from behind Marin.

"I know." *If she didn't think about him*, Marin thought, *Elsbet wouldn't be so sad.*

"Sometimes I think awful things."

"What do you mean?"

"Sometimes I wonder what would happen if Anton's wife died, whether then he'd want me back."

Marin didn't know what to say. The thought of sweet Elsbet having such thoughts stunned her. Is that what loving someone could do to a person? All the more reason not to fall in love.

"I know," Elsbet continued, "it sounds horrible. I don't truly want her to die. I just want Anton back. I know it's not her fault he left me. If he hadn't married her, he would have married someone else. He simply didn't love me as much as I love him."

The emptiness in Elsbet's voice told Marin how much the truth hurt. An old Swedish proverb slipped into Marin's mind. *A wound never heals enough to hide a scar.* "You aren't the only woman whose intended left them behind in Sweden. It happens too often. Men can't be trusted."

"Not all men are like Anton. Some men truly love their wives—men like Fader."

"Yes." Anyone could see how much Fader and Moder loved each other. Marin weighed her words carefully before speaking. "If a woman could be guaranteed a man would love her the way Fader loves Moder, every woman would gladly fall in love. If you believed another man would love you that way, you'd let someone else court you, too, Elsbet."

Elsbet winced. "We're talking about you. You're nineteen, and you haven't started a hope chest."

"I'm too busy teaching." Not for the world would Marin remind Elsbet that her own hope chest, filled with so many hours of loving work, was still under one of the beds, its contents untouched. She linked her arm through Elsbet's. "One day I'll start that hope chest. You and I will need some things when we start our own home."

Elsbet smiled but didn't look convinced.

Time would prove the truth of Marin's intent. For now, she'd just do as Moder said and accept Talif's presence in her classroom. She'd treat him like any other student. Spring was just around the corner. Field work would soon demand Talif's time and require he abandon his plans to attend school. That would be the end of it.

Chapter 6

Teaching had been a heady combination of joy, fear, study, and lack of sleep for Marin before Talif joined the classroom. Now every day challenged her emotions. She was challenged to keep her attention on the other students and their lessons. She was challenged to keep her gaze from darting to Talif whenever she heard his voice or laugh. The greatest challenge came during the part of each day she spent with the older boys on their specific lessons.

Three weeks after Talif began attending class, Marin approached the older boys with dread. Talif, along with Einer, Jems, and Knute, made up the class. Marin kept her gaze carefully away from Talif as she approached them.

"We'll be working on English words with especially difficult spellings and sounds today," she informed them. "We'll start with words that begin with the letter *k*, but the *k* is silent."

Jems, leaning against the wall with his arms crossed, sneered. "Why would a word have a letter that's silent? That's stupid."

"Be that as it may, there are such words." Jems had been challenging her more lately. He'd started school as excited as the other students to learn, but the last week or so his attitude had changed, and she didn't know why. "We'll start with *kniv,* which is spelled *k-n-i-f-e* in English." Marin picked up one of the small board slates, wrote the word, and held the board for the four to see. "It sounds like *nif* with a long *i.*"

"So the *e* is silent like the *k*?" Talif asked.

"Yes." She nodded toward Knute. "If you pronounce the word like we do Knute's name, with a *k* sound, you'll be proclaiming your ignorance of the language."

Knute grinned. "That makes it easy for me to remember."

"For all of us," Talif agreed.

Funny how the simple recognition that she'd made learning such a small thing easier for them filled her with pride. "Another word is the English word *know,* which in Swedish is either *veta,* to know something, or *känna,* to know someone."

"The same word is used for both in English?" Talif questioned again.

"Yes." She wrote the word on the board below *knife.*

"It sounds the same as *no,*" Jems protested, "the opposite of *ja.* How do we know which form of the word to use?"

"By the way it's used in a sentence," Marin explained, trying to keep her patience. Jems should know that rule by now. "Why don't you try using each version in a sentence for me right now? Say the entire sentence in English, of course."

"*No,* I won't." Jems grinned. "I don't *know* how to say it."

Knute and Einer laughed, and Marin could see Talif brush his hand over his face to hide a grin. Marin found Jems's play on words rather amusing, also, but the teacher in her wondered whether the action was inappropriate and disrespectful. Best to let it pass, she decided.

"Very good. Now you, Einer."

Einer and Knute each copied Jems by coming up with

twists on the two words. The boys' laughs soon drew the other students' attention. "Back to work, everyone," Marin admonished in her most teacherly voice.

Some of the students turned reluctantly away. Others continued to watch, albeit in a less obvious manner. *Oh, well,* Marin thought, *at least they may learn something listening.*

Then it was Talif's turn. When he didn't speak at once, Marin glanced at him. He looked like he was struggling to come up with the sentences. She was about to ask if he needed her to clarify something when he said, "He know she will say no if he asks to court her."

The class erupted into laughter. Marin felt her cheeks grow warm. Was he teasing her? The other students obviously believed he was speaking of himself and her. His eyes glinted with poorly suppressed laughter.

At least his grammar error allowed her to correct him rather than address the meaning of the sentence. "In that use, you would need to add an *s* to the word *know*, Mr. Siverson. 'He knows she will say no.' Please repeat the sentence using the word correctly." Anger cooled her voice.

"He knows she will say no," he repeated, his eyes still laughing though not his voice.

"Correct." *Let him wonder whether I mean he said it correctly, or whether he's correct in thinking I'd say no,* she thought, triumph overcoming the anger.

She proceeded to explain the way the word *know* changed depending upon singular or plural references, and how *knew,* the past tense of *know*, also had a sound-alike word in *new.* She instructed Talif and the boys to work together using the words in more sentences and practicing pronouncing and spelling the words.

When she finally turned to go back to the younger children and begin an arithmetic class, she gave a sigh of relief.

Talif watched Marin walk away from himself and the older boys, and over to a group of younger children. Her shoulders, which inched closer to her ears while talking with his group, lowered back to their normal position.

Did she always feel uncomfortable teaching the older boys? Certainly it couldn't be easy trying to teach her brother Einer. Brothers didn't often like to learn from sisters, especially in front of other boys.

Marin probably worried that Jems and Knute were too close to her in age to respect her knowledge. That would make teaching them tough for her. Lately it seemed Jems was testing her. Not a lot, just pushing a little more than was proper. The situation would bear watching. Talif wasn't about to let Jems or any of the other students cause problems for Marin.

She'd been a good sport about the humorous sentences they'd come up with today. He'd considered using a less volatile sentence, but to subtly tease her had been too tempting in the end. He smiled, remembering how she'd responded with an even more subtle jibe. It was the first time he'd experienced her wit.

After his first day at school, he'd more than half expected Marin to recruit her father and insist he demand Talif quit attending the school. Instead, she taught him every day just as if she didn't wish him gone. Of course, her cool reserve and her reference to him as Mr. Siverson instead of Talif told him clearly that she hadn't changed her mind about his attendance.

The clang of the oven door drew his gaze from where Marin bent over young Eva. Mrs. Nilsson was preparing the stove for baking. Her face looked tired in the dim light of the soddy. The realization of how difficult it must be for Marin's family to go about their daily business with the house filled with students jolted through him. There was barely a minute during the day for the Nilssons to relax and spend alone. Not many families would so graciously disrupt their lives for that of other people's children to have the opportunity to learn.

A memory slipped into his mind: Marin telling him how she hoped to have "a true schoolhouse one day." His gaze slipped back to her. Her earnest expression as she explained an arithmetic problem to Eva caused a little catch in his heartbeat. Marin's dedication to the students never ceased to amaze him.

She deserved that schoolhouse. But how, since neither the county nor church could afford one?

His heart sent up a prayer. *Dear Lord, please provide the schoolhouse for which Marin longs. If there's any way I can help, please show me. Amen.*

A picture of the homesteader's old shack flashed into his mind. Was that meant as an answer to his prayer? He dismissed the thought. That tumble-down place wasn't fit for skunks, let alone a school, and nowhere near as large as this little soddy.

An elbow nudging his side caught his attention. "You plan to study these words with us like the teacher said?" A glint in Jems' eyes added sly innuendo to his question.

"Of course. Just remembering something that needs doing." Talif turned back to the group, disgusted at letting himself get caught by a student, especially Jems, watching Marin.

At noon, the students relaxed and talked while they ate the lunches they'd brought from home. Some children had only buttered bread, others had baked potatoes they'd carried hot to school and left on top of the stove to stay warm. The Nilssons waited to eat until the students were done. Then the family sat down at the table while the students went outside for fresh air.

Talif let Eva and Sophie sweet-talk him into playing fox and geese with the younger children. He'd forgotten the joy of simple play in snow under a blue sky, with cold temperatures crisping the air and wood smoke adding a pleasant, warm fragrance.

Marin's ringing the cowbell brought an end to the games. Talif entered the home-turned-school with the children. Students took advantage during the last minute or two of chatting and laughing together while they removed their coats, mittens, and scarves.

As always, Talif's glance caught sight of Marin. She was picking up the small board slates the ten-year-olds had been using before lunch, nodding and smiling as Sophie regaled her with exaggerated tales of Talif's attempts at fox and geese.

Marin's face changed suddenly from a smile and a pleasantly distracted air to frozen shock. She stared down at the small slate in her hands, the color draining from her cheeks.

Shocked at the sudden change, Talif slipped up behind her and looked over her shoulder at the slate. He was dimly aware of children snickering. "What is it?" he asked, his voice discreetly low.

"Nothing." Marin flipped the board over and stepped briskly away.

But not before he saw it. Someone had drawn a heart, and inside, the words "Teacher + Talif."

He swallowed a groan. This wasn't going to do his cause any good at all.

Chapter 7

One evening two weeks later, Marin rested her elbows on the table, her chin on the palms of her hands, and stared at the open New Testament. She was so weary that the words seemed to swim in the wavering light from the kerosene lamp. The warmth from the stove behind her only made her more tired.

Her gaze slid to the small board slate beside the book. She'd meant to make notes on the slate for tomorrow's lessons, but it remained blank. Her mind refused to follow her intention to plan.

Elsbet sat down opposite her. "You look exhausted. Perhaps you should go to bed."

"No." Marin shook her head. "I haven't planned tomorrow's lessons."

"You'll be too tired to teach if you don't get some sleep. Something will come to you for the lessons tomorrow. It always does."

Did it seem so easy to everyone else, Marin wondered, *to find ways to teach?* "It would be easier if we had proper supplies. I'd like to teach geography, but how, without maps or a globe? I draw maps on the blackboard, but there isn't a way to save them so the students can study them again later. I considered asking the students to write letters to people back in Sweden telling them in English about their new life here. How can they do that on these small board slates? Paper is too precious to expect their parents to allow them to use any for just a lesson."

"Maybe you can have them work on a letter together and write it on the large blackboard."

"But I wanted them to write the words themselves, to practice writing English."

Elsbet's eyebrows lifted in question. "Can't you have a different student write each sentence? Or have them write a sentence on their slates and then you write the sentence on the large board so they can see whether they've written it correctly?"

Marin smiled wearily. "You came up with a solution so easily. I should have asked you for help earlier. Perhaps you should be the teacher."

"Oh, no." Elsbet shook her head, smiling. "That's not for me. I can help you with the simple, everyday things children need to learn, but I haven't the head for schooling you've had since you were a wee one. I wish I could be more help to you. I've noticed Talif helping lately."

"Yes. He's quite smart and completed his schooling in Sweden. He only needs help with his English. Since he can spend more time during these winter months away from his farm, he offered to help teach the older boys arithmetic. It's such a help. Knute is usually a conscientious student, but Einer and Jems prefer to tease and cause trouble sometimes. I suppose they're bored or don't like to learn from someone so close to their own age, and a woman at that."

Elsbet casually brushed at a bread crumb that had escaped

the after-dinner wipe down of the table. "So perhaps Talif's insistence on attending school is a blessing in disguise."

Marin's back tensed. "Not such a blessing that it overcomes the difficulties he brings along. At least no more hearts have shown up on students' slates since that awful experience a couple weeks ago, but I hate the students' sly looks and snickers every time I need to talk with Talif."

"Children are like that. Anything which looks like possible romance amuses them. You know that. It will pass."

"I hope you're right. Teaching isn't nearly as much fun as before the innuendoes began."

"What advice would you give a student in a similar situation, Marin?"

"To ignore it. That to give the teaser a reaction only increases the teasing." Marin laughed, realizing Elsbet's point. "See, you're a natural teacher."

"Only in practical, everyday matters, as I said before." Elsbet stood up as a loud knock interrupted them. "Not in reading, writing, and arithmetic," she said over her shoulder as she hurried to open the door.

Talif entered with the winter cold. Marin was only dimly aware of their greetings as her gaze met Talif's across the room. Annoyance slipped through her veins. Since Talif began attending school, his evening visits with Fader had almost stopped, and from the look in Talif's eyes, he wasn't here to see Fader now.

Marin felt herself tense as Talif removed his hat and gloves and crossed the room to the table. A cylindrical object under one of his arms caught her attention. "*God afton*, Miss Nilsson. I mean, good evening."

"Good evening, Mr. Siverson." Marin straightened her

spine and allowed an invisible wall of reserve to slide over her face. "What can I do for you?"

He shifted his weight from one booted foot to the other. "I'd like to do something for you and for the other students." He took the roll of cloth from beneath his arm and handed it to her across the table.

"What is this?" Suspicion made her frown. She accepted the material reluctantly when he didn't respond. Pushing aside the New Testament and slate to make room, she began to unroll the object. It was rectangular in shape and only two-thirds as long as the table's width. The off-white material contrasted sharply with the rough pine boards of the table. Bright-colored embroidered letters began to appear. "A sampler?" When the whole was revealed, she gasped. "Oh!" She covered her cheeks with her fingers.

A picture of a small, white cottage with a thatched roof and a barn decorated the top of the sampler. Beneath the picture the Swedish alphabet marched primly, and beside that the English alphabet. Marin ran her fingers lightly across the finely wrought, colorful letters. "It's beautiful. Where did you get it?"

"My sister, Karin, made it for me before I left for America." Talif pointed to the picture at the top. "That's our parents' place in Sweden."

Marin's conscience struggled for supremacy. The sampler would make a wonderful teaching aid, and the school desperately needed such things. Yet. . .

"I can't possibly accept this." Setting her jaw as firmly as her determination, she began rolling the sampler back up. Such mementoes from loved ones in the homeland, people who might never again be seen, were precious, even priceless. "A gift from your sister. . ." She shook her head.

Talif reached out and stopped her from continuing to roll the sampler. "Now it's her gift and mine to you and to the students." He glanced at the curtain that hid the beds and behind which Elsbet and Mrs. Nilsson had discreetly disappeared. He leaned closer and lowered his voice. "You give of yourself every day to others who have come to this new land, to help them have a better life. Please, allow me the pleasure of giving to the students, also. *Var god.*"

"But it must be so special to you."

"It is." A grin lit his blue eyes. "Isn't that the best kind of gift to give?"

Marin ignored the question. "This sampler is part of your family's heritage now. You should keep it to pass it down to your children and their children."

A strange, almost hurt look filled his eyes for a moment, then disappeared behind a thin reserve. "Perhaps by the time I have children of my own, the students will no longer need the sampler." He cleared his throat. "I promise you, my sister will love knowing her sampler is helping students in America."

Marin gently held the sampler against her chest. "Just before you came, I told Elsbet how badly we need supplies for teaching." She tried unsuccessfully to keep tears from welling up in her eyes.

"You keep adding to that prayer list of things you need for the school, and pretty soon there won't be anything left God hasn't provided."

It seemed to Marin that God supplied most of the things through Talif. The thought ran through her mind that perhaps God found it amusing to do so, to keep bringing the one man who attracted her into her life. Had God also brought this man into her life because she was meant to be attracted to

Talif? Her heart skittered away from the possibility.

"Thank you, Talif, for your thoughtful gift." She couldn't simply dismiss him after this, couldn't say "thank you, and good-bye now." She gestured toward the table. "Let me get you a cup of coffee and a cookie before you go."

"*Tack.*" Talif sat down on one of the upended packing boxes beside the table.

Marin set the sampler down and turned to the stove. She reached for the large graniteware kettle, which still held warm coffee from dinner. Marin poured some for herself and Talif, then took from a tin in the homemade pine cupboard some of the eggless cookies Elsbet had made earlier in the day.

When she finally seated herself across from Talif, he said, "I overheard some of the students' parents speaking to you at church last Sunday, telling you that you're doing a good job."

"Yes, it's nice they think so."

"They're right."

His praise pleased her, and she realized it meant more to her than the parents' praise. After all, he saw her teaching every day. None of the parents had visited the school.

The thought of Sunday meetings brought less pleasing recollections of comments by the adults in the congregation. More than one student's mother had asked her whether she and Talif were courting. Of course, Marin denied it in emphatic terms, but the questions made it obvious students and parents alike found Talif's presence in the classroom curious.

"The Linders told me their children are helping them learn English at home," Talif told her. "I suspect the same is happening in the other families. Your teaching is touching lives beyond your classroom."

Marin had never thought of that possibility. She lifted her

cup to take a sip of coffee and, looking over the rim, found Talif's blue-eyed gaze intent on her. Suddenly, unexpectedly, she felt shy.

"Moder, Elsbet," she called out, "come see what Talif brought for the school."

The women admired the sampler, then sat down to have coffee with Talif and Marin. The embroidered picture of Talif's home in Sweden stirred the Nilssons' memories, and soon they and Talif were sharing stories of life in the homeland.

While the others talked, Marin discreetly studied Talif. Why hadn't she ever noticed the smattering of freckles on the bridge of his nose, or the way little lines—were they from laughter or squinting against the sunshine while working in the fields, or both—fanned out from the corners of his eyes? She'd never considered him a handsome man, but he had a fine, broad, honest face. He'd grown obviously stronger since they met, likely from plowing never-before-plowed land with its tangle of prairie grass roots.

Maybe she'd reacted too strongly to his choice to study with her class. After all, he only wanted to learn to better speak and write English. What was so awful in that? He'd helped her get the school started, made the blackboard and slates, assisted with teaching the other students arithmetic, and now given the school that wonderful alphabet sampler. Surely, if anyone deserved to take part in her class, Talif Siverson did.

After all, just because she wasn't in love with the man was no cause to be unfriendly toward him, was it?

Chapter 8

Talif ran the palm of his hand over the board he'd been smoothing with a piece of broken glass. His lips stretched into a tired smile of satisfaction. No students would end up with slivers in their backsides from this bench seat.

He laid the board on the packed-earth floor and rubbed his right shoulder. Working on that board for hours left its mark on his muscles.

Talif let his gaze wander about his small sod house, lingering on one homemade bench after another. He'd spent hours and hours the last month tearing apart the departed homesteader's shack, hauling the wood home, cutting and pounding it into small benches for the school. He'd made good progress on his plan for Marin's schoolhouse. . .or rather, on the plan he believed the Lord had given him for the schoolhouse.

Rain spattered against his only window, in front of which he sat on one of his homemade benches while working, taking advantage of the little sunlight the clouds and rain let in. If this spring storm kept up, the roof would be dripping water and mud soon.

Mud. April's warmth had melted the last of the snow,

chased the frost from the ground, and turned solid ground into squishy, boot-sucking mud. Too wet for planting or for building sod houses. When the rains stopped and the ground dried out somewhat, he and the other farmers could get into the fields.

It would be late summer or early fall before the school-house became a reality. Impatience tugged at him as though he were a puppet with annoying strings tied to his limbs. Through each step of preparing for the school, he daydreamed of the expression he'd see on Marin's face when she first viewed the building.

There were still things to do—ordering the window glass and the wood for the window frames and door, for instance. He'd need to do that in Benson, thirty-odd miles across the prairie, the nearest town with a sawmill. There wasn't enough wood left from the homesteader's shack to use for the frames and door, and what was there wasn't good enough quality for such use anyway. No telling when the land would firm up enough for the Benson trip. He'd need to work the trip in after planting. Some things in life couldn't be put off, and planting fields was one of them.

He wished he could put all his energy into building Marin's school, but that wasn't possible. It would all come about in God's timing, of course, but waiting was difficult.

Marin's heart pounded as she looked about the crowded building at the congregation. She could barely believe this day had finally arrived: the first Sunday in May, the day of the school program signifying the end of the school year.

It seemed a good time for the school year to end. Spring heralded an end of the old and beginning of the new. Hadn't the community just celebrated the coming of spring on April

30, with the Swedish Walpurgis Night celebration? Everyone had gathered about bonfires and enjoyed good food while singing and talking about plans for the warm months ahead.

Students would be busy preparing fields and gardens soon. Too busy for school work. The longer, warmer days had already melted the snow cover and left the land so muddy many of the students found it difficult to traverse the prairie to school. Yes, it was time to end the first school year.

The Skarstedt family owned the largest sod house in the area, and they'd graciously offered it for this special Sunday. In spite of its size, parishioners filled it to overflowing. Unlike most of the sod houses, this house had a separate bedroom. There the students gathered after morning church service, waiting for the program to begin.

Marin's gaze wandered over the students, meeting their bright, eager gazes, noting the cheeks red with anticipation, admiring the Sunday-best clothing, and listening to the excited whispers. She knew the importance of the choice of clothing, how it made one feel better about oneself and more capable. She herself wore her best dress, with a new lace collar made by Elsbet especially for this occasion and Moder's precious silver pin, which had been passed down for three generations.

Even Talif wore a suit today. It wasn't new. *My*, Marin thought, *he looks handsome.*

Talif hadn't much part in today's program. She'd thought it might appear improper to the parents or at the very least cause more speculation by adults in the congregation. He'd agreed to help her keep the program running according to plan and take a small part in one skit. To her relief, he seemed satisfied with that.

She lifted an index finger to her lips. "*Shhh.* It's time for the program to begin. We'll do everything just like we practiced.

When others are performing, those of you waiting here are to show them respect and keep quiet. No more whispering. If you've any questions while you wait, ask them of Talif. When it's your turn to perform, don't forget your curtsies and bows." Marin took a deep breath and gave the students a big smile. "I'm so proud of each of you. You will all do wonderfully."

Talif, moving to stand beside her, reaffirmed quietly, "*Ja,* they will."

Marin glanced at him. The calm certainty in the gaze which met hers spread sweet serenity through her. In spite of her assurance to the students that they would all do wonderfully, her desire for them to make her look good had caused her to worry. Now the knowledge hit her that whatever the students did would be fabulous in their parents' eyes, truly wonderful simply because the students had worked so hard to learn and to put on this program.

Yes, of course everything will go well, she thought. "Now, Eva, Sophia, and Stina, since you're the first to perform, come stand here by the door and wait while I introduce you."

Faces beaming, the girls hurried forward.

Sophia, blue eyes sparkling, put her plump hands over the coiled braids above her ears. "See my ribbons, Teacher? They match the black stripes in my dress."

"The ribbons are very pretty, Sophia, and so is your dress. You look beautiful." Marin smiled at Eva and Stina, then turned the smile on the rest of the class. "All the girls look beautiful, and all the boys look handsome." She winked at Sophia and dropped her voice to a whisper. "Be very quiet now while I go tell the parents what you and Eva and Stina are going to do, all right?"

Sophia nodded, her hair ribbons bouncing against her shoulders.

Marin entered the other room, walking over to the square oak table covered with the fine lace cloth. The table served as the altar during the church service. She could smell the comforting scent of the candle that had burned on the altar during the service.

She stood beside the table and faced the congregation, her hands folded primly in front of her green dress with tiny white lace edging the collar. Off to one side sat a special guest, Miss Allen, the teacher from town who had so kindly given Marin advice and encouragement months earlier. She'd made the long trip today to see the students' program. Marin hoped she could return the favor in a couple weeks when the town students gave their own program.

The parents' faces look as excited and proud as the students', Marin thought. She greeted them in Swedish. "Welcome to the first program of our congregation's school. The students have worked hard over the last months, and each one should be proud of what he or she has learned. They've also worked hard on this program. We hope you'll enjoy it. For our first presentation, Stina and Sophia Linder and Eva Skarstedt will sing a song in English about the days of the week."

The song set the program off to a good start. Marin had written the song with its simple tune. The lyrics told of common housekeeping duties for each day of the week. The students performed actions indicating laundering, baking, and such, which made it apparent to those in the audience who only spoke Swedish which day of the week was represented.

When the ditty was over, the audience burst into applause. At the appreciation, the little girls smiled widely and curtsied again and again, bringing enchanted laughter from their admirers.

Knute Linder, one of the most intelligent of Marin's students, read in Swedish an essay on the beginnings of their new country. The congregation listened wide-eyed and intent while he told of the Stamp Act, the Boston Tea Party, and the Revolutionary War.

The lesson on the United States continued with Orpha Stenvall and Viola Linder, thirteen and ten, reading the Declaration of Independence in Swedish. Marin had spent many long hours, working long into the night by the wavering light of the kerosene lamp, translating the work from English into Swedish. She and Talif had debated whether it should be presented in the new language or the language of the homeland, and Swedish won. Learning to speak English was important, but the adult immigrants—and even Marin's students—hadn't enough knowledge of the language to understand such a long and involved presentation. More important, Marin and Talif decided, that the audience understands one of its new country's most important documents.

When Orpha and Viola were done, the listeners affirmed Marin and Talif's decision by not only clapping but also cheering. Obviously they agreed with the sentiments of their new country's founders. Marin lifted her gaze above the crowd and searched out Talif where he stood at the bedroom door. His grin and wink made her laugh from the joy of sharing in the wonder of this special moment.

Other students followed with songs and recitations. Finally it was time for the largest event. Marin introduced it. "Next is a skit. The class wrote it as a joint project, and they did a fine job indeed. It involves situations in which we all find ourselves, simple things like greeting people, asking for directions, and buying things in stores. You'll hear common English phrases,

phrases we will all use many times in the years to come. Every student in the class will take part. Talif Siverson will play the part of a store clerk. And now, the Prairie School Players perform for your pleasure."

As Marin walked away, she passed eight-year-old Sture and ten-year-old Anders Skarstedt as they headed to the stage area. She knew her own brothers, Einer and August, were coming from the other direction. The four would begin the first scene, greeting and introducing each other.

"Good morning. How are you, Anders?" Marin heard Einer ask as she reached her place in the back of the room behind the audience.

As she watched, contentment at her students' presentation filled her heart. *Did all teachers feel this incredible sense of satisfaction at their students' accomplishments?* she wondered. Her gaze rested on Miss Allen. She didn't speak Swedish, so she couldn't have understood everything. Yet judging from her expression, she was enjoying the program. Marin hoped this experienced teacher felt the students were doing as well as Marin did.

At the end of the skit, Marin joined the students. They all faced the congregation and recited together Psalm 23 in English. Then Marin invited the audience to join them in reciting the psalm in Swedish.

Before they were done, tears glittered in some of the parents' eyes, and tears blurred Marin's sight as well. Marin thanked the audience for coming and the students for their hard work. She spoke of the things the students had learned during the months of schooling, of how far they'd come, and of the goals she hoped the school could help students achieve in the future. Her own parents' faces gleamed with pride, making Marin feel humble in response.

She was about to dismiss everyone when Talif stepped forward. "Excuse me, Miss Nilsson. There's something I and the other students would like to say."

Surprise kept her from speaking, but she nodded at him and began to step back. Talif touched her elbow, stopping her, then moved his hand away.

"You came today," he said to the audience, "to honor the students for the efforts they've put forth over the last few months and to listen to examples of what they've learned. They deserve your respect, and it's easy to see they've received it. There's someone else here today who deserves your respect and that of the students, as well as all our thanks. Miss Marin Nilsson, one of the finest teachers on the prairie."

The congregation rose as one, clapping and smiling. Calls of "*Ja*," and "*Många tack*, Miss Nilsson" reached Marin's ears and heart.

Before the ovation died down, Talif faced Marin and continued. "The families wanted you to know how much your devotion to their children means to them, so they've bought you a gift." He looked over at Jems Stenvall. "Jems?"

Her heart lodged in her throat, Marin watched Jems walk over to the stove and pick up from beside it what appeared to be a packing box covered with a woven rug. He brought the box over and held it in front of her. His expression was sober, his eyes serious as he spoke. "Miss Nilsson, all of us students thank you for all you've done for us. We can't truly repay you, but we hope this will show you how grateful we are for your teaching."

Marin covered her lips with her fingers and swallowed twice before she could respond. "Thank you, Jems." She recognized it as an extraordinary speech from the often rebellious student. Who had selected him as the gift giver? The choice was a lovely gesture.

She reached out shaking fingers and lifted the brown-and-tan striped rug. At the sight of the gift beneath it, she dropped the rug to the floor with a cry.

Jems, Talif, and the other students laughed, and Marin, recognizing their laughter as joy at her response, joined them. She lifted out the gift: a globe of the world. She held it high to show the crowd.

Turning to Talif, she asked, "How did you ever. . . ?"

She didn't need to finish the question. Talif grinned. "All the families contributed to it. Miss Allen sent for it. More than that, she told the county school superintendent about our plan. He decided that since the students' families went to such trouble to start a school, the county could spare a little of their funds to make up for what we hadn't raised in the cost of the globe."

Marin's gaze darted to Miss Allen. The town teacher rose and joined Marin and Talif. "You and the students deserve this gift. You are to be commended, Miss Nilsson. Your dedication to the students is inspiring. I feel privileged to know you."

Marin murmured her thanks as the congregation once again broke into applause.

Marin could barely keep her emotions in control while the parents, one by one, thanked her before leaving, and the girl students stopped to give her hugs.

Standing in the background, Talif watched it all, sharing in Marin's happiness from afar. Miss Allen's words rang true: Marin well deserved the praise.

The rest of spring and summer loomed long ahead of him, months without seeing Marin in class every day. But the thought of the surprise gift awaiting her before classes resumed next fall made his heart quickstep. The next school program wouldn't be held in anyone's home but in a school, as was proper. In Marin's school.

He'd spoken with Einer, Knute, and Jems after the program, and they'd agreed to help. Their eyes had shined with excitement at the idea. He knew they'd find time to slip away from their chores and field work to help him when the time came.

Talif leaned back against the wall, arms crossed over his suit front, a smile on his face, joy in his chest, and Marin in his sight and heart.

Chapter 9

Marin knelt in the late August twilight, weeding the garden in the cool of the evening. She was grateful for the light breeze that rustled through the corn and kept the mosquitoes away. Crickets and cicadas sang their songs for her as she worked. Scents of moist earth, green plants, and humid air surrounded her.

Standing up, she stretched, pressing her hands against the small of her back as she lifted her gaze and stared over the land toward Talif's home. His roof was barely visible over the tall prairie grass and her father's field of corn. Grasshoppers had invaded the county again, destroying many crops but for some reason sparing the Nilssons', Siverson's, and other nearby fields.

Talif's plowed land lay on the side of his home opposite the Nilsson farm. A small rise hid his fields from her view even in the early spring before the wild grasses and crops grew high. Sometimes on windy days during the spring, she'd seen thin clouds of dirt in the air and known he was working his fields. Now no such signs disclosed his actions.

She hardly dared acknowledge to herself that she missed seeing him every day as she had during the school term, hardly dared acknowledge the ache that tugged at her heart when she remembered all his kind assistance with the school. Last winter, even before school began, Talif had stopped at the house often to visit with Fader. Field work kept all the homesteaders busy during the summer. She knew Talif was no exception. They all worked late into the evenings. Only when rain kept Talif from the fields did he stop by the house to see Fader now. Talif always greeted Marin pleasantly when he stopped, asking after her, but it wasn't the same as when they worked on his lessons or he helped with the class in some way.

Would he join the class again this fall? He hadn't said, and she wouldn't ask.

Soon she'd need to begin planning lessons again. Likely fieldwork would prevent any but the youngest boys from attending the first fall classes. She expected the parents would allow most of the girls to come to school except during harvest when all female hands were needed to bake and serve the men when they came from the fields.

The black-and-white dog came running out of the cornfield and across the garden rows, eager to greet her. "Sven!" Marin grabbed at the dog. "Come. The garden is no place for you. If Moder sees you among the beans. . ." She let the warning stay unfinished as she urged the dog across the furrows.

"Where've you been, Sven? Did you go with Einer? You're as mysterious as he's been, heading off every night as soon as the evening meal is over, refusing to tell me where he's going. I can't believe Fader lets him go like that."

It wasn't like Fader to let Einer leave that way. The cows needed milking each evening, and Fader and the boys often worked in the fields late. Besides, where could Einer possibly go? They lived too far from town for that to be his destination.

She'd asked Fader where Einer went, but he hadn't told her.

Petting Sven's head, she looked out over the prairie, then up at the sky where the love star announced the coming of night. Something strange was going on, that was certain.

※

Talif lifted his hat with one hand and wiped the sweat from his forehead with his opposite forearm. Einer, Knute, and Jems imitated him.

Talif grimaced to hide a grin. Almost nine in the evening and still warm enough that he and the boys broke a sweat working on the building. Of course, cutting prairie sod into three-by-two bricks and laying them up two layers thick to build a house would probably make a man sweat in the midst of a Minnesota winter.

He took a tin dipper of water from the bucket beside him and drank down a refreshing swig. Einer followed suit.

Talif rested his hands on his hips, surveying the building. "You've done a good night's work, boys." Talif studied the cloudless sky. "If the weather holds, we can start the roof tomorrow. Once that's on, we should be able to finish the school by this time next week."

Einer wiped his hands on the back of his jeans and grinned. "Marin's going to be mighty surprised."

"She'd better be." Talif looked from boy to boy. "You've all kept your word? Haven't told anyone but your fathers?"

They all nodded.

"Good. It'd be a crying shame if Miss Nilsson caught wind of what we're doing."

"I haven't told anyone else, but. . ." Knute cleared his throat, "Fader told Moder."

Talif wasn't too surprised. "Well, that's to be expected. Seems men can't keep secrets from their wives no matter how hard they try. Besides, I imagine your mothers insisted on knowing where you boys have been going each evening."

Knute nodded, looking relieved by Talif's response. "Moder wants to help. She's a Dala painter. She thought, if it's all right with you, Talif, she could paint pictures on the door and window lintels."

"Sounds like a great idea. It would sure make the school more attractive. I'll talk with her about it at Sunday service."

Knute leaned over to grab the water dipper, but Talif figured the boy did so more to hide his pride in Talif's response to his mother's offer than because Knute wanted the water.

Soon the boys left for home, leaving Talif alone with the soon-to-be schoolhouse. He walked inside the roofless building, imagining it filled with benches, students, and the most beautiful Swedish teacher on the prairie.

He sighed deeply. "Oh, Lord, please let her love it as much I think she will."

❦

Marin sat with her brothers and sisters in the bed of Fader's spring wagon as they bounced across the prairie under the Sunday morning sun. The straw beneath her softened the jolting somewhat but poked through the blanket she sat on and through her stockings, making her calves itch. The back of her head hit the side of the wagon with a *thump* as the wagon went over a particularly rough bump. "Ouch." She winced and pressed the palm of her hand against the back of her favorite blue sunbonnet. "How much longer before we're there, Fader?"

"Soon. Have patience."

She could hear the laughter in his voice. She wasn't amused. She glanced at Elsbet, who sat beside her, and didn't bother to disguise her disgust. "I don't know why it's such a secret where services will be held today. It's never been a secret before."

Elsbet smiled and patted Marin's calico-covered knee. "May as well enjoy the ride and let Fader enjoy his secret."

They'd passed Talif's home minutes earlier, so obviously the meeting wouldn't be held there. The Linder and Stenvall families lived in the direction they were headed. She hoped the meeting wouldn't be the Stenvall home, which was more cramped than most of the congregation members' houses. Immediately she felt ashamed for her attitude. What could be more crowded than her own home when she taught school?

Marin stretched her neck, trying in vain to see over the wagon's side. The sounds and smells didn't help. The prairie was filled with the scent of earth and sound of wind rustling through crisping leaves of corn. With a half sigh, half inelegant snort, she gave up and let her mind drift to lesson plans. She mentally listed English words for the everyday lives of her students: fields, plows, crops, farm, farmer.

She felt a smile tug at the corners of her mouth. Talif would say this showed she was a God-made teacher. A trickle of sadness slid through her. She missed his presence in her life, missed his encouragement for her teaching. Well, no sense dwelling on that. She forced her mind back to the list. *Trädgård*, garden; *växa*, grow; *grönsaker*, vegetables; *ko*, cow.

Entertained with the list, she didn't notice the wagon slowing and stopping. "Everyone out," Fader called.

Marin stood, looking about. In front of them sat a sod house, one she'd never seen. Rectangular, it had a door in the middle and a window on either side. Someone had cut down the prairie grass in front of the house, and half-a-dozen horse-drawn wagons stood in the yard. She recognized a number of the teams as belonging to church members.

"Who lives here?" she asked as Fader helped her from the wagon.

"No one."

She opened her mouth to question further, but the twinkle in Fader's eyes told her it would be useless.

The planks making up the door stood unweathered against the prairie winds and still held the smell of newly cut wood. Fader held the door for the family, Marin entering last. She paused a step past the threshold, her gaze wandering over the congregation-filled room as curiosity grew stronger instead of lessening.

The freshly whitewashed walls added light and cheer. The unusual luxury of a window on each end of the building let in additional sunlight and warmth. On the wall facing her hung a painted blackboard like the one Talif had made for the school. Below it, a crate stood on end, three books on the only shelf as though the crate were intended as a bookcase. A metal stove stood square in the middle of the room. Primarily women and children sat on the crude benches facing the far wall. Men and older boys with hats in hands stood along the walls. A small table between the benches and far wall served as an altar. A white cloth with a cross made of hardanger embroidery covered the table. Two silver candlesticks held candles for the service, and a Bible lay between them. The pleasant scent from the warm candle wax mingled with the odor of fresh earth.

"Good morning, Marin." Talif's whispered greeting came from beside her.

She turned her head to smile at him but didn't think to answer, her mind still attempting to understand where this place came from and why Fader had kept it a secret.

"Come, Marin." Fader's hand against the small of her back urged her forward. She followed her mother and siblings to the front row of benches, which for some reason remained empty in spite of the standing members.

Marin found it difficult to keep her attention on the service and the pastor's words about the Lord bringing all things to a time of harvest. Her gaze and mind kept wandering about the room, noticing every little thing, trying to figure it all out. When the service was over except for the final blessing, the pastor finally mentioned the building.

"The Lord has brought much to harvest in our little congregation this year," he began, "including this wonderful new *kyrka*, church, in which to worship. One day we will have a building of wood or brick, but for the moment, we have a temple filled with love and devotion, and I am sure that makes it a magnificent temple in the eyes and heart of the Lord."

Murmured *amen*s and nodding heads showed agreement.

"Our gratitude goes out to the one who conceived the idea for this building, who gave the land for it, and who gave of his own labor and funds to build it. Talif Siverson, please accept our thanks."

Marin whipped her head around in stunned surprise to look at Talif, who still stood beside the door, his face now a ruddy red from the attention and applause of the congregation. Talif had done this, created this place, given it from his own land and labor?

"Every family has contributed something," the pastor continued. "I especially want to honor Einer Nilsson, Knute Linder, and Jems Stenvall, who helped Talif build the church."

Marin's gaze found Einer's face with its pleased but embarrassed expression. This was where he'd disappeared all those evenings!

The pastor lifted his right arm in a sweeping motion. "Mrs.

Linder decorated the lintels with Dala painting."

Marin liked the cheer added to the otherwise plain walls by the typical Dala-picture elements: a simple, almost childlike style, oversized flowers, bright colors, and people wearing traditional Swedish outfits.

"The Stenvalls contributed a water bucket and dipper," the pastor continued. "Mrs. Nilsson and Elsbet made curtains for the windows and Mrs. Skarstedt sewed a curtain for the bookshelf. The women brought their gifts today."

Marin stared in amazement as the women carried the items to the front and laid them reverently on the makeshift altar. When had Elsbet and Moder found time to make the curtains without Marin's knowledge?

After thanking the women, the pastor said, "There are some here who still don't know of this building's complete purpose."

Marin brought her gaze to his and was surprised to find him smiling at her.

"Specifically," he continued, "Miss Marin Nilsson and most of her students. Einer?"

Einer stood and, carrying a rectangular plank, walked to stand beside the pastor. Then he held the plank for everyone to see.

Marin gasped. Prairie Church and School, she read. The words were in script, in two lines, the top in English, the bottom in Swedish. She covered her lips with her fingers. Tears blurred her vision. Through her wonder, she heard the pastor's words. "This building began as a school, a place for our children to learn, a place for our own dedicated Miss Nilsson to teach them."

She missed the rest, the few additional words or phrases, the final blessing. She wanted to turn, to look at Talif, to thank him. How could he possibly have done this marvelous thing? She'd scorned his attentions. In return he'd only given good back to her, encouraged her dream, assisted with teaching ideas, and now built a school.

The wonder of the new school paled beside the other thoughts and feelings flooding her, crumbling the walls she'd built around her heart. Such a man as Talif would never betray a woman as Elsbet's fiancé had betrayed her. A man like Talif would remain devoted to the woman he chose to love.

Marin caught her bottom lip between her teeth. Had she given away any chance of Talif's love? Her chest felt as though squeezed in a vise. She'd hardly seen him the last few months. Had he lost interest in her? But he'd built this school. Had he done so because he loved her or because he, also, cared deeply for the students? Hope fluttered in her heart. If she received another chance at Talif's love, she wouldn't be so foolish as to refuse it again.

🐝

Early the next morning Marin hurried down the ruts that formed a road between the Nilsson farm and Talif's place. She breathed a sigh of relief as she passed his home apparently undetected and continued along toward the new schoolhouse.

She saw the sign hung above the schoolhouse door long before she reached the building: Prairie Church and School. It sent joy humming through her.

A long piece of carved wood rested on the large flat stone Talif had placed for a doorstep. The sight of the wooden piece brought Marin to a breathless stop six feet from the house. She recognized the piece. Not that specific piece, but the design, like a long, beautiful chisel. Any Swedish woman would recognize the traditional courting request. Bring it inside, and she agreed to be courted by the giver. Leave it on the doorstep, and the giver knew his heart's request was rejected.

Her breath came short and quick as she walked toward it, step by slow step. She stared at it long and hard before kneeling to examine the intricate carving of hearts and flowers with a trembling index finger. It was Talif's work, of course. She lifted the piece and hugged it to her heart, whispering silent thanksgiving to the Lord for the second chance.

Marin carried the courting board inside with her, began to set it down on the desk, then changed her mind. With one hand, she untied her bonnet and laid it on the desk, then began slowly walking around the room, glad to at last be alone to absorb the wonder of this school built for her and her dream.

Talif leaned against the doorframe of the open door, watching Marin walking about the room, lost in her own thoughts. He'd known as soon as he saw the courting board gone from the doorstep that she'd accepted his request, but his heart stumbled in joy at the way she clutched it to her. Warmth spread through his chest at the reverence with which she ran her fingers across the simple desk and the back of the barrel chair he'd made her.

Even knowing she welcomed his courting, he felt tentative stepping inside, as if entering new territory. And weren't they? A territory filled with new joys, and new challenges, as well. He walked slowly across the packed-dirt floor toward where she stood with her back toward him. "Marin?"

He'd spoken quietly so as not to startle her, but she swung about like a frightened bird, her blue eyes first wide with fright, then shining with welcome and something similar to embarrassment. Instinctively he reached to comfort her, his hands on her arms. "I didn't want to frighten you."

"You didn't. I mean, you did, but only for a moment."

His touch made her nervous, he could see. Disappointed, he removed his hands from her arms, reminding himself they were only beginning the move from friendship to courtship.

Marin's lashes hid her eyes from his view as she glanced down at the board she still carried. "I–I'm honored you wish to court me. Thank you for this. It's beautiful."

"You're welcome. I'm honored you agreed."

Her gaze darted about the room. "And this. . .the school. . . everything. I don't know how to begin to thank you."

"By using it for the teaching God created you to do." He took the board from her and set it on the desk. Then gently, he brushed the fingers of his right hand over the curve of her cheek, rejoicing when she didn't flinch from his touch. "I wish it could be a wooden building, but I couldn't afford that now and neither could the congregation."

"That will come in time."

He saw belief in her eyes, and it reinforced his own. Would they help build that school one day together? Would their own children attend it? He swept the thought away. Moving too fast again. She'd only just agreed to court.

Yet unless he was mistaken, there was more than belief in the school to come in her eyes. There was joy at the thought of *them*, of the two of them as a couple. Anticipation? Faith?

His hand slid to the back of her neck, and he leaned close until, an inch away from her lips, he locked her gaze in his and whispered, "May I kiss you, Miss Nilsson?"

"Y–yes."

He touched his lips to hers tenderly, lost in wonder at the gift, the treasure that was Marin, at the hope that she offered him in agreeing to court. One kiss grew to two, gentle, questioning. Then to more, exploring, thanking. Until with a sweet sigh, she leaned against his chest, and his chin rested against her hair. And forgetting all over again not to move too quickly, he said, "I love you, Marin Nilsson. Is that all right?"

Marin shifted her head until he could see the joy shining in her eyes. "It's perfect."

As he drew her into another embrace, he could only agree.

Epilogue

June 1874

The summer breeze tugged playfully at the wildflowers tucked into Marin's coronet braid and tossed the heads of the flowers she carried as she stood outside the church and school, waiting impatiently for the ceremony to begin. Delicate blue, pink, and yellow flowers dotted the prairie grass surrounding the building and growing from the roof.

Marin smiled at Elsbet. "Was any chapel or home ever decorated so beautifully for a wedding?"

Elsbet's gaze held laughter, but she agreed as she smoothed the arms of Marin's dress of dark green silk.

Lovely strains from a violin inside the building reached them, and Marin took a shaky breath. She smiled at Sophia. "Time to begin. Are you scared?"

Wide-eyed, the little girl shook her head no. "Mother says I've the most important job of the whole wedding."

Marin bit back a laugh and avoided looking at Elsbet. "Your mother is right."

Sophia grinned and started toward the church to spread

wildflowers from her basket onto Marin's path. At the door stood Fader, waiting to accompany Marin to the altar.

Elsbet slipped her arm about Marin's waist in a quick hug. "I'm so happy for you. Talif is a good man. Seeing his devotion to you. . ." Her voice broke. Marin waited patiently while Elsbet took a deep breath and continued. "Seeing the way he treats you. . .it makes me believe that maybe. . .maybe there's a man somewhere who might love me that way."

Elsbet's hope caught at Marin's heart. She hugged her sister close. "Of course there is," she whispered fiercely. "Can't the Lord do anything? Isn't love His favorite gift?"

Marin saw tears glitter as Elsbet broke away and followed Sophia toward the church.

Moments later, Marin's vision was free from tears as she stood beside the altar and the man who would become, in only minutes, her husband. Seeing the love in Talif's eyes, standing with him before the Lord and her family, and the congregation in the church and school built by Talif's love, she knew her words to Elsbet were true.

That truth sang inside Marin's heart as she and Talif vowed the love they had for each other would continue forever.

JOANN A. GROTE

JoAnn lives in Minnesota where she grew up. She uses the state for most of her story settings, and like her characters, JoAnn seeks to serve Christ in her work. She believes that readers of novels can receive a message of salvation and encouragement from well-crafted fiction. An award-winning author, she has had over thirty-five books published, including numerous novellas, several novels with Barbour Publishing in the **Heartsong Presents** line, and novels in the **American Adventure** and **Sisters in Time** series for kids.

The Reluctant Schoolmarm

by Yvonne Lehman

Dear Reader,

When I was a child and someone asked what I wanted to be when I grew up, the thought occurred to me that other children would say, "A nurse" or "A teacher." Wanting to be different, I said, "I want to write books." I said that only because I loved reading books but hadn't the slightest notion I could be a person who put stories on paper to become a book.

Now that I do write books, I have an entirely different view of nurses (there being several in my family) and of teachers (having taught college courses and creative writing classes). Teaching an hour course takes many hours of preparation and planning. Getting to know and care about students takes time, as does grading papers. Much effort goes into teaching in spite of modern conveniences such as computers.

Therefore, I can look with respect and admiration to the time when teachers taught in one-room schoolhouses, all subjects being taught to children from age five through their teen years. These teachers had limited supplies, and they often contended with parents who thought caring for the crops was more important than caring for young minds. My "Reluctant Schoolmarm," who teaches in the mountains of western North Carolina in 1910, will come to understand and appreciate such dedicated professionals.

—*Yvonne*

Study to shew thyself approved unto God,
a workman that needeth not to be ashamed,
rightly dividing the word of truth.
2 TIMOTHY 2:15, KJV

Chapter 1

As Christa Walsh started down the steps of the train, the man in front of her turned to race back up. She reached for her hat lest it be jarred off.

Male voices began singing, "For He's a Jolly Good Fellow" accompanied by a harmonica. Looking ahead, she saw two men, one tall and one short, beneath the sign above the depot, confirming this was Grey Eagle, the closest she could get by train to her destination high in the Blue Ridge Mountains of western North Carolina.

The man in front of her cast furtive glances over his shoulder while stammering, "Pardon me. . . I. . . " The greenish cast on his face wasn't caused by the reflection of the vest he wore over his white shirt. Maybe he was motion sick. The train had chugged higher and higher around curves. The smoke and people odors in the coach hadn't been all that pleasant either.

A man's voice behind her sounded annoyed. "Ma'am, sir, could you step aside, please?"

The tall singer rushed to her. With a slight bow, he held out his arm. She had the strange feeling she should respond by placing her hand on it. The green-vested man now held her suitcase. The short singer grabbed his arm.

At least the strap of her smaller bag still lay across her shoulder. Her arm pressed the bag closer to her body in case the singers weren't as innocent as they seemed. She'd heard tales about highlanders not liking their territory being invaded by flatlanders and referring to city folks as highfalutin' with their 1910 conveniences that hadn't reached the mountains.

The logical explanation for the singers, however, was that they were welcoming some important personage. No thanks to her fellow passenger, they stood in the way of others trying to exit the train.

Christa placed her gloved hand on the tall man's arm and moved forward, not wanting to mess up their parade or this welcome.

She and the panicky-looking man were being escorted across the yard toward the depot, where the bearded man in overalls was still playing the "Jolly Good Fellow" tune.

The welcoming committee was quite small—only three people. The depot was small, too, compared with her hometown of Hendersonville. A welcoming committee there would have been a band of a dozen or more men in uniform and perhaps a chorus of women and children. Horse-drawn taxis would meet an important personage. Men and women would dress in their finery. These men wore simpler attire—everyday work clothes.

When they reached the depot porch, Christa took her bag from the strange man. Now that they were out of the way, she thought it exciting that she might see a celebrity while waiting for Uncle John to show up.

The short singer began talking to the weird man, but before Christa could catch what he was saying, the tall singer said, "Jeb Norval here. Ah!"

His "Ah!" kept her from introducing herself. Her gaze followed his. Coming up the road, raising a cloud of dust, was a horse-drawn wagon with a big red ribbon tied around the horse's neck.

"Whoa!" The driver drew up and looked down at her. "Black Bear Mountain, next stop!"

Christa looked up. He nodded like he knew her. Was this her transportation? "You. . .know John McIntyre?"

He looked as if the question were an affront to his intelligence. "Why, ma'am, I don't just know him. I beat him in a game of checkers ever now and then. Can outhunt 'im, outshoot 'im, and if need be outrun 'im." He laughed heartily, jumping down from the wagon.

Christa thought he might have out-aged 'im, too, considering his head of snow-white hair and the cottonlike puffs on his jaw.

He bowed, then stuck his thumbs behind his red suspenders. "Clem Carmichael at your service, ma'am."

Christa responded favorably to the smiling man with his twinkling eyes. He obviously enjoyed life. She hadn't. . .in a long time. But this was not the time for thinking about that.

She offered her gloved hand. "I'm Christa Walsh. So pleased to meet you. This is some taxi service."

"The least we can do, ma'am. Here, let me help you up."

"I need to get my suitcase."

"Which one?" the weird man asked. "I'll get it for you."

Surely this man wouldn't want to steal a woman's luggage. "The tweed one."

Clem Carmichael took her small bag and set it in the wagon, then held out his hand to help her up. She lifted her skirt slightly, stepped up, and took the seat behind the driver's. The man who'd gone for her suitcase hoisted it and a black bag into the back of the wagon, then jumped up and sat beside her.

She stumbled on her words. "You. . .you're going to Black Bear Mountain?"

"Don't have much of a choice." He made it sound like a fate worse than death.

Clem Carmichael spoke briefly with the singers. Christa wished she could stay longer to see the important person emerge from that train. Why would they come here? From the few things she'd heard about Black Bear Mountain, she'd concluded it was a backwoods place.

Well, for whatever reason, her uncle John couldn't meet her, but he sure made nice arrangements by sending his friend to fetch her. How sweet of him to think of the red ribbon.

To her surprise, when the driver climbed up into his seat, the two singers and harmonica player went to the side of the depot, unhitched horses, and rode out in front of them.

She looked back. The conductor shouted, "All aboard!" and a couple got on. The train began grinding away, puffing smoke from the stack. Leaving the station.

Had she missed something?

"Giddy-up," Clem Carmichael said, flicking the reins. "The real celebration is at Bear Cove," he explained, looking back over his shoulder. "You know my Dora, Doc."

Now what did that mean? His doradoc? Was that a name? A person? Place? Or was. . .

She slowly turned her head toward the green-faced man, who quickly turned away. "Are you ill?"

He took a deep breath and faced her. His dark eyes seemed to say that was an understatement. He exhaled heavily. "Quite!"

"Perhaps," she said with a lift of her chin, "you should see a doctor."

His growl was not happy. Looking worse by the moment, he leaned back against the seat and mumbled, "I can't believe it. This can't be happening."

She had to ask. "He called you Doc?"

He nodded.

"You. . .are the celebrity?"

His gaze met hers. "No," he said. "You are."

Chapter 2

D r. Grant Gordon had seen varied responses to all sorts of injuries—broken bones and even the insides of a man blown away by rifle shot. But he wasn't sure he'd ever seen a more baffled expression than was on the face of this woman.

This should not be whatever her name was. This should be Adelaide Montgomery, his beautiful blond, blue-eyed fiancée from Asheville. Or—he corrected his thought—his fiancée-to-be. The only thing lacking was a ring on her finger. That would happen after he made the final payments to the jeweler.

His fellow passenger wasn't really the celebrity, of course, since she was not Adelaide Montgomery. A little scrutiny revealed she was likely a couple years older than Adelaide. Definitely darker. Medium-brown hair, wide surprised-looking eyes. Would her dark eyes dance with golden fire if he obeyed his sudden urge and asked her to be his fiancée?

He understood that crazy impulse—it was the product of desperation. This situation could ruin his career in the cove. Over the past few years while waiting for Adelaide to be ready for marriage, he'd won the people's trust. He'd started out as one of them, but after going away to university and medical school, he had to prove he didn't have highfalutin' ideas.

In Asheville, he had to do the opposite and prove himself intelligent, competent, and without backwoods ideas.

He'd given the impression that he and his intended would come to the cove because that's what he wanted and what Adelaide had implied. Promised, in fact!

What he hadn't counted on was the predicament that had delayed Adelaide's arrival. He'd determined to return to the cove and explain things. That was before these greeters had assumed this woman seated next to him was Adelaide.

He drew in a deep breath and prepared to explain. However, the only words he uttered were, "I'm truly sorry."

Sorry? Christa thought a more apt word would be *crazy*.

Or else she was!

Her brother, William, had said she was doing a dangerous thing, traveling alone on the train to a backwoods place she'd never seen.

Her sister-in-law thought her motives noble, but Christa had a feeling Bettina would be glad to have her out of the house and shop. The woman had wished Christa well and warned her not to talk to strangers.

Now, Christa sat behind a stranger in a wagon that was taking her to Uncle John's and taking this strange man. . .where?

She was about to ask when he took a letter from his pocket. She tried to see what was on that pink sheet of paper upon which was scrawled a feminine script. As if aware of her intent, he tilted the paper, studied it, then returned it to his pocket. He sighed heavily.

Whatever his problem, it wasn't hers!

She would not respond to his "celebrity" remark, in case

he wanted a discussion of whether being the preacher's great-niece gave her celebrity status and rated a couple of singers, a harmonica player, and a horse with a red ribbon.

Dear Uncle John was treating her as special, so she would simply enjoy it. With that resolve, she looked at the scenery.

Everything was lushly green in mid-June. The air cooled the higher they went. At times, the thick forest prevented the midafternoon sun from filtering down on the road. She wouldn't want to be out here alone at night. Her previous thought resurfaced. She was in this secluded place with two men she didn't know—strangers!

She had seen nothing but trees and mountains for quite a while, one piled behind another until they faded into the horizon. Where were the houses? She'd noticed a few near the train station at Grey Eagle, and farther out she'd noticed a few buildings making up a small town with a main street, a hotel, and several houses.

Occasionally she glimpsed a log cabin or a plank-board house, or smoke curling from a chimney back in the forest.

She began to wonder how far back into these mountains they were going. She leaned forward. "Mr. Carmichael!"

Wearing that friendly smile, he looked over his shoulder. "You'll have to speak up. I'm a little hard of hearing."

She leaned closer. "I was wondering how much farther to Uncle's John's?"

"Oh, a few miles as the crow flies. 'Course we don't take the same route as the crows." He laughed. "But we'll be there directly."

Clem Carmichael then described what a fine preacher her uncle John was. "Too bad he can't be here for the festivities."

Christa looked at the doctor, whose gaze lifted to the sky as if pleading for help. She leaned forward again. "Festivities?"

"I don't want to give anything away. I guess John was in too big a hurry to get down to Flat Creek Community for their revival meetings to tell me you're his niece. But we sure are glad to have you here in the cove."

Christa wondered why. A light began to dawn. Of course! Uncle John must have told him she wanted to find unique mountain-made handcrafts to sell at the shop in Hendersonville.

"When is Uncle John coming back?"

"Later tonight. Has to preach here tomorrow, it being Sunday and all."

She was disappointed it wouldn't be sooner but understood her uncle had obligations. At least she had a place to stay.

"Did Uncle John leave a key?"

"Don't need no keys around here, Miss Walsh. Nobody's got anything anybody else wants, 'cept maybe some food. John would give anybody his last bite. No need to steal it."

Christa leaned back and tried to relax.

That wasn't easy. The weird man beside her had just learned she'd be at Uncle John's alone—and without a key to lock the door.

※

Grant realized he had another problem after hearing that John McIntyre wasn't in the cove. The depot hadn't been the place to explain the mix-up because, yes, Grant did know Clem's Dora. Sending Clem and the singers to the station indicated this was only a preliminary welcome.

Nevertheless, a hope grew within. Maybe this would be a quiet dinner for Clem and Dora, Grant and his fiancée. He would explain the mistake, and they would laugh. Dora would be pleased she could do this nicety for the preacher's niece.

Soon they rode out into a clearing. The horse trotted along on level ground. A line of children held a long WELCOME TEACHER banner. In front of the church stood women and a few men who began to sing "She'll Be Comin' 'Round the Mountain" to the sound of the harmonica and the rhythm of their hands.

No, this would not be a quiet dinner for four.

Chapter 3

"Whoa, Nelly!"

Christa knew this was no welcoming party for her, although "Doc" had implied so.

She could not explain this situation, so she might as well stop trying. Clem was thoughtful to bring her to this celebration instead of to her uncle's empty house. Besides, this was a good way to meet people and ask about their crafts.

The doctor stepped down and turned to assist Christa. His strong hands easily encircled her waist. By the time her feet touched the ground and he had moved aside, a regal-looking woman with silvery gray hair stood in front of her, smiling. She hugged Christa. "I'm Dora Carmichael, dear."

Christa thought the woman must have been a friend of Aunt Sadie's. They were about the same age. Maybe as a tribute to Sadie, who had died six months ago, and to their beloved preacher, the celebration really was for her. Back here in the cove, any change might be an excuse for a celebration.

"I'm pleased to meet you, Mrs. Carmichael. I'm Christa Walsh. I'm here—"

"Finally!" Dora Carmichael gushed. "Just follow me!"

With a flourish, the woman turned and strode up a path bordered by at least fifty people. They applauded, and the children chanted, "Teacher, teacher, teacher" in unison.

Dora must be a teacher.

Dora looked over her shoulder. "Come on, Grant, and get your dues. You're responsible for this."

Grant stepped up beside Christa. She realized he must be the teacher. He had admitted he was a doctor, and she had thought his degree was in medicine. But it must be academic.

"This is the worst day of my life," he said. "I'm sorry to drag you into it."

She tried not to feel scared. "Are they going to tar and feather us?"

He drew in a deep breath. "Worse."

When she stopped, he shook his head. "Not you. I'm the one who's going to be run out on a rail."

"You just came in," she said.

"That's where I made my mistake."

Christa followed his gaze. They stood in front of the church, and the others were following.

Dora loudly declared, "We have waited a long time for this. Our dear children have suffered from the lack of a teacher for more than a year. Now our prayers are answered."

Grant's eyes met Christa's for an instant before he shut them and shook his head. If he didn't want to be a teacher, why was he here? Come to think of it, why was she standing beside him?

"Grant told us he would persuade his intended to come and teach our children."

His intended? Where was she? Christa could only stare at Dora, who said, "Let's thank Grant and welcome the new teacher, Miss Christa Walsh."

"Hip! Hip! Hooray!" the crowd cheered. "Hip! Hip! Hooray! Grant! Grant! Christa! Christa!"

"Miz Dora," the doctor choked out, just as Christa said, "I feel rather faint."

Dora ignored Grant and addressed Christa. "Oh, my dear, you've had a long trip, and this hot sun doesn't help. You don't need to make a speech now. You can talk to the people during our potluck."

Dora led her around the side of the church.

Christa wondered if the train ride up the mountain had done something to her mental processes. Perhaps she had caught whatever disease Doc had. Amidst the women welcoming her, children trying to talk to her, and Dora gushing about her, she tried to figure this out.

Doc. . .or Grant. . .was the teacher.

Christa was John McIntyre's great-niece.

But Dora Carmichael hadn't said that. She had said that Christa was Grant's. . .intended?

She had to do something. "Do y'all know John McIntyre?"

Dora stopped in her tracks. "Oh, honey, he's our preacher. You know him?"

"I'm his niece. Great-niece, I should say."

Dora placed her hand over her heart. "Oh, my dear. If you're kin to John, you have to be great. He's the dearest man. We all just love him."

The other women nodded, expressing similar sentiments.

Dora huffed. "I could just box that Grant Gordon's ears. He wouldn't say much about you. But word got around that he was bringing his fiancée here to teach. Now we have a double reason to celebrate. A teacher! And kin to John McIntyre. Just wait 'til the others hear this. You're balm to a sin-sick soul, child."

Christa wondered whose sinful soul Dora referred to. Before she could say she was not a teacher and could not be, they had reached white cloth-covered tables supported by sawhorses.

"Say grace for us, Clem," Dora said.

"Let's bow our heads," Clem said in a loud voice, "and thank the good Lord for the blessings of this day and what it means for our children's future."

They bowed their heads. His prayer echoed across the mountains as if the entire cove was being blessed. When he said, "And thank You, Lord, for this young lady who has come to fulfill Your purpose," Christa sneaked a peek at the doc.

His glance met hers. He grimaced and shut his eyes tightly.

"Here, dear. Take a plate. You go first behind the children."

Christa raised her head and looked into Dora's eyes, which held a hint of mischief. She must have seen Christa and Grant peeking at each other. She would think. . .what everyone already seemed to think. . .that they were. . .promised to each other. Feeling flushed—and not from the sun—Christa took the empty plate and followed the children and their mothers.

A woman on the other side of the table spoke. "We think the world of Pastor John." The man behind the woman nodded. Christa smiled. She could not explain the teacher part, but she was glad they were accepting her as Uncle John's kin. Without further hesitation, she filled her plate with fried chicken, green beans, sliced tomatoes, corn on the cob, and corn pone.

"Let's go over to that table," Dora said. "You're the guest of honor, and we don't want your pretty outfit to get messed up."

Christa followed her to a table shaded by a tall oak. She sat on a bench facing tombstones in the cemetery beyond the backyard. Grant strode up. It took all her strength not to ask what in the world he thought he was doing.

Dora patted the place across from Christa. "You sit here, Grant. Across from your sweet lady."

Since none of the other women were wearing hats, Christa removed hers. She looked steadfastly at the man, then glanced at the graveyard, hoping he got the idea that if he continued this farce, he might end up there.

Something flickered in his eyes as if he found the idea amusing. At least he got her point! He looked slightly repentant. "Could I get you ladies something to drink?"

"I'm going to need something to be able to swallow this," Christa said.

He held his breath.

Dora laughed. "They do know how to put on a spread. Some of the girls managed to get some tea and make it for this special occasion. We know city girls like tea."

"Thank you." Should she partake of this hospitality? Wouldn't refusing be cruel after all the trouble they'd gone to? They obviously accepted her as Uncle John's niece. Doc could explain the rest.

She stared at him. "I would like tea, please."

He glanced at Dora, who nodded and took the seat next to Christa. Dora gasped. "Oh, look. Just in time."

Christa looked up to see Uncle John on a fast-galloping mount. He hopped down, tied the reins to a stake, and rushed forward.

Clem and some other men stopped him and talked. He reared back at one point as if hearing something unbelievable. His smile broadened, and he strode toward Christa, chuckling, his thumbs at the lapels of his suit coat.

Christa scooted off the bench, ran, and fell into his arms. Now they could put an end to this charade.

Her uncle's embrace felt warm and comforting, reminding her of her daddy's hugs. She wanted to nestle there and bask in the feeling. However, she stepped back, and he placed his hands on her shoulders.

"My, it's good to see you," he exclaimed. "How long has it been? Two years? Sorry I didn't meet you, but I didn't know you were coming. I just got your letter on the way back from Flat Creek," he explained. "The mail had been held up because of storms last week." His eyes twinkled. "They don't deliver to your door up here."

Christa felt her smile was stuck. He didn't know she was coming? Then the welcome at the depot had nothing to do with her.

"And to think, my little niece is a teacher. And engaged. Well, glory be!"

Before she could protest, he looked beyond her. "And here's the lucky fellow."

Chapter 4

Grant felt helpless. He should have known better than to confide in Clem that his fiancée would graduate from college this year and might become the cove's teacher after their marriage.

He should have had better sense than to go to Clem's son, who was a jeweler in Asheville. He should have known the son would tell Clem about the ring, Clem would tell Dora, and Dora would turn possibility to fact. That woman had a way of turning a kitten into a bobcat.

The pastor would know how to ease things without upsetting this crowd. Grant set the glasses of tea on the table and hurried toward Christa and Pastor John.

John spread his arms wide. "Well, you ol' rascal. Who would of thought we'd end up kinfolk?" He laughed jovially, then added, "Son!" Obviously, someone had already given the pastor the news.

Grant suffered through the embrace while staring into Christa's eyes. Her chagrin had changed to amusement. She had an ally in her uncle. He could see his well-planned future dissolving before his eyes.

John released him long enough to put an arm around his shoulders. "I need to get me some of those victuals, son. Have you eaten?"

"No. But I'd like a word with. . .um. . ." Miss Walsh hadn't given him permission to address her by her first name. Instead of saying "Christa," Grant finished, "your niece."

John chuckled. "I understand. She's a beauty like my Sadie was. Has that same reddish-gold hair when the sun shines on it."

The brown did have a reddish-golden sheen. Quite. . . impressive. But Grant had no business looking at her as his fiancée. She was not Adelaide.

Pastor John went off toward the food, chuckling. Grant turned to Christa. "How are we going to handle this?"

🎀

"We?" Christa crossed her arms. "I have no idea how you're going to handle this."

She kept her voice lowered and spread a smile on her face for the benefit of onlookers. The doctor looked like he might have a heart attack. "All I want is for you to tell them that I am neither your fiancée nor the schoolteacher."

He nodded. "Before this is over, I'll tell them."

"Think they'll be sorry they fed me?" She gazed longingly at her plate. "That is, if I ever get to eat."

"Go ahead," he said. "I'll fill my plate. I'm sure Pastor John will sit at our. . .your. . .table. I'll relate the situation to him and the Carmichaels. The custom is to have a few welcoming speeches. They will expect me to introduce you since I know you best—"

"You don't know me!"

"What I mean is, they expect me to introduce Adelaide. Instead, I will explain the mistake."

"How will they take it?"

192

"They'll be disappointed. Especially the children."

Christa frowned at the food. They had prepared it for the person they thought she was. She had to eat. She had to show appreciation. Besides, she was starved. She returned to her seat at the same time Dora Carmichael stood.

"I'm going to get some of FannieMae's blackberry cobbler." Dora picked up her plate. "You'd better eat, young lady. You can't live on love. And you're going to need your strength."

Christa needed some now. She tackled the food before anything else could interrupt. Her solitude didn't last long. While children ran off to play, women and a few couples came by to greet her.

Dora returned with cobbler for them both. Uncle John and Grant were talking with several men.

"From what I could overhear," Dora said, "there's trouble up the mountain. Rifle shots rang out. Jim thinks the revenuers might have found the still."

Christa perked up. This was more like the stories she had heard about these people. But she mustn't judge. Likely, they'd heard unsavory stories about city folk, too.

She finished her dinner and tasted the dessert. "*Mmmm,* this is good."

Dora nodded. "FannieMae is the expert with blackberries. She picks 'em all over the cove. Makes pies and cobblers and sells some down at Grey Eagle."

"Is she here?"

"No. Her daughter, LulaMae, is expecting a baby any time now."

Christa noticed fewer children running around. The crowd had thinned. "Grant said there would be speeches."

"That's the practice if a visiting preacher comes. And when

Grant came back to us, we wanted to hear what he had to say. Oh, don't look so worried." Dora patted Christa's arm. "We won't do that since everybody has already met you, and your being John's niece is recommendation enough. We're just hoping you're going to like us."

"Oh, I do like you," Christa said. "Everybody is so nice."

Uncle John joined them, holding a plate piled high with food. "I'm sorry, Christa. Grant's gone up the mountain with Jim."

Christa gasped. "He's. . .gone?"

"Now don't you fret none, child," Dora soothed. "He'll be just fine. Neither the revenuers nor the moonshiners want to hurt Grant. He'll be there to help in case anyone gets shot."

That wasn't what worried Christa. She feared that if this tangled situation dragged on, Christa Walsh or Grant Gordon—or both—would get shot.

❧

Two hours later, horse's hooves sounded outside Uncle John's door. Christa opened it before the doctor had a chance to knock. At least this glum man took things seriously, unlike Uncle John, who had gone from a hearty laugh to intermittent chuckles over the misunderstanding about her being Grant's fiancée and the schoolteacher.

When Grant stepped inside the cabin, Uncle John's laughter started again.

Christa closed the door. "Uncle John, it's really not that funny."

"Now, Christa, don't deprive me of this. I haven't had such a good laugh since before Sadie got sick. She got her dander up at the slightest thing, just like you."

Was that a compliment? She folded her arms across her waist. "I don't consider this slight, Uncle John. Unless the doctor here. . .sets this straight, I can't face these people again. They're going to think I'm as devious—"

Grant straightened. "Now wait just a minute."

Uncle John chuckled again. "Let's discuss this over supper. You eaten, Doc?"

"Nothing all day."

Uncle John turned toward the kitchen. "Dora made us bring home enough to last a week."

Grant motioned for Christa to precede him.

Uncle John set a plate and milk on the table.

Grant closed his eyes to pray.

Christa waited for him to look up, then spoke. "It's time for an explanation."

Uncle John held up his hand. "Now hold on a minute. Did anybody get shot up the mountain?"

Grant chewed, then swallowed. "Nope. A black bear came down where children were playing. Men were shooting to scare it away. Apparently no revenuers are nearby, and the still's intact."

"They weren't trying to kill the bear?" Christa asked.

"Just scare him away."

"Then maybe we won't get shot."

Grant's eyebrows lifted. "They'll probably chase me up Rattlesnake Ridge or shoot me—whichever they have a hankering for."

Did the doc have a sense of humor? On second thought, maybe that was no joke.

Christa watched Grant eat. He had manners, unlike a few people she'd seen at the potluck. After several bites, he took a gulp of milk.

He licked his lips, then spoke. "The only explanation I have," he said, "is that I went to Asheville to get Adelaide and instead was given a letter saying she couldn't come today." He stabbed a bite of tomato.

Christa's words halted his fork in midair. "When is your fiancée coming?"

"In about a week when she and her parents return from Charleston." He poked the tomato into his mouth.

Uncle John leaned over the table. "Christa graduated from college."

Christa's suspicions were alerted. "What are you saying, Uncle John?"

Spreading his hands, he looked deceptively innocent. "You could teach for a week, Christa. That would keep both of you in these people's good graces, and later they can laugh about the whole situation."

Christa could hardly believe the expectant look on her uncle's face and the gleam of hope in the doctor's eyes.

"Well, I'm here for crafts, not teaching. Explaining the truth is"—she pointed at Grant—"his responsibility."

Uncle John spoke softly. "The Lord brought you here for a reason, Christa."

She slapped her hands against the table. "If the Lord brought me here, Uncle John, then He smokes a lot, chugs loudly around the mountains, and doesn't smell too good."

Any other time, she might have thought the doctor had a nice laugh. But she didn't want to give any indication she would consider Uncle John's ridiculous suggestion. After the men's laughter subsided, Uncle John said what one might expect from a preacher. "God doesn't always do what we presume, Christa. He often works in mysterious ways His wonders to perform. That's what the Good Book indicates anyway."

Rather than respond, she stood and walked to the window

above the sink, taking in the view of red tomatoes on stakes, green cornstalks, and yellow squash peeking through huge green leaves.

She'd tried to believe verses that said if you ask you'll receive. She'd asked that Roland would come to his senses. She'd asked that she find crafts that would make her brother and sister-in-law think she could be an asset to the business.

But that had all gone by the wayside.

Chapter 5

That blackberry cobbler seemed to call Grant's name, however, his desire for a solution to his problem was greater. Christa's reaction to Pastor John's suggestion that she teach indicated she wouldn't provide the answer.

John's next question presented further complications. "Just what is the situation between you and your intended, Grant?"

Grant looked at a spot on the table. "Pride is part of it. I bragged too much to Clem's son, Frank, when I bought that ring." He looked up. "You see, Frank and I were rivals in our younger days, whether it was over school, coon hunting, or girls. Then Frank went to the city, got married, and got a good job."

He might as well admit the whole truth. "I told Frank I was marrying the prettiest girl in Asheville, the daughter of a well-known doctor. To prove it, I took Adelaide to pick out her ring."

John spoke kindly. "You mean you stretched the truth, Grant?"

"I didn't lie about Adelaide being lovely and charming, or about her dad's status. But when I'd go to make payments, I gave the impression she'd definitely be coming to the cove to teach." He unclasped his hands and felt the coolness of the wood beneath his palms.

"The reality is that Adelaide was to come to Bear Cove to see the school and meet the people before making a decision. But when it became known that Adelaide was coming to the cove today—probably through Frank to Clem and Miz Dora—the news got around, and everyone assumed she was coming to start teaching."

John stroked his chin. "Generally, I'd say this was not a church matter. But it's come about because people jumped to conclusions. I can allow for your explanation after Sunday's service. They're expecting school to start Monday morning."

"Thanks." Grant breathed easier. "I'll be at school Monday morning in case anyone doesn't get word."

John huffed. "The way news travels around here, I suspect they'll hear."

Christa walked over to the table. "Not everyone will take this well—and those little children who were introduced to me. . ." She touched her forehead. "Oh, I can't do this. I'm going home tomorrow."

Grant leaned back. "Afraid you can't do that."

She had a pert way of lifting her chin. "And who is going to stop me?"

He tried to conceal his amusement. "No train comes into or leaves Grey Eagle on Sunday. Unless you hitch a ride or walk, you'll have to wait until Monday."

Her eyes sparked flaming arrows. She apparently did not find him amusing.

Pastor John looked up at Christa. "Don't make any decision until after church tomorrow. Why, I'll even let you announce your purpose in being here. They'll be disappointed about the school, but they've waited over a year already. Another week won't hurt."

She shook her head. "I can't do that. This was not my doing."

John sighed. "I think the good Lord just gave me a new sermon for tomorrow—on bragging, gossip, rumor, and jumping to conclusions." He nodded, then gazed at Christa. "They'll look upon you just as warmly as they did at the potluck. Many of them would love to sell their crafts in the cities. If this is the Lord's will for you, Christa, it will work."

Grant watched her mouth open, but no words came. Was she about to cry? Suddenly, she walked past the table. "Excuse me. I'd like to take a walk before dark."

"Don't go far, Christa," John said. "As soon as the sun goes behind the mountains, darkness falls quickly and so does the cool night air."

Christa looked out the window and up at the sky, where the light was already fading.

John's gaze followed hers. "You have about thirty minutes or so of daylight. A nice walk would be up to the church and along the creek that runs behind it. A few cabins are out that way, belonging to some of the people you met today."

Grant heard the front door close, then brought the bowl of cobbler closer. "I'm sorry I've brought this on your niece, John."

"Give it all to the Lord, Grant. He works in mysterious ways. But do me a favor. Soon as you finish that cobbler, go find Christa and make sure she's all right."

※

Christa walked from marker to marker, reading inscriptions. Many bore only a name and the dates of birth and death. She stopped at a larger tombstone that marked Sadie McIntyre's grave.

A twig snapped. She turned. Grant stood there.

"If you want me to leave, I will."

"No." She faced the tombstone again. "It's all right."

"You must have loved her very much," Grant said. "The cove people did."

"I didn't know her well," Christa confessed. "Before she became ill, they visited a couple times. She wasn't able to come to my parents' funeral, but Uncle John came. I was surprised and honored when he came to my graduation."

She touched the tombstone. "We couldn't come to Sadie's funeral because of the snowstorm."

"Yes," Grant said. "We were isolated here for several weeks."

The tombstone felt cold to her touch. "All this reminds me of how different things would be had my parents lived."

"How different?"

She saw no reason not to confide in him. They'd have no more than this brief encounter. "Had they not died, my brother would have remained in Charlotte as an accountant. But he felt obligated to take over the family business. According to him, a mere coed couldn't handle it."

"It's a crafts business?"

"Yes. More tourists come in each year now that the trains run from major cities. They like to take back souvenirs."

"So your brother doesn't let you work in the shop?"

"Oh, I can work. But he manages it, and he has a new wife." She looked toward the treetops.

Grant's "Hmm" seemed to confirm what she thought. A new wife would easily replace a sister in her brother's heart.

"Don't get me wrong. William and Bettina are good to me.

I get to live with them, help with the cooking, cleaning, and running the shop." She regretted the resentment in her voice.

"I see," he said. "Your trip here is to make them sit up and take notice."

"Well, to show that I'm not just another hired hand. I have a better idea of how to handle that shop than Bettina."

"Bettina is your brother's wife?"

"Yes. She's lovely and charming." As soon as she said it, she recalled it was how he had described Adelaide. She turned quickly and tripped over a stone.

He reached out and grasped her arm. "Charm has its place," he said. "But you could match anyone in the lovely department."

Christa stepped away, and his arm fell to his side. This man who had ruined her chances to prove herself in this cove implied she was. . .lovely? He likely was trying to redeem himself for all the trouble he'd caused.

For an instant, she was speechless; then she focused on the grave markers. "Most of these are for babies and young children."

"Too many children die because of ignorance, superstition, or lack of a doctor's care. I want to help these people."

She looked at a marker. "This bears the name of Gordon."

"My little brother died of scarlet fever. There was no doctor to attend him."

"I'm sorry," she said.

"Thank you. That was many years ago. Pastor John says the Lord works in mysterious ways. I don't understand all that God allows. But I know my brother is in heaven. His death helped strengthen my resolve to become a doctor. Good comes from the worst of things, if we trust in the Lord."

She gave a short laugh. "That's great advice from a man who can't find a way to tell people his fiancée has been delayed. Where was your trust today, Doctor?"

Chapter 6

G rant stared at the ground. The changing light began to bathe the markers with color. "Come with me," he said.

A slight hesitation preceded the lift of her chin, but she walked beside him out of the graveyard and along the creek. Water rushed over the rocks, making small waterfalls and white foam, emitting a clean, fresh scent.

Surefooted, he stepped on a rock and held out his hand, unconcerned with city protocol that a gentleman wouldn't touch a lady's hand without her wearing gloves.

For an instant, her gaze rested on his hand; then she reached out. With one hand in his, and the other lifting her skirt to her ankles, she stepped out in her dainty shoes. They eased their way across the creek.

On the other side, he let go and led the way through the thick forest, heady with the smell of pungent pine.

"Oh my," she said, when they walked out into a clearing. "This is so unexpected."

She steered clear of thorny stems to touch wildflowers in the glade. She stopped at a great outcropping of rocks that revealed treetops and other mountains far below and beyond.

Her face lifted toward the brilliant sky where yellow became gold, orange turned red, and blue deepened. The orange sun peered over a mountain. The glow touched her face, shone in her eyes, and caressed her brown hair with a halo of reddish gold.

All the emotions he had seen in her face—chagrin, resentment, hurt, irritation—flew away like the few birds in the sky. Her expression held perfect peace and awe.

She whispered, "I've never seen anything so beautiful." She found a level spot on a boulder and sat down.

He sat near her, drew his knees up, and rested his forearms on them. "This is my favorite place. I can relax and be in tune with God. Remember how insignificant I am and how great He is. Coming here renews my trust in Him."

Her face turned toward his. With a slight movement, their shoulders would touch. He remained quite still, seeing the deepening color in her eyes, on her face, and the way the cool breeze blew a few strands of hair against her cheek. She had a perfect nose, lovely lips. They were slightly parted. He thought he knew why her eyes held a question and a challenge.

"You asked me about trust," he said. "When I was in Asheville and things didn't work out the way I wanted, I failed to trust, to stand up like a man and speak out. I let pride get in the way."

Feeling her fingers lightly on his arm, he glanced down, and she moved her hand away.

She spoke softly. "You were brave to go up the mountain, knowing your life could be in danger."

"That's easy. It's those women with their potlucks who scare me."

Christa laughed. Grant joined her and marveled at the

sound echoing against the mountainsides.

"Well, Doctor," she said. "I'm afraid, too. They were pleasant, but when they find out I'm not the teacher, I'm afraid there's going to be some righteous anger."

"They've already accepted you, Miss Walsh."

"Christa," she said softly.

"Christa." The name tasted clean and cool in his mouth, like sparkling spring water.

"What are you thinking?"

He told her what he was thinking about her name.

She opened her mouth in surprise, then looked out at the darkening landscape as the sun hid its face behind the mountain. "Thank you."

He stood. "It's getting cool and will be dark soon. We should go back." He held out his hand and helped her stand.

Strange, he had planned to bring Adelaide here. Instead, she was more than three hundred miles away. Perhaps she had watched the sky change colors over the ocean.

He didn't mean to compare Christa with Adelaide, but the comparison lay in his thoughts. Adelaide wouldn't walk with a man she didn't know or hold his hand to cross a stream. He couldn't image her stepping out onto those rocks or sitting down on the boulder in her fine dress. Adelaide would not travel alone on a train.

Christa had an entirely different lifestyle. She had no parents to whisk her off to Charleston. Even if she had, he doubted she would go anywhere with her parents instead of visiting the man she planned to marry.

Adelaide should be here with me.

❦

Adelaide should be here with him, Christa thought.

But she wasn't. And Christa was enjoying this male companionship. Her impression of Grant Gordon had changed. He was a capable man with an honorable profession. Yet he was vulnerable to hurt and uncertain about some things. She could identify with that.

She wondered if something like this had happened with Roland. Had he taken an innocent walk and noticed the attributes of another woman, just as she was doing with this man beside her?

She could imagine how easily one might find another appealing. Were Grant Gordon not engaged, she might entertain serious thoughts.

He led the way back through the forest and took her hand again as they stepped on the rocks to cross the creek. His hand felt warm and strong.

Twilight had come. Stars twinkled in the darkening sky, and a silvery moon appeared. The evening was pleasantly cool. The leaves in the maples and oaks whispered.

Upon passing the graveyard, Christa realized something. "Most of the graves are marked several years ago. Are there fewer deaths now?"

He looked down at her. "Yes. For several years the cove had no doctor."

She liked the way the moonlight laid on his hair and on his rugged face. "So your being here has made a difference."

He smiled. "Having a doctor nearby does that. Also, education helps. Parents are eager for their children to be educated. That's why they jumped to the conclusion that you're the teacher and why I was reluctant to disappoint them. Would you like to see the school?"

"Uncle John—"

"He knows I came looking for you. He said he'd had a long week and was going to turn in."

"Oh. Then yes, I would like to see the school."

The shadows lengthened as the moon brightened. They walked past the church and onto a dirt road. Faint light glowed from the windows of several cabins. "That one is mine," Grant said. "The bigger one across from mine is the Carmichaels'. Teachers have always had a room in their cabin."

"There were more than one?"

"Not at one time," Grant said. "Sometimes the teacher borrowed a horse and rode to homes way back in the cove. Sometimes he stayed with a family for weeks and taught the children. But. . ." He drew in a deep breath. "Most teachers couldn't handle that for any length of time. Teaching here takes a lot of time, and there's very little pay." His gaze met hers. "In terms of money, I mean." He looked ahead toward the trees. "The pay comes in different ways."

Christa could understand that. A doctor, a teacher, or a preacher could feel proud of making a difference in people's lives. "Do any of them send their children away to school?"

"The closest is at Grey Eagle. That's too far to take children in all kinds of weather, and it costs too much to board them there. And too, the children in Grey Eagle stay out of school when their parents need them to help with crops, cattle, pigs, chickens. They're needed for that here in the cove, too, but these people will take what teaching they can get when they can get it."

"That's admirable," she said.

"Wasn't always like that, Christa. The railroad coming as close as Grey Eagle has brought an awareness of a world outside the cove." He gestured ahead of them. "There's the school."

The land had been cleared. She could imagine children playing there. Moonlight bathed the small building on the rise of the hill. A couple of wooden swings hung on long ropes tied around the limbs of two tall oaks.

She followed Grant up the steps and onto the narrow porch across the front of the building.

"Just a minute," he said when they reached the doorway.

He went inside, struck a match, and lit a wick. Light from a lamp on a table in front of the chalkboard brought the room into view. A narrow aisle separated the two sides. Several desks were reminiscent of ones Christa had used in the early grades. She suspected they were donated. Men of the cove likely had built the benches and narrow tables.

Two windows were on each side. She couldn't find anything to comment about and felt no need to walk around. The impression lodged in her mind was "bleak."

"There on your right," he said, "is the bell that summons the children to school."

A bell no larger than a good-sized pear sat on a narrow ledge. "I wouldn't think the sound of that little bell would travel far."

He smiled. "You could stand in this doorway, yell, and your voice would travel over these mountains and return to you. God knew what He was doing when He created echoes. He knew people back in these coves wouldn't have the advantage of things city-folks have like timepieces and telephones."

She should say something. "I–I see this is only one room."

"The cove men built it several years ago. Before that, school was held in the church." He turned down the wick, leaving the room in shadows created by moonlight filtering through the windows. Christa walked onto the porch. Grant joined her and braced his hands on the banister.

"After the last teacher left, Sadie taught until she became ill. Years ago, the Carmichaels sold their house in the city to come here as missionaries. They're responsible for bringing your aunt and uncle here, as well as teachers. But age and illness have limited their activities. They are encouragers and have servant hearts. Their main income now is from raising chickens and selling them here and in Grey Eagle."

What about this place made people like Uncle John, Aunt Sadie, the Carmichaels, and Grant want to spend their lives here? She looked out at the schoolyard with its two big oaks. "It's certainly beautiful."

His voice was soft as moonlight. "You're a city girl, Christa, like Adelaide. I know this schoolhouse is backwoods compared with those in the city. Do you think she will like it here?"

Christa looked at the mountain vistas beyond. Would Adelaide like it? To be around people who put service to others ahead of themselves? To be in a place where so many anticipated her coming? To be loved by children eager to learn? To have an attractive man with an honorable profession love her? Would she like it?

Christa looked at the moonlight on his handsome face. "Yes," she said softly. "I think she will love it."

She walked down the steps and into the yard. She heard his voice behind her. "Christa."

She turned to face him.

"We got off to a bad start. But I hope you have forgiven me. Do you suppose we could be friends?"

Chapter 7

The scene looked liked Saturday reversed. The forest that had swallowed up people and kept them overnight, now released them back onto the lush green lawn and into Sunday morning sunshine. The children looked freshly scrubbed—boys with their hair parted and plastered down, and girls in pigtails or curls. Most of the men wore coats despite the warm temperature.

They came quickly, eagerly, holding children's hands. They nodded to each other or spoke with dignity and reverence. The women wore plain hats or scarves on their heads. Miz Dora, strolling beside Clem in a suit coat and top hat, wore a fancy hat that complimented her frilly blouse, cameo broach, and black skirt. Christa breathed easier at the sight of her, having feared she looked too fancy in her store-bought dress and hat with its colorful silk band and small flowers.

From her place inside the church at a window, she saw a couple wagons pulling up. Grant came riding across the clearing. Christa hastened to the bench where Uncle John said she should sit—up front.

The church reminded her of the schoolhouse—small

with one aisle down the middle. The differences were a pulpit instead of a teacher's table and benches with high backs.

Uncle John stood at the doorway, greeting people. She had come early with him to ring the first bell, as he called it. When he rang the second bell, people had about five minutes until the service started.

Christa wanted to see the church in case she didn't have another opportunity. Her gaze moved to the wooden cross on the wall behind the pulpit. She looked down to her gloved hands rather than think about what took place on that old rugged cross. She believed Jesus had died for her as He had for the entire world. But did He really work in one's daily life? If so, what had she done to cause Him to withhold His blessings from her?

A tap on her shoulder brought her attention to her surroundings. "Oh, good morning, Miz Dora."

"Good morning, Christa, dear. Your outfit is adorable."

"Thank you. So is yours."

Dora leaned forward and whispered, "I bought this in Asheville. I believe in wearing my finest to the Lord's house."

Christa smiled and glanced around, wondering if she'd be able to meet these people's eyes after Grant made his announcement. She heard his voice along with Uncle John's.

Soon, he sat beside her. She glanced over, and their eyes met. Her breath caught. Why did he sit beside her? She supposed it would look strange for him not to sit beside his supposed fiancée. And he had an announcement to make.

Besides that, they were friends.

Last night, when he'd asked, she had held out her hand in agreement. But friends. . .for how long?

After Roland told her about his change of plans, he had said, "We can still be friends, can't we, Christa?"

"Of course," she'd said and forced a smile. That had been followed by half a day in her room, drenching her pillow with tears. Bitterness had taken root in her heart. The feeling she had for Roland was not friendship.

And now, although she and Grant shared a songbook and she thrilled to the sound of his baritone voice, she wondered what kind of friends they could be after his fiancée arrived.

Adelaide would fill his time, heart, and mind.

Christa would go back to being a woman past marriageable age who had no purpose in life beyond taking a few highland crafts back to the city.

But for the moment, she sat beside a most appealing man. Everyone else other than Uncle John thought the two of them were in love, would be married. For the few minutes of this service, she would bask in that thought while being conscious of the warmth of his arm brushing against hers as they shared the songbook. She was this man's fiancée.

She would be. . .until he made his announcement. She slowly turned her face toward Grant. His head turned toward her. Their eyes met. For an instant, he seemed startled, then an expression like that of a dear friend crossed his face, and she thought a trace of color tinged his bronzed cheeks.

She saw him swallow as he again faced the front. His shoulders rose slightly.

So what if he thought her brazen. He had allowed these people to think she was his fiancée. For however long Uncle John preached, that's what she would be. When all one had was memories, she would savor this one. And for the first time, she hoped the sermon would be quite long.

❦

Grant wondered what Adelaide would think of his taking

213

Christa to his private place. To have held her bare hand, looked into her eyes, and asked for her friendship.

Adelaide had had a conniption fit when he'd commented that her cousin was quite attractive. She would never accept Christa being his friend. How could they be friends, anyway? She would be here a week. A few days. Until the train left tomorrow.

Could people be long-distance friends?

Sure.

Just as there could be long-distance fiancées. If someone was in the heart, it didn't matter if one was in Charleston and the other in Bear Cove. Was Adelaide in church thinking of him?

He could tell John was winding down. Grant had planned a speech. There'd been a mistake, he would say. This woman whom you have taken to your hearts is not my fiancée and she's not the teacher. No! That would never do—saying what Christa Walsh was not.

He would have to keep the attention focused on himself, not Christa.

Was that possible when during the entire service his eyes had been on Pastor John but his sensibilities had focused on the smartly dressed, lovely young woman beside him—his. . .friend?

Pastor John finished. He asked anyone who had anything to get right with the Lord to come and kneel at the front of the church.

Everybody stood. They were singing about when we all get to heaven what a day of rejoicing that will be.

Grant kinda wished he was there already.

John stared at him. Grant willed himself to stand.

"Pastor! Doctor!"

The singing stopped. A man with blood covering the front of his shirt ran down the aisle. Fear filled his eyes, and his breath was shallow. "Doc, it's my son." Both men ran up the aisle. The bloody man looked wild. "He nigh got his hand cut off down at the sawmill. He's out in the wagon."

Uncle John spoke loudly. "Let us bow before the Lord."

He prayed for Birr Morgan and his son as Grant ran out to the injured boy.

At the *amen*, everyone rushed out. Grant jumped down from the wagon. "Take him to my cabin." The boy looked deathly pale and rocked back and forth in the corner of the wagon, holding on to a bloody rag wrapped around his hand.

Birr Morgan jumped up onto the wagon, picked up the reins, and commanded the horse to go forward. Grant mounted his horse, calling out, "I could use some help."

Dora turned to Christa. "I'm sure Grant would appreciate your help. You'll be called on many times."

Here they were, the two best-dressed women in the crowd, picking up their skirts and racing across the yard. Soon they reached the dirt road. Christa looked at the older woman, who might have been a track runner. "Nobody else seemed eager to help."

Dora raised her eyebrows. "That's Birr Morgan. He had a bad experience with a churchgoer who got lumber from him, then left town without paying. He's had nothing to do with churchgoers since then. Makes them pay before he'll load their wagons. They take that as an affront."

"But surely they won't hold that against the boy."

"They'll say if Birr had been in church, this wouldn't have happened."

The doctor's cabin was spotless. He began telling the women what to do at the same time he calmed the boy and his dad.

After giving the boy something to dull the pain, Grant cleaned the wound.

"How bad is it, Doc?" Birr Morgan kept asking.

"I'm trying to determine that," Grant said more than once. The boy looked scared. "It's gotta be all right, Doc."

"Yeah," Birr said, "I'll need him at the sawmill."

"Then I don't want it well," the boy said. "I told you, I'm no good at the sawmill."

"You'll learn, boy."

Christa wondered about Birr Morgan's stern look. Was he only concerned about work?

When Grant asked, Dora handed him the sterilized instruments. He talked while examining the wound. "Looks like it cut the flesh across the palm. The cut on the thumb is deeper but not into the bone. That will heal just fine." He sutured the wound, then wrapped the hand in gauze. "Todd, we'll have to keep close watch on this. You need to follow my instructions about keeping it clean."

He addressed Birr. "You have him working at the sawmill before this is healed, and he could get an infection. Then there's a real problem." He paused. "Understand?"

Birr nodded.

Uncle John stood by the doorway.

"If you don't need us anymore, we'll leave, Grant," Dora said.

"That's fine. Thank you two, very much."

Birr Morgan interrupted. "I want to say something, and it's fine if you womenfolk hear it." He glanced around. "You, too, preacher."

He shifted uncomfortably, then stuck his thumbs behind his suspenders fastened to the waist of his worn pants. "I'd like to trade for your services, Doc."

"Sure," Grant replied without hesitation.

"Don't have any extra money right now," Birr said. "Need some supplies and repairs. I know you and Miz Dora here always wanted this boy in school. He learned a lot of foolishness that time I sent him. But he ain't no good to me in the sawmill like this."

Todd's eyes lit up, and all traces of pain left his face.

His dad continued. "He's got these highfalutin' notions Miz Sadie put in his head a long time ago. I don't need no education to run my mill. But things are changing, and my boy will have to deal with them townspeople. So, as a favor to you and your woman here, I'm gonna let my boy come to school."

The quick nod of Birr Morgan's head indicated he'd sacrificed his son as payment for his medical treatment. "His cutting his hand and all, pertnigh scart the daylights outta me. And I'm responsible. Just because I don't attend church don't mean I can't say when I'm sorry." He nodded at his son.

"Thank ya, Pa."

Grant and Birr Morgan shook hands on the deal.

"I. . .need air." Christa hurried from the cabin.

Dora followed. "Are you all right, dear?"

"I'll be all right." She would. As soon as she could get out of this place where she'd become a living lie.

Chapter 8

Christa stopped when Uncle John called her name. He caught up with her. When they were out of earshot of others, she could hold back no longer. "Uncle John, how could you and Grant let Mr. Morgan make that kind of deal? Have you forgotten? I am not the teacher, and I'm not. . . anybody's woman."

"It's a breakthrough for Birr Morgan to allow his son to get some schooling. To turn down Birr's offer would destroy that man's pride. It was a favor to Grant, and to—"

"His woman!"

Uncle John sighed. "Well, Christa. Sometimes it's best to remain silent. Grant will answer for his actions or lack of them."

"He certainly will."

Uncle John chuckled. Christa looked at him sharply.

He took on an innocent look. "That accident is working to change Birr's hardheadedness. Yes, indeed. The Lord works in mysterious ways."

So did a few people around here. Namely, her uncle and Dr. Grant Gordon.

When they reached the door of the cabin, Christa faced

her uncle. "Maybe I should write to Adelaide and tell her not to bother coming to the cove. Tell her we already have a teacher—and Grant has his woman!"

She expected her uncle to tell her to ask the Lord's forgiveness for such an outburst. Instead, he laughed heartily. "You do remind me of my Sadie. Put spark in our lives, she did." He sighed and grew serious. "You bring joy to me, Christa. I stay busy, but I get lonely. It's good having a woman in the house."

Uncle John liked having her here? She liked being here. . . except for the deception.

They ate lunch, then Uncle John said he was going to his bedroom. "Sunday's the only day I can take a nap and still sleep all night."

She was washing dishes when Grant arrived. She offered him the leftover vegetable soup and corn pone.

He ladled soup into a bowl and sat down. Christa wiped her hands and sat across from him. If she had married Roland, they would be sitting across from each other like this.

She corrected that thought. Roland would never live in a rustic cabin in a backwoods cove. He wanted and needed attention. He was a banker now, married to the bank president's daughter. He wore suits with a watch's gold chain hanging from his vest pocket. He was fast becoming a man of means.

She did not want to sit across a table from such a man.

That idea startled her. Was she getting over Roland?

Grant looked over at her. He must have heard her intake of breath.

He wiped his mouth with a cloth napkin. "I'm sorry. I must have been eating like a pig. I eat fast. Most of my meals are interrupted by someone needing help."

"I like seeing someone enjoy a meal I fixed, even if Uncle John insisted I open a jar of vegetable soup Sadie put up instead of taking time to cook from scratch."

He ate more slowly and kept peeking over at her. This mature man had a way of looking like a lost little boy. "Did John explain the importance of my accepting Birr Morgan's trade?"

"Enough to make me know you find it of the utmost importance. But something else is troubling me. I'm wondering—Grant, do you really have a fiancée?"

That's not what he expected her to say.

Did he have a fiancée?

He thought so.

He was making payments on a ring. Adelaide had said she'd come to the cove to check it out. "Of course I have a fiancée. Surely you don't think that's not true."

The look on her face reminded him that he hadn't told the truth in two days. But emergency situations had prevented his confession. He continued to stare at Christa when she took his empty bowl and carried it to the dishpan.

He picked up his glass, downed the rest of the milk, then went over to her. He picked up a towel and took the dishes from the rinse pan, dried them, and set them aside. "While I was eating, Christa, I was thinking of a solution."

She scrubbed a dish. "You mean there is one?"

"Sure. I'll be at the schoolhouse in the morning before eight o'clock. I'll tell everyone as they come."

"They're going to be terribly disappointed, aren't they?"

"Yes," he admitted. "But they'll handle it, Christa. And when Adelaide arrives, they'll be captivated by her charm."

She stiffened. "You think these people need charm?"

He realized his mistake. Christa must think he meant that she had no charm. She didn't have the kind of charm that Adelaide had. She had different qualities. "They're already captivated by your enthusiasm for life, Christa. Your outgoing nature. Your—"

He'd almost said, "your appeal." But it wouldn't be fitting for an almost-engaged man to speak that way to another woman.

She scoffed. "Oh, Grant. You don't have to flatter me. I know I'm not the kind of charming young lady who bats her eyelashes, has honey in her mouth, and makes a man fall at her feet. I'm a spinster in her early twenties."

He shrugged and grinned. "The attributes you mentioned are not the only ones that attract an old man like me—in his midthirties."

He picked up the bowls and put them on a shelf. He had been in his early thirties when he'd fallen for Adelaide. He had to admit that eyelashes and honey weren't a bad combination.

He glanced back at Christa. He must not contemplate her attributes, however.

He closed the cabinet door. "Christa, meet me at the schoolhouse in the morning. After I tell the parents you're here for crafts, you can talk with them."

She lifted her chin. "Dr. Grant Gordon, even if I have to walk, I'll be out of this cove tomorrow before the school bell rings."

❧

Clang. . .ang! Clang. . .ang! Clang. . .ang!

Christa couldn't believe she was standing in the doorway of this one-room schoolhouse, ringing the bell. It not only rang; it echoed around the mountainsides and returned as if the sound were trapped, reminding her of exactly how she felt.

How was she going to tell these people to take their children home?

Grant had come by early, saying LulaMae was having her baby. The midwife sent word that it hadn't turned right. She needed the doc and the preacher.

Christa stepped into the front room just in time to see Grant and a boy disappear from sight. Her uncle turned to her. "I have to go."

"What about school?"

"Maybe Grant or I will return before school starts. If not, you can. . . ." He lifted his hands helplessly. "I honestly don't know, Christa."

She stared at his disappearing back, then at the wooden door. The quiet was deafening, until the hoot owl scared the wits out of her. No, she'd already had the wits taken out of her by Dr. Grant Gordon and his inability to speak up. Now her uncle was in cahoots with him.

So, here she stood in the schoolhouse doorway, swinging this bell as if she were the schoolmarm. Once they knew, these people would never forgive her.

The sun rose over the mountain in all its glory, and the forest thrust forth children, all sizes and ages. They came across the clearing and from down the road. They hastened up the road from the direction of the doctor's cabin, and some came from behind the church, through the graveyard.

Why had she rung that bell?

Facing a black bear would be easier than facing the parents of these children.

Parents?

"Wh–where are your parents?" she asked as several children came up to her with expectant faces.

"School ain't fer them, ma'am," said a red-headed, freckle-faced boy who looked to be eight or nine years old. "And we ain't babies. We can come by ourselves."

"Of course," she said.

His smile spread from ear to ear. "Name's BillyJoe Davison, ma'am."

Christa hoped the children mistook her grimace as a smile. She felt no joy.

A girl as big as Christa came holding the hands of a younger boy and a girl who didn't look a day over four years old.

They kept coming.

She kept willing Grant or Uncle John to show up.

They didn't.

A fair-haired boy of about seven came right up to her. "The preacher said to tell you Ma had a baby girl. The baby's doing fine, but Ma ain't feeling so good."

"Well, I'm sure the doctor and the preacher will take good care of her."

"Yes, ma'am," he said. "Ma shore is proud to have a girl. She named her FloraMae. Right purty, ain't it?"

"Very pretty." Christa was glad he focused on the baby instead of his ma, who wasn't doing too well. Maybe she should tell the children she wasn't doing too well and send them home.

She saw a wagon in the distance. A child wouldn't be driving a wagon to school. But explaining to one parent wouldn't solve anything. She could at least give the impression she was a teacher. "Children, go in and take your seats. Um. . .little ones in front and bigger ones in back."

They obeyed as if she knew what she was doing.

She recognized Birr Morgan in the wagon. "Here he is, ma'am. Just like I said."

She tried to smile. "I see." Todd climbed out of the wagon, careful not to use his injured hand. "Thank you, Mr. Morgan."

He touched the edge of his floppy brimmed hat and nodded, then went back the way he'd come.

"Teacher."

Christa looked at Todd. In the doctor's cabin, she hadn't paid attention to his looks. Before her stood a young man taller than she. He had the most vibrant blue eyes, and his blond hair gleamed in the sun like corn silk.

"Teacher, this is one of the happiest days of my life. If I'd known cutting my hand would get me in school again, I would have done it on purpose." Color blushed his cheeks. "That is, if we'd had a teacher here."

Christa had to tear her gaze away from him. His resonant voice was as impressive as his looks. She remembered that Uncle John, Miz Dora, Sadie, and Grant had wanted this boy to get an education. She didn't know what his abilities were, but she couldn't imagine that he should be hidden away in a sawmill.

Hours later, she had to admit she'd enjoyed getting to know the children and their interests and making lists of their names, ages, something about their families, how much education they'd had, and what they knew. They sang a couple songs together, and Christa was struck by the pure beauty of Todd's voice.

At noon, she dismissed them for recess and to eat the lunches they'd brought. She had no lunch. She couldn't imagine what had detained the men unless LulaMae had grown worse.

Excited voices sounded from the schoolyard. She reached the doorway as BillyJoe rushed up. "Teacher. Come look."

She hurried onto the porch. Children were gathered around. BillyJoe pointed to the ground. Her breath caught at the sight of a man slumped over at an odd angle.

"Grant!"

Chapter 9

"Huh! Wh—what?"

Grant sat up, groaned, and began massaging his numb leg. He waved away the giggling children.

Christa stood in front of him. "What are you doing on the ground, Grant?" She looked at his leg. "Are you hurt? Shot?"

My, she was pretty in that white shirtwaist and red skirt. "I was sleeping." He stood in spite of his tingling leg. "When I heard Todd singing, I couldn't interrupt. I closed my eyes to thank God that Todd has this chance, and I fell asleep. Christa, we can't let him go back to hiding away in a sawmill."

"We?" Christa crossed her arms.

Grant blinked. "I mean the people in the cove. The boy has great talent."

"I agree."

He yawned. "Um, you want me to teach the rest of the day?"

"You're dead on your feet, Grant. Go home and rest. Apparently, you don't get much of that."

"You're right. I am sorry about all this, Christa. I'll set it straight. Just wait and see."

"I'm waiting." She tapped her foot.

He grinned, climbed on his horse, and looked down at her. "You look like a schoolmarm."

"I am not a schoolmarm."

"You still look like one. All stern, as if you'd like to give me a whack with the ruler."

He rode on home. Yes, she did look like a schoolmarm. But next week, Adelaide would be standing there.

He supposed he was just too tired to feel elated about that.

❧

Christa dismissed school at 3:00 p.m. She found Uncle John in the backyard, where he'd wrung a chicken's neck and was pulling out white feathers. His smile was warm. "I had to take a nap after being awake most of the night, Christa. The least I can do is fix you a hot supper. You must be tired."

"Honestly, Uncle John. I haven't felt so exhilarated in years. Oh, Uncle—"

He held up the chicken by its legs. "If you're going to talk about school, go fetch the doctor. Invite him to supper. He and I can finish out the week. Dora claims she can only teach Bible and music, but she always pitches in wherever needed. We should know what you did today."

"Yes, you're right."

She walked quickly up the dirt road to Grant's cabin and knocked.

"Just a minute," he called. He opened the door, buttoning his shirt. His hair was damp from being washed. A mass of dark curls fell over his forehead. She liked the looks of this. . . friend.

He readily agreed to come to supper.

They walked down the road in the late afternoon sunlight.

"How are LulaMae and FloraMae?"

"The baby's perfect." The softness in his eyes turned serious. "But LulaMae has been fighting a bronchial cough. I couldn't give her strong medication until after the baby was born. I needed to stay and make sure she would be okay. You understand, don't you, Christa?"

She nodded. "I hope the parents understand when they learn their children were taught by an imposter."

"Do you know what your uncle John said?"

She grinned. "That God works in mysterious ways?"

Grant chuckled. "Well that, too." He stuck his hands in his pockets. "He said that you're a lifesaver."

"Maybe a lifesaver for myself, Grant. Today, I stopped thinking about what's gone wrong in my life. I thought about the children. They're bright and talented. But their abilities will go to waste if they're not trained. When you didn't speak up, it wasn't because you're a coward, but because you care."

His glance met hers. "I do care, Christa."

They reached Uncle John's cabin and were greeted by the wonderful smell of chicken frying. Grant and Christa set the table, then pulled out chairs and sat down.

"Todd wants to write songs," Christa said. "He brought some with him written on old scraps of paper. He hides them from his dad, who thinks songwriting is a waste of time."

Uncle John turned from the sizzling chicken. "You seem to have found out a lot about him, Christa."

She smiled. "He volunteered that information after class today while waiting for his dad. He left the papers with me. He has the tunes in his head but can't put notes on paper." She sighed. "I don't know how to help him with that."

"I don't know music," Grant said. "But I'd like to see what he's written."

Christa nodded. "We got to know each other. The children are eager to hear about city life—what the houses are like and the kind of work people do. I wrote down their names and what I thought important." She laughed. "Except the boy who said he's not supposed to tell what kind of work his pa does."

Grant laughed and nodded when Uncle John said, "Must be the Spiller boy."

Christa assumed the boy's reluctance had something to do with moonshine—and not the kind that comes from the sky.

After supper, Uncle John insisted on washing the dishes. "You two talk over that schoolwork, and I'll listen."

Grant refilled their coffee cups. "I'd like to see your notes, Christa, since I'll be teaching tomorrow." He motioned toward her notepad. "Let's take a look."

She took a sip of coffee, then opened the notepad.

The sun's rays were slanting through the kitchen windows by the time they finished. Grant had moved closer to her to better see her notes. She had written students' names, a rough description of where they lived, how much schooling they'd had, who could read, who knew their ABCs and numbers, their hobbies, and what their parents did.

Grant studied her pages for a long time, making Christa feel defensive. "I tried to make it a fun day so the children would like learning. A child should show respect but not be afraid of a teacher." She hoped she'd done something right. "Do you think this will help Adelaide?"

Both men stared at her as if she'd spoken in French or Latin. Uncle John rubbed his chin and glanced at Grant.

Grant looked thoughtful, then said, "Unequivocally." He leaned back in his chair. "Do you have any suggestions about what should take place tomorrow?"

"Well, yes. I thought I'd test them. Not grade them, but tell them the spelling bee and the numbers quiz is practice for the real tests after they study. That way I—I mean you—can divide them into grades. Also, you should find out what they know about life beyond the cove and about history."

He pushed away from the table. "I'd like to check on Todd's hand. Would you go with me?" She hesitated, and he added quickly, "We can discuss how we might help him."

❧

Grant returned to John's front yard with his horse and medical bag. Christa had changed into a riding skirt and had taken the pins from her hair. It fell in waves below her shoulders. Her face glowed with happiness as he reached down to scoop her up behind him.

He glanced at John, who stood looking at them with raised eyebrows and a finger against his lips as if holding back words, such as the Lord and His mysterious ways.

Grant acknowledged John with a nod and turned the horse in the opposite direction. Whether it was the Lord or the day at school, he knew John was pleased with Christa. She was learning, as Grant had after losing his parents, that getting involved with the problems of others lessened your own. She had taken over the school quite successfully.

He liked the change in her. And he liked the feel of her behind him, holding onto his shirt, and the sound of her voice telling him about the need for books, writing materials, and lesson plans.

Earlier, he said she looked like a schoolmarm. Now, she talked like one.

The Morgans lived a couple of winding miles away. Several hunting dogs greeted them. Todd came onto the porch, and

Elvira Morgan stood in the doorway. She invited them inside.

Elvira kept a clean cabin. Maybe because she had only one child. After having Todd, she had had several miscarriages.

Elvira poured tea for them at the kitchen table. Grant unwrapped the bandages from Todd's hand. "It's red and raw, but that's to be expected. Keep it clean, and no lifting."

Elvira sat at the table. "Oh, Miz Christa. Thank you for coming to teach. I know what this means to Todd. I once had the kinds of dreams he does about singing." She blushed. "My voice wasn't near as good, though."

"Now, Mrs. Morgan," Grant said, "your voice stood out above the others in church."

"I always did love singing." She looked at Christa. "It's no secret, Miss Christa, that my pa left Ma with a passel of younguns and went off and joined a band down in Tennessee. We heard he done real good. I vowed I'd never do a thing like that." She glanced at Todd. "And I told my boy he has to mind his pa 'cause family's more important than singing."

"Some people manage to have a family and enjoy their music, too, Mrs. Morgan," Christa said.

Elvira looked surprised. "They can really do that?"

Christa nodded.

Grant wrapped gauze around Todd's hand. "It sure would be nice if you and Todd sang in church again."

Elvira agreed. "I learnt Todd all the songs I know. He makes some up, and we sing them to the tunes of church songs. But we don't let Birr hear us. He says them churchgoers ain't no count since that one done 'im wrong."

Christa spoke up. "Does he feel that way about Uncle John and Grant and the Carmichaels?"

"Oh, no. But he says they have to be decent, being the

preacher and missionaries and a doctor." She touched Christa's arm. "And I know you're good, Miss Christa, just by what you done for my boy today. You give him hope."

Grant tied a knot around the gauze. "Does he feel the same about the women at church?"

Elvira leaned back. "Well, no, Doctor. He don't do business with no women. But they's married to the men."

"If you were there, I reckon there'd be one good woman who was married to a good, honest man."

Grant watched her eyes light up. "I could say that to Birr. I can up and tell 'im what the church needs is some good woman like me." She laughed. "You know I'm funning with ya."

"You have a nice way about you, Mrs. Morgan," Grant said. "I wouldn't be a bit surprised if you have that husband of yours back at church in no time."

Todd grinned.

Grant's good feeling left after they left the cabin. Christa walked so fast, he feared she might ride off and leave him stranded. "Did I do something wrong?"

"You encouraged them to come to church where there are good, decent people like you and me." She got up behind him on the horse. "So how will they feel when they find out we're liars and deceivers? The good teacher won't even be at school tomorrow."

The mountain air cooled as the sun set, but the coldness he felt was from the stiff figure seated behind him.

They returned to John's cabin beneath a darkened sky. She didn't protest when he raised his arms to lift her down. Maybe she, too, missed their earlier togetherness.

She stood in front of him. He gently turned her face up toward his. "There's no way I can tell people the truth until they're gathered in church on Sunday."

He braced himself for her reaction before adding, "Is there a chance, Christa, that you would consider teaching for the rest of the week?"

Chapter 10

C hrista hardly heard the *clang. . .ang* of the bell. A different tune sounded in her heart and mind. Last night, she'd looked into Grant's face bathed in soft moonlight. How could she say anything else? "Grant, I will be honored to continue with the children because. . .we're friends."

After an interminable moment, he had pressed her hands gently. "I'm grateful to you."

Christa felt pleased that she could let go of resentful memories of Roland and replace them with thoughts of a man who had shown her that he was competent, confident in his work, yet vulnerable when it came to disappointing adults and children.

The first child came bounding out of the sunlit horizon, bringing Christa back to her own sense of mission. She would give her best efforts to being a schoolmarm.

The week went all too quickly. Grant came a couple times and talked to the children about science and chemistry. Uncle John commented on a Bible story before lessons began. Dora helped Todd lead the hymn singing. Christa wrote the words on the blackboard with chalk so they could see how the words looked. The children were like sponges soaking up everything being taught.

Dora helped her plan the Friday exhibition for parents.

Friday dawned clear and warm. They practiced most of the day.

Grant and Uncle John set up tables outside for refreshments provided by Dora and Clem. Adults arrived before 3:00 p.m.

Christa told the children they had nothing to be nervous about, despite her shaking hands and tremulous voice. At three o'clock, she had the children stand on the porch, the steps, and the ground. Parents stood opposite them.

Todd led the other children in a welcoming song. The parents applauded, then Christa greeted them. She had the younger children sing the ABCs. Older children recited the multiplication tables. They all quoted the Twenty-third Psalm. Christa didn't want any child to perform alone in case they become embarrassed by making a mistake. That is, no one but Todd.

He sang "Amazing Grace." His high tenor reverberated around the mountains as if an entire chorus of angels had joined him, and nature itself had decided to praise the Lord. The adults didn't move a muscle or blink an eye. Tears streaked many faces.

When Todd finished, complete silence followed. Finally, a man shouted, "Amen." Others began saying "Amen" and "Praise the Lord" and applauding.

Todd smiled. He had told Christa he was going to sing to the Lord, no matter what his pa might do.

Christa gave out report cards for the week's work. She wrote only praise for what each child had accomplished, whether learning no more than "ABCDEFG" or as much as the older girl who did long division.

The program was a huge success. Children and parents

glowed with pride and happiness.

Then came the moment Christa had been dreading. First, she told the parents how much she appreciated them letting her teach. "I've never had a more fulfilling week in my life." She paused, feeling tears threaten her eyes.

The faces in front of her expressed respect and admiration. That would soon change. She looked at Grant. "The doctor has something to say."

Grant had prayed and thought but still wasn't sure what to say. He faced the adults. Christa stood by Pastor John, who put his arm around her shoulders.

Grant began. "I have an announcement."

All sound faded except the gossiping birds in the big oaks.

The words came easy when he praised Christa for what she had meant to the children during the past week, how the program reflected her love for the children and her efforts to discover their capacity for learning. "There could be no finer teacher," he said. Applause erupted.

Silence returned when he said, "However, there has been a misunderstanding."

He reiterated what happened from the moment he got off the train, and how he'd wanted to find the right time to tell the truth. He'd been called away for emergencies both times.

Their gazes remained fixed on him. He prayed their anger and disappointment would be toward him and not Christa.

"Christa Walsh is not my fiancée, which means she's not the teacher you expected."

He heard a few gasps but continued. "She came to visit her uncle John and to find crafts for her brother's shop in Hendersonville. She thought her uncle had sent Clem to fetch her. She had nothing to do with this deception, and I hope you won't blame her."

He lifted his hand to silence the escalating mumbling. "Adelaide Montgomery is my fiancée and a teacher. She and her parents will arrive tomorrow."

Pastor John came and stood beside him. "My niece told me about the situation that first night at the cabin. Doc planned to set things straight on Sunday morning." He reiterated some of what Grant had said. "But if the misunderstanding hadn't happened, then the children would have been without a teacher this week. And nobody can deny Christa has been about the best teacher we could have."

Grant doubted anyone would take issue with that. A little of his confidence returned. "What Miss Walsh has done will be turned over to Miss Montgomery. Miss Walsh came here for crafts. So to show appreciation for her week of teaching, maybe you will want to share with her."

Uncle John laid his hand on Grant's shoulder. "And we can thank the Lord for Grant's not speaking out sooner. Otherwise these children would still have been underfoot this past week."

The people laughed.

Uncle John continued. "The Lord works in mysterious ways. Let's bow for prayer."

At the *amen* Miz Dora stepped up. "Now it's punch and cookie time."

Grant expected to receive a few verbal punches. He hoped Christa would be spared. Just then, he saw Birr Morgan making a beeline toward her.

❧

Christa could hardly believe it. Children stopped to say they wanted her to be their teacher, then ran off to play. Women told her about their crafts and about people who made the finest quilts, whittled beautiful wooden animals, tatted the fanciest doilies, dried the prettiest flowers, and made souvenirs from rocks.

Birr Morgan walked up, staring at her. Elvira and Todd hurried to stand next to him. Others stepped back.

Christa thought Birr's removing his hat and holding it in front of him was a sign of respect. But she dreaded what might follow when he said, "Miss Walsh. I'm plumb dumbfounded." At least, he wasn't toting his rifle.

He looked her in the eye. "I knowed Todd could sing but not like that. I ain't never heard anything so beautiful. My woman could sing pretty, too, and I don't normal say things like this, but she needs to hear this. Todd, too."

Christa identified with the uncertainty in Elvira's and Todd's eyes.

"That singing today wasn't like guitar and banjo singing. Or even church singing. It was citified. I've heard citified singing so I know what I'm talking about. I was mighty proud of the way my boy stood up there, waving that stick I made 'im, and them children singing in time with it. I think maybe I've been selfish, taking Elvira away from the music she was fond of."

Elvira caught hold of his arm. "Oh, no, Birr. I made my choice. You was it. I loved you more than I loved singing. And there ain't a thing wrong with your banjo picking. I sing to that."

Birr stood a little taller. Then he looked away from the softness in Elvira's eyes. Christa thrilled at the love they had for each other. "So," he said. "I think my woman is right. She made her choice, and it was me. I reckon Todd needs to make his choices hisself. But he's only sixteen, and first I want him to know a trade in case he don't make it in the city with singing."

"Oh, Birr." Elvira's arms went around him.

"Now hold on, woman. People's looking."

She stood close. "You're just the best man I ever knowed, Birr Morgan."

He cleared his throat. "Well, anyway, Miss Christa. Feel free to help my boy. And if you ain't going to be here, you can tell that new teacher." He spoke softly. "You might want to know. I make a few craft-like pieces out of my wood."

Christa felt she must surely look as happy as that family. How mistaken she'd been thinking that Birr Morgan was the meanest man she'd ever seen. He had a tender heart, and dearly loved his wife and son. The way some things turned out sure was beginning to look. . .mysterious.

When the crowd dwindled, Dora came up and handed Christa a glass of punch and a cookie. "You're such a hit, Christa, with everyone. I don't know how they'll get along without you. And I tell you this. . . ." She leaned closer. "We're not having another welcoming like we did for you."

Christa didn't know if she should thank her for that. "I appreciate all you've done for me. And I didn't mean to deceive anyone."

"Oh, we know that. We're just glad to have you here. Maybe you can help the new teacher."

Being a substitute would make her feel like she had after Roland jilted her and all her friends were getting married.

After she and Uncle John went to his cabin, she told him that the women, and even Birr Morgan, were eager to share their crafts. "But Uncle John, I've imposed on you long enough."

"Imposed? Girl, it's a joy having you here. And I'm selfish enough to want you to stay."

"Oh, Uncle John, I'll spend a day or so gathering a few things to take back for William. Then I should leave."

He nodded. "You'll have to stay long enough to see what Miss Adelaide looks like, now won't you?"

Chapter 11

C hrista chose the royal blue suit she'd worn when she came to the cove, the dressiest outfit she'd brought. Even so, she'd be no match for the lovely, charming Adelaide.

She sat in the front row at church. Would Grant escort Adelaide down the aisle and seat her beside Christa? Everyone must be as curious as she to see the woman who had won their doctor's heart and would be the real teacher for their children.

Where were they? Church was no place to make a grand appearance after everything started. Uncle John asked Todd to stand up front and lead the singing.

When they stood, Grant slipped in beside Christa. A quick glance didn't reveal any charming woman standing with him.

During the service, his hands moved to his knees and he'd lean back and take a deep breath. At times he crossed his arms.

When Uncle John asked for those who had a decision or special request to come forward, Grant walked to the front. "I have an announcement," he said.

❦

Grant didn't like speaking about his personal life in public, but he owed these people an explanation. He'd simply state the facts.

"The Montgomerys didn't arrive yesterday," he said. "Instead, a telegram came. Adelaide's grandfather suffered chest pains. Dr. Montgomery can't make the trip until he's sure his dad is all right. Adelaide can't travel alone all the way from Charleston."

Only Christa could help in this predicament. "Miss Walsh," he said, "Could you stay on until Miss Montgomery arrives?"

With her head held high beneath that pert little hat, she walked up and stood beside him.

When Christa said, "I am reluctant," Grant felt the disappointment in the room. "Because," she continued, "I love it so. I will be honored to substitute until the real teacher comes."

The congregation broke into applause.

Uncle John stepped up. "The Lord. . ."

When they returned to their seats, Grant whispered, "How can I ever thank you?"

Christa tried to reject the words from Browning's famous poem. "How do I love thee? Let me count the ways."

Grant's words and her thoughts had nothing to do with love.

He was thanking her for saving him from humiliation. For a while longer, however reluctantly, she would be a schoolmarm.

❦

Christa made up her lesson plans and continued to use Uncle John, Dora, and Grant to help. She didn't think she rated any praise. The important thing was teaching the children as best she could.

She'd never before felt so useful. Others could probably do the job much better than she. But they weren't here.

And she was.

The following Sunday when Grant sat beside her in church, unaccompanied, Christa supposed Adelaide might never come.

She reprimanded herself for that selfish thought. Adelaide's grandfather could still be ailing. . .or worse.

Uncle John must have had a similar thought. "Instead of waiting until the end of the service for the doctor's latest announcement," he said from the pulpit, "we'll have that first. Otherwise if he were called away early, we wouldn't know what's going on in his life."

Grant stood and announced that Adelaide's grandfather was improving. Adelaide and her parents would arrive on Monday.

Christa peeked at him. He didn't look at her. There was no applause. He said, "Well, um, that's it."

He returned to his seat. Uncle John motioned for Todd to lead the singing.

When Christa and Grant stood, sharing the songbook, he didn't sing. She supposed his mind was with his Adelaide.

❧

Grant stared at the dark clouds hanging low in the sky. A storm was rapidly rolling over the mountains. It would be gone by morning. Weather would not prevent the Montgomerys from arriving. He would meet them tomorrow and rent a carriage to bring them to the cove.

Would Adelaide fit in the way Christa had?

Would Todd and his parents feel as comfortable with Adelaide?

A week ago, Grant had written to Adelaide that a teacher was filling in for her. He'd mailed some of Todd's songs and told her of the boy's exceptional talent.

The dark clouds moved closer. Grant turned to leave. Walking into the woods, he heard a rumble of thunder, saw a movement.

"Christa?"

"Oh!" She tugged. "I'm caught."

Grant loosened her skirt from the thorny twig. "A wild-berry bush."

"Thank you." She smoothed her skirt and stepped away from the bush. "Sorry. I didn't mean to intrude. I thought you would be home, making arrangements. I just wanted a last look."

He should have said there was a storm coming. But that was no way to treat a friend who had done so much for him. He took hold of her arm and smiled. "You could never be an intrusion. Come look."

They walked out into the glade.

"It's even beautiful with a storm approaching," she said.

"Yes. You should see it when the clouds are below this glade." He knew that might never happen. "I was just thinking about the house I want to build here."

"Oh, this belongs to you?"

He nodded. "This is directly behind my cabin, separated by the woods. I've thought my cabin could be a clinic someday."

"I suppose you were thinking about your cabin and your life with Adelaide."

He stared at the mountains below. "Yes," he said finally. "I was." He took a deep breath. "Dr. Montgomery was my mentor and entrusted his daughter to me. I owe him everything."

All was quiet except the wind rustling in the trees.

He knew this was difficult for Christa. She loved the school and the children. "Will you stay in the cove? You've come to mean so much to. . .everyone."

"I'm glad I got to teach. I'm going to miss it."

Shadows on her face reflected the darkness he felt at the thought of not seeing her, teaching with her, sitting with her in church, watching her relate to the children. "I don't want to lose y—"

A crack of thunder stopped his words. He'd almost said he didn't want to lose her. He now said, "I don't want to lose your friendship."

He barely heard her voice above the rising wind. "You'll be busy with Adelaide, and I'll return to Hendersonville."

He felt like a tree, rooted to the ground. He wished she would turn, run away from him, before. . .

Following another loud roll of thunder, she stated the obvious. "It's raining!"

"You're kidding," he said as the cloudburst showed no mercy.

They ran through the forest and across the creek, not bothering with stepping stones. They laughed and sloshed past the graveyard, splashed beyond the church, and hurried to John's cabin.

As if having a mind of their own, his hands came up to her shoulders. Her rain-spattered face lifted toward his. He didn't intend it, but their cool, wet lips touched.

Then as if lightning had struck, they pulled away.

She said, "Bye," and fled inside. He remained staring at a closed wooden door, getting soaked.

How could he ever forget this storm?

This storm that raged within his heart.

Chapter 12

Christa and Todd stood outside the school as the newcomers strolled across the schoolyard. Christa glanced at the middle-aged woman and Dora but could not take her eyes from the lovely young woman walking with them. Blond curls peeked out beneath a pink-flowered bonnet that matched her pink and white dress.

The pretty girl came right up to Christa and reached for her hands. "You have to be Miss Walsh. Grant and the Carmichaels think the world of you. They told me about your being mistaken for me. It's so funny. But I must scold Grant for not telling me how pretty you are."

Christa couldn't help but respond favorably to the compliment accompanied by the sweet smile and shining blue eyes. "And you'd be Adelaide Montgomery. Grant did say how lovely you are. I'm pleased to meet you."

Adelaide turned to the other women. "This is my mama, Jane Montgomery."

The woman hugged Christa. "We're all so grateful to you, my dear. Grant told us how disappointed the people in the cove would be without all you've done."

Christa could see where Adelaide got her charm. This smartly dressed, congenial woman reminded her of her own mother. "I'm sure I've benefited more than the children. Let me introduce Todd Morgan."

Adelaide shook Todd's hand. "Oh, you're the talented young man Grant told us about. I have shown your songs to a music teacher in Charleston. He is so impressed that he has made this trip with us."

Todd's eyes sparked with excitement. "A music teacher came all the way from Charleston?"

Adelaide nodded. "He's with my papa and Grant right now, and he wants to talk with your parents."

By Todd's adoring look, Christa felt he had lost his heart to Adelaide. With their blond hair and blue eyes, they could pass for brother and sister. His smile broadened. "There's my pa now."

Adelaide did not seem put off by Birr Morgan's rugged looks. He climbed down from the wagon and took his hat off before shaking her pink-gloved hand.

Birr, Todd, and Adelaide engaged in conversation. Christa would have liked to listen, but Miz Dora spoke. "I've managed to convince Adelaide and her parents to stay with me and Clem tonight. That way, Miss Adelaide can get an early start with you in the morning."

Adelaide bade the Morgans good-bye and turned to Christa. Apparently she had overheard Dora. "Oh, Christa, I do want you to tell me all about the children and what you've done. Grant says it's remarkable." She smiled delightedly.

Dora invited them all for supper. "Christa, you and Pastor John are welcome to join us. Dr. Montgomery, Mr. Warren, and Grant will be there."

"Thank you," Christa said, "but I'm sure Uncle John is already fixing our supper. And I need to make sure I have everything ready for Miss—"

"Miss nothing," Adelaide said. "I'm Adelaide to you. I think we could be great friends."

Christa couldn't imagine that anyone would turn down an offer of friendship with Adelaide.

But she also couldn't imagine sitting at supper watching Adelaide and Grant glow with love for each other. How could she consider staying here and have her mending heart break again?

At the depot in Grey Eagle, Grant and Adelaide had kissed each other's cheeks. She was so beautiful. He felt guilty. Not only had he betrayed his fiancée, he'd betrayed Christa's trust in him. Mrs. Montgomery hugged him, and Dr. Montgomery shook his hand. Then Adelaide introduced a young man in a dark suit as Charlie Warren, the music teacher from Charleston.

Grant was pleased that the man was impressed enough with Todd's song to visit him in the cove but thought him young to have much experience. However, as Charlie and Dr. Montgomery rode along with him on their rented horses ahead of the carriage in which Adelaide and Mrs. Montgomery rode, Grant soon discovered the young man's accomplishments.

Charlie had been a child protégé and traveled as a concert pianist, but his love was teaching music. "I feel that the Lord wants me to give back to others the kinds of opportunities I have had. I want to see if Todd is one I should mentor." He addressed Grant. "I understand that is what Dr. Montgomery did for you, and now you're of tremendous value in this cove."

Grant admired Charlie Warren's dedication to the Lord and to others.

After the three men toured the cove, they visited the Morgans, where Charlie talked to Todd about his music. Upon returning to the Carmichaels, Clem and Dora insisted the Montgomerys and Charlie stay with them instead of riding back down to Grey Eagle after supper.

"Charlie's welcome to stay with me," Grant said.

Charlie accepted the offer.

Adelaide linked her arm through Grant's and teased, "You didn't tell me your Miss Christa was so young and pretty."

Grant felt warmth rise to his face. "Well, yes, I suppose she is."

Adelaide surprised him by saying, "I like her. Very much. I'm eager to observe her tomorrow in school."

During supper, Grant halfway listened to the conversations. He kept reminding himself of Adelaide's attributes. Yet he couldn't keep his mind on Adelaide. When he needed words most, they didn't come.

What could he say?

That while promised to one woman he found another. . . appealing.

Appealing?

To say the least.

But he must face facts. His feelings for Adelaide had grown over time. His feelings for Christa had come suddenly, unexpectedly.

Things weren't working out the way he'd planned—in his life or in his heart.

☙

Christa lay awake. The past weeks had been wonderful. She'd

gained a purpose, a love for children, a new confidence in her abilities. She'd replaced her bitterness and resentment of Roland, William, and Bettina with an admiration, respect, and even love for so many.

Grant and Adelaide were now together, and Christa thought Adelaide would be a wonderful teacher. The Morgans and the Carmichaels liked her. So would the children.

She prayed that God would forgive her for ever harboring a hope that she might be the one in Grant's heart. She never wanted to feel sorry for herself again, be selfish, or wallow in negative thinking.

She finally slept but awakened several times and prayed about her apprehension concerning the day to come.

At breakfast, Uncle John prayed that she might have courage.

After he said, "Amen," she poured maple syrup on a flapjack. "Thank you, Uncle John. I'm afraid I don't have much courage."

"You have more than you think, Christa. You see, courage isn't bravery. Courage is taking action even though you're afraid or apprehensive. You've faced fears head on, and God has used you in a wonderful way."

"I've resisted all the way."

"No, Christa. You acted in spite of your reluctance. You've put others ahead of your fears. You put Grant's reputation ahead of your own. The Lord answered your prayer for help."

"Oh, Uncle John. For so long I didn't trust Him to answer. I wanted Him to bring Roland back, to make William and Bettina see that I was responsible and make me the proprietor of that shop."

Uncle John smiled and put his hand on hers. "He had

something better in mind for you."

She nodded. "Yes, but why would He do this for me when I was not trusting Him?"

Uncle John leaned back. "To prove that He loves you. You're His child."

That was a good feeling. To know that God loved her. Uncle John loved her. "I've learned a lot, Uncle John. But it's over now."

"Don't worry about that." He pointed his fork at her. "God has a way of teaching us new lessons all through life."

Christa smiled. Lessons could be hard. Sometimes you didn't pass the test.

On the other hand. . .sometimes you did.

"Don't worry," Uncle John said. "I'm coming to school with you this morning. As pastor, I need to meet these people."

Shortly after ringing the school bell, Christa's commitment to courage almost failed. Walking across the schoolyard were the Carmichaels, June Montgomery, and two men who would be Dr. Montgomery and the music teacher.

Behind them was Grant, giving his full attention to Adelaide, who had one hand tucked around his arm and the other holding a sunshiny yellow parasol above her pretty face. She looked like everything in her world was just perfect.

Chapter 13

C hrista abandoned her careful lesson plans. The visitors should see for themselves what the children had learned.

The children performed much as they had for their parents. Having an audience brought out their best. She asked the music teacher, looking handsome in his citified suit and tie, to speak to the class. He accepted graciously and talked about various kinds of music, from banjo picking to opera to his own instrument—the piano.

Charlie Warren asked Todd and Adelaide to sing with him a song he and Adelaide had sung at church in Charleston.

Todd's voice was by far the best of the three, but the trio sang beautifully. Christa was again struck by the fair hair and blue eyes of Adelaide and Todd. Their appeal was enhanced by the tall, dark-haired man. Todd was dressed in everyday clothes, but Christa could visualize him dressed up, singing on a stage before a huge audience, delighting them with his voice.

Christa stood near the doorway and stole a glance at Grant along the wall near Dr. Montgomery. Both men seemed entranced as the trio gave a theater-worthy performance in a one-room schoolhouse.

She was thankful she had been a part of Grant's life during the past weeks, helped make things easier for Adelaide, and played a part in the life of a boy with exceptional talent.

She had done her best, in spite of her reluctance.

Now, she must step aside for those who could do better than she.

❦

Christa dismissed school at noon so she could talk with Adelaide. Charlie Warren took Todd home. The other adults praised her for how well she had taught the children.

Grant came over and thanked her. Christa nodded, afraid to do more than glance at him.

Uncle John moved to her side. "I think it's lunch time," he said.

Dora heard him. "All of you are invited to my house for lunch."

Adelaide spoke up. "Grant, why don't you make yourself useful and bring a plate for me and Christa. We need to talk about things."

He looked as if a weight had been released from his shoulders. "I'd be glad to."

"And I'd be glad to accept your lunch invitation, Miz Dora," Uncle John said. He turned to Christa and winked.

Christa stared at the adults walking between the two oaks. Why did Grant seem as strange and unresponsive as the day she first met him? Did he think she would fall apart because she'd no longer be teaching? Did he suspect how she felt about him? Likely, he was regretting that brief kiss. She thought he'd regretted it the night it happened.

Adelaide spoke. Christa turned. "I'm sorry. My mind was elsewhere."

"Oh, I understand," said Adelaide. "I was saying that you obviously love these children and have done a wonderful job with limited resources. How do you like cove life? I know this one-room schoolhouse is quite different from what you've experienced in the city."

They walked toward the classroom. "It's hard," Christa admitted. "The living situation is rustic. No electricity except closer to Grey Eagle. No stores to buy food or clothes. Pump water for a bath."

A part of her wished it would seem too hard for Adelaide. But she wanted to be honest. She stopped on the porch. "I love it here. You will, too, I'm sure. The benefits are seeing these children so eager to learn."

Adelaide's face lit up. She did a fancy little dance step. Her blond curls swung around her pretty face. Then she rested her hand on the banister. "I know Grant loves this place. It's closer to his heart than anywhere. Can you see that his work is making a difference?"

Christa looked away from the light in Adelaide's eyes. She answered as truthfully as she could, trying not to feel the emotion that welled up in her.

Grant needed a helpmeet to welcome him home. He needed someone to talk to, to understand, to care, to have supper ready, to warm his bed. She turned back to Adelaide. "The graveyard out back of the church is just one testimony to the effectiveness of his work here. The mortality rate for babies has decreased by half in the past few years. Oh, Adelaide, you can teach women about hygiene. That will make such a difference."

She saw the pleasure on Adelaide's face. She almost expected the lovely girl to shout. She had done some good after all. She had helped settle in Adelaide's mind that she was needed here, would love it. Yes, she had done something good for the man she. . .called friend.

Adelaide grabbed Christa's hands. "Oh, thank you, Christa."

They continued talking about everything. Christa would love to have a friend like Adelaide. But she knew that would be possible only if her feelings for Grant vanished. That seemed about as unlikely as the mountains ahead of them disappearing.

They were laughing and talking about city life when Grant brought their food.

"You're not eating with us?" Adelaide asked.

His brow furrowed. "I'm talking with your dad about the medical needs here."

"Hmmm, I see. That's more important than us."

"No, but it is important."

"I'm teasing you, Grant."

He nodded and glanced at Christa. She smiled down at her plate. Instead of thinking about what she might want for herself, she thought of how she'd felt when Roland had jilted her. She would not wish that kind of experience on anyone, particularly the lovely Adelaide.

While they ate lunch, Adelaide surprised her. "Christa. Could I ask a favor? Could you finish out this week for me? I'm just not ready to jump in and teach. But I would love for you to show me the church and a little of the cove."

"I'll be glad to. But don't you want Grant to do that?"

"I learned a long time ago that Grant and my dad forget everything else when they discuss medicine."

Christa and Adelaide spent the afternoon walking through

the cove. They talked to adults and children. After they returned late that afternoon, Christa was afraid Adelaide might not completely understand how busy Grant was as the cove's only doctor. She relayed some of that information.

"Oh, I'm aware of how much the people here need him, Christa. Last night he had to go help a cow deliver her calf." She laughed. "I guess Grant has to be a veterinarian, too."

"The animals are important to these people. Milk isn't delivered to one's porch."

"Christa, don't you think Grant is about the most wonderful man a girl could want?"

Christa feared the warmth flooding her face must be visible. But Adelaide kept talking. "I'm so glad we spent this time together. I've had questions about teaching here. Now, I'm sure of where I belong and what I should do." Her blue eyes shone. "Friend to friend, will you tell me something?"

"If. . .if I can."

"Do you believe in love at first sight?"

This girl was obviously very much in love. Adelaide had known Grant for years. Christa had known him for a short time.

"I don't know about just a look," Christa said. "But I do think love can happen very quickly."

Adelaide laughed delightedly. "Sometimes in spite of ourselves, right?"

Christa nodded

Adelaide took Christa's hands in hers. "You can't imagine, Christa, what our conversations today have meant to me. Now, I need to go see Grant." Her pretty yellow skirt swirled gracefully as Adelaide turned and hastened down the road.

Christa would have preferred Adelaide to not have asked

about falling in love. And she wished she could have said, "No, you need to know a person for a long time."

But Adelaide, offering her friendship, had deserved the best answer Christa could give.

Chapter 14

When Christa came home from school on Wednesday, Uncle John set a cup of coffee for her at the kitchen table, sat adjacent to her, then said the Montgomerys, the music teacher, and Grant had left the cove.

"What? Why?"

Christa had thought it strange that Adelaide hadn't made an appearance at school but supposed she and Grant had a lot of plans to make. That would be why Adelaide asked Christa to finish out the week of teaching.

Maybe something wonderful had happened for them—like their deciding to elope.

Or maybe something terrible happened. "Is it Adelaide's grandfather?"

He shook his head. "I don't know. Grant said they had to catch the train and he'd explain when he returns. Dora and Clem visited later. They only know the Montgomerys graciously thanked them for their hospitality."

On Friday, Miz Dora stopped by to say Grant had returned, but before she could get anything out of him, he was called away to a logging accident.

Determined to be useful, Christa spent Saturday visiting those who made crafts.

When she sat in the front row of church Sunday morning, she thought she heard Grant's voice, but he did not sit beside her. Perhaps he sat farther back with his fiancée—the real schoolmarm.

Uncle John stood up and announced, "After the service, some matters need to be addressed. I hope you'll all be able to stay. Now, let's get on with our worship."

Todd led the singing. Uncle's John's sermon seemed shorter than usual. No one came forward for special prayer. Uncle John said, "Our doctor has an announcement."

Grant walked to the pulpit. Christa prayed she'd conceal her emotions, particularly if he announced that his fiancée had become his wife.

She looked up when he described an important doctors' meeting in Asheville. Dr. Montgomery hadn't planned to attend, but a situation arose that changed his mind. At the meeting, the doctor made an impassioned plea for funds and equipment to turn Grant's cabin into a clinic. They would appeal for a doctor just out of medical school to come and train under Grant.

Christa joined in the applause. She was happy for Grant. His dreams were coming true. Oh, how she wished she could see these things materialize.

"I'll need men to help renovate the cabin," he said, "and women to help with furnishings."

Birr Morgan spoke up. "We'll do what we can at the sawmill. Free of charge."

"It'll be hard with crops coming in," Jeb Norval said, "but me and my boys will help."

Other offers sounded throughout the church.

"One more thing," Grant said. "The Montgomerys have a commitment from the Asheville church to send school supplies. Mr. Warren, who is eager to mentor Todd when the time is right, has also promised help from Charleston schools."

After taking a deep breath, Grant cleared his throat. "Miss Montgomery plans to take a teaching position in Charleston."

Christa stared. What did that mean? Would Grant leave the cove after he trained another doctor?

"I think, if Miss Walsh will continue at our school, we need to make a bigger commitment to her than one day or one week at a time. She deserves better."

Others agreed, but Christa focused on her gloves when Grant walked past her up the aisle.

Dora stood. "Christa, do you have something to say? You know we want you here as teacher."

Christa had thought this was what she wanted. Now, she wasn't sure. "I need to think this over."

Dora smiled. Uncle John looked tenderly at her.

Clem nodded. "Jeb had a good point. We were so eager to have a teacher, we wanted the children in school even though it's summer. But you men want to help with the clinic. Children are needed to help bring in the crops. A few weeks off school might be good."

Grant spoke up. "That would give Miss Walsh time to get her crafts and think about teaching permanently. Since she has been so gracious to teach for us, we should let her make the decision about the school schedule."

Sounds of affirmation sounded.

Christa stood. "At school tomorrow, I'll send notes home with the children about the schedule."

The meeting ended. Adults expressed their wish for her to be the teacher.

When Christa went out into the yard, a few men were walking away from Grant. He acknowledged her with a nod, then headed toward his cabin. She supposed he had plans to make that didn't include her.

❦

Men came at daybreak to start renovating the cabin. Clem and Dora, who insisted Grant live with them while the work took place, left on Monday morning for Asheville. Christa left on the same train with craft samples for the shop. She had sent notes home with the children that school was dismissed until further notice.

"Will she come back?" Grant asked John when they stopped for the lunch that women brought to the work site.

Christa's uncle gave Grant a long look. "I didn't ask." He proceeded to fill his plate.

Grant sensed that a lot of meaning lay behind that simple statement. He followed John and absentmindedly spooned food onto his plate. "I haven't asked, Pastor John, because I didn't want to influence her decision."

"What decision, Grant?"

Grant stared after him, feeling the impact of that question. By his silence, he'd gotten Christa into teaching. Now, by silence, he'd likely driven her away.

For the rest of the week, he worked with the other men from daybreak 'til dark, then spent the nights in the Carmichaels' cabin, wondering where they were. What was Christa doing? Should he go to Hendersonville and find out? Or wait here forever, wondering what might have been?

He felt lonely in church Sunday. The Carmichaels hadn't

returned. Christa wasn't sitting in the front row.

On Monday morning, he told the men to quit working on the clinic at noon and tend to their crops and businesses.

In the afternoon, he stood outside the depot when the train pulled in. Holding his bag and a ticket to Hendersonville, Grant headed for the train. He stopped when Dora and Clem exited, followed by Christa, wearing the same questioning expression he'd seen when he first ran into her.

"You going somewhere, Grant?" Dora asked

Where he was going depended on Christa.

He took Christa's suitcase from her hand. "For now, let's just say I've come to welcome each of you home."

His heart skipped a beat when Christa smiled at him and said, "It's good. . .to be home."

Chapter 15

G rant remembered his first ride with Christa in Clem's wagon. Out of desperation, he'd wanted to ask, "Will you be my fiancée?"

Now he wanted to ask the same question from a desire to spend the rest of his life with her.

If he did, she would likely get that suspicious, confused look again. However, when he stopped by Pastor John's and asked if she'd like to see the progress on the clinic, she agreed to go.

He asked about her trip to Hendersonville. She answered politely. They even talked about the weather. Had she lost trust in him because he'd kissed her while engaged to another woman? Was she leaving the cove, meaning the end of their relationship before it really had begun?

The tension vanished when they reached the clinic. Her enthusiasm rekindled his as he explained each room. She walked across the hardwood floors, commented on the waiting room, looked into the treatment room, and touched cabinets. He led her to the addition at the back that would be sleeping quarters for his assistant.

"This is fine, Grant. Even if you don't get an assistant

right away, this is so much better since patients will be able to come here."

He agreed. "And the cove people will appreciate it because they helped build it. That's the difference between here and the city. We don't take things for granted."

"I learned that from teaching," she said. "No one takes teachers for granted. That makes it so worthwhile."

Hope sprang in him. He opened the screen door, and they went out into the backyard, smaller now because of the extension to the cabin. They walked toward the gurgling creek. Maybe she wouldn't hear the pleading in his question. "Does that mean you will stay on as teacher?"

He stepped on a stone in the creek and held out his hand. She hesitated, then tilted her head and smiled. "I can do it." She lifted her skirts slightly and stepped from one stone to another. His foot slipped. Hers did, too, and they grabbed each other's hands. Laughing, they reached the other side without filling their shoes with water.

"I could have done it," she said, "if you hadn't done that silly dance on the rocks."

Ah, it felt good to have her behave in that spunky manner again. "Sure you could." He couldn't resist adding, "But holding onto someone else helps one's balance."

Maybe he shouldn't have looked into her eyes then. She ducked her head slightly and walked ahead of him into the woods. In the coolness and the shadows, he tried to regain that sense of togetherness.

"For your information," he said, "I plan to build a bridge over that creek. Since I'll be living in the glade, I'll be called upon come hail or high water and don't want to wade neck deep in the creek."

She laughed. "Good idea." How grand that he and Adelaide would have a beach home in Charleston and a mountain home in Bear Cove.

They walked into the glade. He watched her look out over the lush green mountains beneath a deep blue sky where the late evening sun hid behind a distant cloud. He wondered if she'd come here to say good-bye—to the cove and to him.

He stood beside her, and she looked at him, a gleam of gold touching her eyes. "Being here has been good for me, Grant. I love the people, the children, and the sense of purpose I've gained. When I arrived, I wanted to do well and make a difference, but it was mainly about me."

She turned toward the tranquil view. "I needed to know what was best. I asked God for a sign."

"And He gave you one?" That sounded like he doubted, so Grant added, "Of course."

She nodded. "I realized William and Bettina's acceptance was genuine. They loved the crafts and want to purchase them. And I no longer resent Roland. Maybe he did fall in love with the banker's daughter instead of her money." She shook her head. "I thought the Lord giving me insight into my own self-centeredness and taking away my resentment was the sign."

Just as he figured she would say her place was in Hendersonville, she added, "But it wasn't."

The sun hadn't brought that glow to her face; it came from inside. He needed to pray for what was best for her, in spite of what he wanted. But what she was saying made him want her even more.

She faced him. Amazement tinged her voice. "Dora contacted me. Their former church invited me to talk about the school. I was scared but knew they might sponsor a teacher, so

I told them about the children and about Todd. They were so impressed. Oh, Grant!"

She pressed her hands to her chest. "I am now the official cove missionary-teacher, sponsored by a church in Asheville."

Emotion flooded Grant's eyes. "Christa, this is wonderful. You're perfect for this. I knew it that first week."

She looked down. "Even with that, it wasn't easy. I had to ask myself if this was God's will. I had to be able to say I would teach even if those I. . .those close to me were not here. Suppose Uncle John and the Carmichaels left. And you. . . ."

Was she about to say, "Those I love?"

His heart thudded. "Christa, I'm not going anywhere."

Her gaze met his. "But Adelaide's in Charleston."

He nodded. "She's in love with Charlie Warren."

"Oh," she said. "Are you. . .heartbroken?"

"I was concerned, Christa. I didn't want to hurt her. I do love her. But when you came into my life, I began to realize that I'm not in love with Adelaide. When I couldn't seem to get the words out right, she informed me about the difference between loving someone and being *in* love with them."

Christa nodded. "She asked me if I believed in love at first sight."

He dared believe what he saw in her eyes. "What did you say?"

"I said I believed in love coming quickly."

His hands moved to her shoulders. "I think that's something she and Charlie Warren learned. I know it's something I learned, even though I fought it. I'm in love with you, Christa."

She came into his arms. "I'm in love with you, Grant."

After a kiss that, this time, neither ran away from, he drew a deep breath and held her close. "May I tell the world I have a fiancée, she's the schoolmarm, and her name is Christa Walsh?"

"Please do."

He moved away, faced the view, and shouted. "I'm in love."

Christa shouted, "Me, too."

The mountains echoed back, "love, too" so many times that it began to sound for all the world like, "true love true."

※

A week later, Christa and Grant traveled to Asheville and chose her engagement ring. They rode to Hendersonville and visited William and Bettina, who were delighted with Grant and the engagement. They returned on Monday.

A few weeks later, they joined the Carmichaels at Adelaide and Charlie's wedding in a big church in Asheville. The summer sped by quickly. The clinic was finished. A new doctor lived in the addition and studied under Grant.

Whenever they could, the men of the cove worked on the log house in the clearing where Grant and Christa would live after they married.

William and Bettina had placed orders for crafts that gave many a renewed sense of purpose. Christa couldn't imagine getting married anywhere other than in the little church in the cove where Uncle John preached.

She spent what time she could planning for school, which would begin in the fall. The wedding was set for a week before classes started.

The wedding day arrived—a beautiful, clear, warm day. Clem and Dora organized the reception to be held in the churchyard.

The little church was packed with some standing around the walls and others outside looking in the windows. Christa had invited a couple of her married friends from Hendersonville. Some of Grant's acquaintances from Asheville came, including Dr. and Mrs. Montgomery, who said Adelaide and Charlie were living in Charleston and getting ready for the new school year. They sent their love and a generous monetary gift.

After Bettina walked down the aisle and took her place as matron of honor across from Clem as Grant's best man, Todd sang, "O Perfect Love."

Christa couldn't imagine anything more perfect than William walking her down the aisle and saying, "I, her brother, do," when Uncle John asked, "Who gives this woman to wed this man?"

Uncle John then said, "We are gathered here to join this man and this woman in holy matrimony." He cleared his throat and paused, looking from Christa to Grant and back again. "I must add something to this ceremony. The Lord works in mysterious ways. . . ."

Christa and Grant smiled, then gazed into each other's eyes. She was asked a vague question and said, "I do." Grant did the same.

Uncle John pronounced them man and wife. "You may kiss the bride."

Grant and Christa turned toward each other. She felt his arms come around her, and she lifted her face to his, not the least bit reluctant.

YVONNE LEHMAN

As an award-winning novelist from Black Mountain in the heart of North Carolina's Blue Ridge Mountains, Yvonne Lehman has written several novels for Barbour Publishing and its **Heartsong Presents** line. Her titles include *Mountain Man*, which won a National Reader's Choice Award sponsored by a chapter of Roman Writers of America; *The Stranger's Kiss*, a Booksellers Best Award winner; *His Hands*, winner of the Inspirational Readers Choice Award in novella category; and *Coffee Rings*, a women's fiction title published by Barbour, also published in the German language in Germany.

Other of her novels include the White Dove series for young adults published by Bethany House and the widely acclaimed biblical novel *In Shady Groves*, reprinted by Guideposts in their Women of the Bible series. She is founder and director of The Blue Ridge Mountains Christian Writers Conference. *The Reluctant Schoolmarm* is novel number forty-one; and number forty-two, *Moving the Mountain*, is scheduled for release in July 2006.

Visit www.yvonnelehman.com to learn more about Yvonne and her work.

School Bells and Wedding Bells

by Colleen L. Reece

Dedication

In memory of my mother,
who ruled her students with a rod of love,
and all the one-room schoolteachers
who taught lessons in life,
as well as from textbooks.

For my thoughts are not your thoughts,
neither are your ways my ways, saith the LORD.
For as the heavens are higher than the earth,
so are my ways higher than your ways,
and my thoughts than your thoughts.
ISAIAH 55:8-9 KJV

Dear Reader,

In the early 1920s, Mom—Pearl Towne Reece—taught all eight grades in a one-room schoolhouse near my birthplace of Darrington, Washington. The White Pine School was built on land donated by my ancestors. Mom followed a teacher who was notorious for his lack of discipline. She marched in, won the hearts of even the most unruly students, and erased the problem. A few eighth-grade boys actually fell in love with her!

When the Darrington schools consolidated, outlying one-room schoolhouses closed. Grandpa Reece purchased the land and made the old schoolhouse into a dwelling place. Our family moved there in 1936. I was a year old. My bedroom was the original cloakroom.

As I lived and dreamed in the old schoolhouse, I had no idea God would one day grant my childhood wish to "someday write a book." He has multiplied that wish more than a hundredfold; this title is number 140. *School Bells and Wedding Bells* is a tribute to my rich, God-given heritage: thirty-four years of living in a one-room schoolhouse and learning valuable lessons that have lasted for a lifetime.

—*Colleen*

Chapter 1

Boston, Massachusetts—late 1890s

Sunlight burst through spring-gray clouds and streamed through the magnificent stained-glass windows of the anteroom in Boston's most prestigious church. It turned Meredith Rose Macrae into a living mosaic. Blue, green, and rose shimmered on her white satin gown and the coronet of orange blossoms anchoring her bridal veil, then caressed her white prayer book dripping with ribbons and lilies.

A warning growl of distant thunder mingled with the well-modulated tones of the costly organ in the sanctuary, an unwelcome reminder that March—which had come in with lamblike meekness—might well depart with the temperament of a roaring lion.

Twenty-seven-year-old Marcus Macrae, Boston born and bred and a tall, dark-haired replica of his twin sister, clenched his hands and fought the storm of anger hidden beneath his fine wedding clothes. *Lord, how can I tell Merry? Will it break her heart? Her spirit?* He glanced at the young woman who had been a law unto herself from early childhood, then he surreptitiously stole a look at his pocket watch. What little hope he had clung to departed. Herbert wasn't coming.

Herbert. Marcus straightened the strong fingers that had automatically clenched into fists. He'd despised Herbert Calloway from the moment he met him. Marcus shook his head. Not a fitting sentiment for a minister of the gospel, but it was a simple fact of life. How many times had he ruefully muttered to himself, "If I had a dollar for every hour I've spent on my knees asking forgiveness for feeling this way, I'd be richer than Croesus." His outbursts were always followed by, "Too bad I'm not. I'd abduct that sister of mine and hide her somewhere until she could see Calloway for what he really is!" Time and Marcus's many prayers did little to warm him toward his future brother-in-law. Herbert's supercilious manner, slicked-back hair, and dapper black mustache that resembled a misplaced third eyebrow fired Marcus with the primitive desire to mop up the floor with the man. How could Merry love him?

Marcus shook his head and stared at his twin, seeing her not as she was on what should be the happiest day of her life, but the way she had been as far back as he could remember. . . .

Meredith Rose Macrae had charted her life's course before she was ten. School and finishing school. Travel. Love, marriage, children, and a storybook happily-ever-after. Even as a child, the ebony-haired girl with the direct blue gaze had a way of getting what she wanted. Marcus watched with a great deal of amusement as his twin achieved her first three goals right on schedule. Before God called him to higher purposes, he had accompanied Merry on her jaunts all over the world. The hordes of hopefuls who pursued the well-to-do young woman failed to touch her heart. Neither had Marcus met a woman with whom he wanted to spend the rest of his life.

Before it seemed possible, their twenty-third birthday arrived. Marcus would never forget that day in May when his sister came to him in a panic. He had just made a life-changing decision in the seclusion of the richly carpeted, wood-paneled library and was considering how best to break the news to Merry. Would she understand, or would it create the first real rift of their lives, and color the future?

"What am I going to do?" she demanded, wringing her hands and dropping into a tapestry-covered chair beside the massive fireplace with its cozy fire. "It has been wonderful flitting about the world. I never dreamed my traveling would so thin the ranks of eligible suitors! Marcus, if something doesn't happen soon, I'm in serious danger of becoming an old maid."

The idea was ludicrous; laughter spilled from Marcus like water over Niagara Falls. "You, an old maid? Hardly!"

She raised her chin, and her expression chilled. "I fail to find anything humorous about the situation." A quiver in her voice alerted her brother to trouble.

"My word, you're really serious, aren't you?" Marcus could scarcely believe it.

"Yes. Percival Vandevere just got engaged. So did Howell DeWitt and—"

Marcus gasped. "Don't tell me you considered marrying one of those fops!"

"Both are high on the social register," she retorted.

"Neither has ever done an honest day's work in his life and their family fortunes were acquired by less than honorable means," Marcus snapped. "If Father were still alive, he'd squelch that idea in a hurry."

"I have to marry," Meredith Rose reminded him. "It's what women do."

"Why? You can stay single and keep house for me, old dear," he teased. "Besides," Marcus added fiercely, "I'd rather see you marry a working man than anyone like Vandevere or DeWitt."

Disbelief shone in his twin's blue eyes, followed by scorn. "I? Marry a working man?" She delicately shuddered and turned up her nose. "I hope you aren't going to disgrace the Macrae name by taking up with some common girl who doesn't know which fork to use at dinner."

Marcus leaned back in his luxurious chair. "You really are a snob, aren't you?"

Angry color flared in her smooth cheeks, and she leaped to her feet. "I am *not* a snob. I just know what is expected of me. I pray you do, as well."

Marcus knew the moment had come. Not the ideal time for his confession, but it could wait no longer. "Sit down, please, Merry. I have something to tell you."

Apparently mollified by his refusal to be baited, she flounced back into her chair. "I hope it's good news."

Heart pounding, Marcus leaned forward and rested his hands on his knees. "The most wonderful news in the world, as far as I am concerned." He wistfully added, "I hope you think so, too. You said you pray that I will do what is expected of me. For months I have been asking for enlightenment to find out just what that is."

His sister's mouth opened in a little round *O*, but she remained silent.

"Do you remember when we invited Jesus into our hearts when we were very young?" Marcus began, praying that she would understand what had happened to him.

Her eyes opened wide. "Of course, but what does that have to do with—"

"It has everything to do with it, Merry. I believe with all my heart that God is calling me to serve Him by becoming a minister." His ringing voice filled the library. "I also want to learn at least the rudiments of medicine."

"A minister! *You?*"

His blue gaze never left hers. "Yes. I know I'm not worthy, but I intend to be." Unable to stay seated, he stood and paced the carpeted floor. "Until now, I've played the part of an idler." He felt shame suffuse his face. "Don't misunderstand. I've enjoyed our life of ease—of being with you in all kinds of delightful adventures. But through it all, I've felt hollow. Even going to church hasn't filled the emptiness inside me."

She stirred in her chair and looked perplexed. "I've never heard you speak like this before. Are you sure you aren't just bored?"

"I thought so at first. Not now. I've been studying the Bible, especially the lives of the disciples and others whom Jesus called to serve Him. I want to be one of them."

The tick of the ancestral clock on the mantel sounded loud in Marcus's ears. *Tick tock. Tick tock.* Ticking off the seconds while he waited in suspense. *Please, God, help her accept my decision, even if she cannot comprehend.*

Seconds became minutes before Meredith Rose answered. When she did, it was with outstretched hands and tear-wet lashes. "Dear Marcus, if God is calling you to serve Him, serve you must." She smiled.

He grasped her hands and knelt by her chair. "Thank you." It was all he could get out.

After a long moment, a small voice asked, "What about me? Your decision doesn't find me a husband."

For the second time that day, Marcus's laughter swept

through the room. "No, it doesn't, but don't you see, Merry? If God wants us to have mates, He can send them at just the right time. All we have to do is pray and wait."

"Herbert isn't coming, is he?" His sister's voice yanked Marcus from the past back to the present.

"He may just be late," Marcus reminded her.

She shook her head. "That's unlikely. He prides himself on being prompt at all times. Or at least sending a message when he is delayed."

The door burst open. A man Marcus remembered seeing with Calloway stepped inside. "Mr. Macrae? A message for you." He proffered a sealed white envelope and started out.

"Wait. There may be an answer."

The man's lips set in a grim line. "Begging your pardon, sir, but I was told there would be no reply." He went out, closing the door behind him.

"What on earth was that all about?" Meredith Rose demanded.

Marcus tore open the envelope and removed the crested notepaper inside. Fury rose until he thought he would choke. "What a rotter!"

"What does it say?" She snatched the page. Face whiter than her gown, Meredith Rose maintained a remarkably steady voice as she read the message aloud: " 'By the time you get this, Gwendolyn Arlington and I will be married. Although she is much younger, under the circumstances, I am sure you will understand. Herbert Calloway.' " The signature had the peculiar little flourish he always used.

The humiliation in his sister's face struck deep into Marcus's soul. Yet a spark of hope ignited when he saw the flush of anger that crept from the high neck of her bridal gown and drove away her pallor. Perhaps pride was more involved than love.

"What a coward! He didn't even have the courtesy to address this to me." Meredith Rose jerked the lace mitts from her hands and shredded the page. For a moment she stared at her engagement ring with its enormous, sparkling diamond surrounded by a galaxy of lesser stones, then tore it from her finger and flung it to the floor.

"It was always too ostentatious, anyway," she said through gritted teeth. "I wonder how that cat Gwendolyn Arlington will enjoy wearing it." Her eyes flashed. "I'm surprised he sent word before I got to the altar." She paused. "What did he mean by that cryptic 'under the circumstances'?"

Marcus recoiled. His pain intensified. Surviving Herbert Calloway's desertion was one thing. Facing the shattering news Marcus had planned to withhold until she was safely married was another. To gain time, he stooped, picked up the ring, and shoved it in the breast pocket of his tailored coat. "Time enough to talk about that when we get home. Will you be all right until I tell the minister there won't be a wedding?"

"Yes." She stumbled to a nearby chair.

Marcus chucked her under the chin the way he had done when they were small. "Brace up, old girl. Things could be worse. What if you had married the cur, then found out what he really is?" The horror that sprang to Merry's eyes added fuel to Marcus's kindled hope that the blow was more to her pride than the loss of love. He quickly added, "God has delivered you from a lifetime of misery," and strode out—trying to decide whether to throttle Calloway or fervently thank him.

Chapter 2

Marcus Macrae's words rang in his sister's ears. *"What if you had married the cur?"* Then, *"God has delivered you from a lifetime of misery."*

Meredith Rose shuddered at her narrow escape and stared at the floor. She wanted to shriek to the high heavens. If God had really wanted to spare her, why had He sent Herbert Calloway into her life? *Did God send him, or was it all your own doing?* her sense of fair play protested. She squirmed, remembering the aftermath of that fateful May day when she was twenty-three. . . .

When Marcus announced he'd been called to become a minister, she'd known nothing would ever be the same. She and Marcus had clung to one another from the time they could toddle, especially after their parents died in a railway accident when the twins were in their late teens. He was the dearest person on earth to her—and the only one she allowed to call her Merry. "It's too frivolous for my position," she protested.

Marcus only laughed, his eyes crinkling at the corners in the way that always lifted her spirits. He made a low bow. "Your will is my command, Miss Macrae."

"If you are going to play court jester, I suppose you may

call me Merry," she told him in a long-suffering tone of voice. "You will, anyway."

"Yes, Your Majesty." He bowed again.

A rush of love for the brother who always seemed much older than she filled her. "You may call me anything you wish, Marcus." She anxiously peered into his face. "Just so nothing ever comes between us. It won't, will it?"

His mirth fled. "No, Merry. We are two against the world now that Mother and Father are gone. At least until we marry, you are first in my world."

"I feel the same," she murmured, comforted by his promise.

Their deep and abiding love for one another continued untroubled—until Marcus's call to serve. Meredith Rose instantly recognized their relationship must irrevocably change. She would always hold a special place in her twin's heart, yet she would no longer be first with Marcus. God had replaced her. Even though she knew it was as it should be, a sense of loss pervaded the innermost parts of her being. Marcus could no longer be the willing companion in whatever pleasures she conjured up, free as a butterfly in summer to take off at a moment's notice. He must study and prepare.

"What about me?" she asked. "Your decision doesn't find me a husband."

His reply sank deep into her heart. "If God wants us to have mates, He can send them at just the right time. All we have to do is pray and wait."

Meredith Rose secretly pondered Marcus's words, wondering if he could be right. He certainly sounded confident, but she wasn't sure. Why should God do anything for her, when she had done so little for Him? After asking Jesus into her heart, her religious life consisted of attending formal service on

Sundays and contributing to the needy. She also lent her name to various charities. In the light of Marcus's decision to follow the Master, her own contributions seemed insignificant.

Weary weeks became restless months. Meredith Rose chafed at being denied her brother's company because of his need to study but she wisely never let it show. She also began to dream and scheme toward the day when Marcus would occupy the pulpit of a noted Boston church. The Macrae name could open gates padlocked against others less fortunate. In the meantime, her own life had grown dull and flat.

In desperation she turned to God, beseeching Him for favors, deserved or not.

Nothing happened.

She continued to beat on the doors of heaven. "Can't you hear me, God? I really need Your help, now that You've taken Marcus away from me." The prayer sounded childish even to her own ears, so she hastily added, "It's not that I begrudge losing him to You. Well, at least not much. It's just that his involvement leaves me with too much time on my hands. Please, won't You change my life, too?"

A few weeks later, it appeared her prayers were being answered, at least in part. Miss Grenadier, founder and director of the exclusive Miss Grenadier's School for Young Ladies, which Meredith Rose had attended, came to call. "Miss Macrae, I hope you don't find it presumptuous of me to ask, but would you consider teaching for us?"

The woman twisted her gloved hands. "We are in desperate need. Having your name on our faculty will ensure we can attract students from the best families. I remember how popular you were with both fellow students and your instructors. We would love to have you join us."

Meredith Rose's first inclination was to respond with a haughty and resounding no. Before she could speak, a thought stole into her mind. *Don't be too hasty about turning her down. Teaching would at least relieve your boredom while you're waiting for God to send you your Sir Galahad.*

The idea was too strong to be ignored. "What would my duties be?" She laughed carelessly. "It's been a long time since I diagramed sentences or worked fractions."

Miss Grenadier's eyes gleamed with obvious satisfaction. "Oh, we have others to handle those subjects. We need you to teach our girls more important things: elocution, deportment, music, painting—I remember how skilled you were with the pianoforte and brush—that kind of thing. In short, you'd help us turn out real ladies, like yourself."

The flattery piqued Meredith Rose's interest. "How soon will you need to know?"

The woman looked troubled. "We are really shorthanded." She sniffed. "The former teacher was terribly inconsiderate! She resigned without giving proper notice in order to marry. Can you imagine?" She rushed on. "Would you be able to give us an answer in a week?"

When Meredith Rose nodded, Miss Grenadier clasped her hands and said, "I am so thrilled! Just the thought of having you become one of us is. . . " She left rejoicing, as though Meredith Rose Macrae were already "one of them."

"What have I done?" the young woman wondered. "Do I really want to teach, even those enjoyable activities?" She looked around the library, feeling the walls were closing in on her. "At least I'm not firmly committed."

That evening before Marcus began his nightly studies, Meredith Rose told him of the position she had been offered.

"Take it," he advised. "You'll do a great job." He sighed. "I know these last months haven't been easy. You need something on which you can focus, Merry. Something into which you can pour your time and energy. You aren't cut out for sitting idle. You don't care for heading up charitable drives or doing volunteer nursing."

She shook her head in disgust.

He grinned at her. "Why not give it a try? If you don't like it, the school won't be any worse off than it is now."

The next day Meredith Rose became "Miss Macrae" and entered a life as far from her former indolent existence as Boston from Australia.

"I like it," she reported to Marcus at the end of the first week. "I actually like it." She laughed deprecatingly. "Of course, if I had to teach such mundane lessons as grammar and the multiplication tables, it would be a different story!"

"Always taking the easy way out," he teased, but she could see he was pleased that she no longer moped around home. Now when Marcus studied at one side of the beautiful library, she busied herself at the other. She hunted out music for the girls' chorus, who would do her proud in an upcoming presentation. She pictured herself in a rich sapphire velvet gown, bowing before beaming parents and accepting their gratitude. Recitations from the classics as well as original essays from the brightest students would be included. All were designed to bring even more glory to Meredith Rose and show the world how fortunate Miss Grenadier's School for Young Ladies was to have her on its staff.

Despite her new interest, despite the smashing success of the presentation and others like it, prayers for God to send a husband who would change her life even further remained in the teacher's heart and often on her lips.

A year slipped by. Another. No Sir Galahad appeared, although Meredith Rose continued to remind God she was still waiting. Marcus completed his ministerial studies and began his preaching career, studying medicine on the side. To his sister's dismay, he refused a desirable offer from a prominent denomination in favor of working with a small church on the outskirts of Boston.

"I know you had your heart set on my occupying a high position, Merry," he said sadly, "but the people at Community Christian need me. Those attending First Central don't." All her pleading that the powerful and the mighty deserved to hear the gospel as well as the poor and humble didn't change his mind.

Now she saw him less than ever. Whenever Pastor Marcus—who steadfastly refused to be called Reverend—wasn't conducting services, he was counseling families, visiting the sick, or searching out food and shelter for the needy. At his urging, Meredith Rose accompanied him now and then but decided she was too delicate for the sights, sounds, and smells of social work. "Besides," she reasoned, "I'm providing service to the girls I teach."

Once, in a moment of depression, a sigh so deep she felt it began at her toes and crept upward escaped. Perhaps teaching was all she would ever do. All the other girls in her social set had married. Most had babies. Why had God denied her the joy of being a wife and mother? The thought planted itself in Meredith Rose's mind and haunted her. In less than two weeks, she would be twenty-seven years old. Crop after crop of debutantes had entered society and taken her place, leaving her to wither on the vine, an object of pity among those she once called friends.

"I suppose it's Your plan that I become like Miss Grenadier," she accused God in the privacy of her lavishly furnished bedroom one night. Half-expecting a rebuke, she bitterly added, "Deliver me from such a fate! Nothing could be worse." At least she still had her beauty. The mirror above her brocade-skirted dressing table attested to that.

"If only my life would change!" she complained.

The very next day a new dancing master reported to Miss Grenadier's Finishing School for Young Ladies. Single, sought-after by eligible young maidens and their overly eager mamas, Herbert Calloway was reputed to be disgustingly rich. When the black-haired, black-eyed young man met Meredith Rose, he bent low over her hand and clicked his heels together. "Mademoiselle Macrae? It is indeed my pleasure."

His admiration warmed her lonely heart and melted the reserve with which she usually greeted strangers. "Coincidences like this just don't happen," she told herself. "Herbert's coming is surely an answer to my prayers."

A time of enchantment followed. Herbert overwhelmed her with admiration. A few months later the Boston newspapers formally announced nuptials for Miss Meredith Rose Macrae and Mr. Herbert Calloway would be held the end of March.

When the long-awaited day came, Meredith Rose awakened to brilliant sunshine. Distant clouds warned that the capricious month was not yet over, but she only laughed at their gloomy rumblings.

Somehow the hours passed until she reached the church and donned her wedding dress, chosen over the objections of the dressmaker who had trotted out samples of far more elaborate frocks. Gowned in white satin and dreams, she waited in the anteroom, visualizing the moment when Marcus placed her hand in Herbert's and she took the vows that would bind them together forever. Then the note arrived. . . .

"Ready, Merry?"

Her brother's voice calling her back from her thoughts made her feel she had returned from a long journey, one so wearisome she dared not speculate about what "under the circumstances" meant. "Yes. Take me home."

Chapter 3

Every *clop clop* of the matched pair of white horses that proudly pulled the closed carriage from First Central Church to the Macrae home accused Marcus. *You should have told her. Why didn't you tell her?* He impatiently thrust the accusations aside. What was done was done. Self-recrimination couldn't undo the past. He must focus on how to tell Merry what the ominous words *under the circumstances* meant—but not here. Not while she sat stiffly beside him in a wedding gown as crumpled as her former dreams.

When they reached their spacious home, he silently helped Meredith Rose from the carriage and waved the driver away. She started up the walk, paused, and glanced at the scowling, gunmetal clouds that had changed from warning to reality. A bolt of lightning split the sky, followed by window-rattling thunder. Glad for the diversion, Marcus threw his arm around his sister and called above the tumult, "Quick! We need to reach the porch before the rain starts!"

They made it with only seconds to spare. A silver torrent of rain that changed to hail descended. From the shelter of the wide porch, the twins watched the storm. After it passed on and a patch of apologetic blue sky appeared, Meredith Rose said in a shaken voice, "Look." She pointed to a shimmering rainbow above them that arched across the city of Boston. They watched until it disappeared, then her blue gaze turned to Marcus. "As soon as we get out of these abominable clothes, you can tell me what else is going on. It would be nice to think the rainbow is a good omen, but I know you too well not to recognize Herbert's desertion is only part of something bigger." Before he could reply, she slipped inside and hurried up the stairs.

With a prayer for wisdom, Marcus slowly went to his room and changed into comfortable clothes. "Abominable is right," he muttered, flinging his wedding apparel onto his bed, then hastily retrieving it and hanging it up properly. Under the circumstances, he couldn't indulge in recklessness of any sort, even discarding despised clothing. *Under the circumstances.* Strange. He had never hated the words until today. Now they stood for heartbreak and the rocky road ahead.

The ring of the telephone shattered his reflections. A few moments later, there was a discreet knock at his bedroom door. "A call for you, sir," a servant announced.

"Thanks. I'll take it here." He picked up the phone on his bedside table. "Macrae. Arlington? You have some nerve, calling me at a time like this!" Marcus paused, trying to make sense of what the distraught man on the other end of the line was saying. "I see. . . Yes. . .A sorry mess indeed, and one you brought on yourself." He paused again. "I understand. God help you, Arlington!"

The line went dead. Marcus didn't know whether to rage or rejoice. Romans 8:28, a favorite Scripture verse, came to mind: "And we know that all things work together for good to them that love God, to them who are the called according to his purpose."

Heart lighter than it had been for days, Marcus went back downstairs to the library.

Meredith Rose was already there, clad in a simple white muslin gown scattered with tiny blue flowers and some frilly stuff around the neck and on the pockets. It made her look more like a little girl than a rejected bride-to-be. A blazing fire cast dancing shadows on the walls, and the soft lighting lay like an aura of peace over the room. Marcus dropped into his favorite chair, passionately wishing it could be like any other day when they gathered by the fire to share secrets, joys, and woes.

"Marcus, do you know why Herbert did what he did?"

He drew in a deep breath, held it, then slowly released it. This was no time for evasion. "Gwendolyn Arlington's banker father betrayed client confidence. She evidently passed the news on to Calloway."

Meredith Rose's white brow wrinkled. "What does that have to do with us? What on earth could Mr. Arlington say that would cause Herbert to elope with Gwendolyn?"

Marcus gritted his teeth. The dismay and anger that had attacked him when Arlington first summoned him and broke the news that figuratively blew things to bits returned. "Money. There's no easy way to tell you this, Merry. A few days ago, I learned our trusted family solicitor had been ill. Wanting to make sure our holdings would be well cared for, Mr. Simpson turned them over to his brother. He didn't dream what kind of man he was putting in charge." Marcus paused in an effort to control his feelings and continue with the story.

Meredith Rose's face turned to parchment. Shock filled her face. "You don't have to say what happened. The brother absconded with our funds."

"Yes." Marcus pounded his knee with one hand. "If I'd only known sooner I might have been able to salvage at least something—"

She acted as though she didn't hear him, but her eyes darkened to the color of the night sky. "So when Mr. Arlington found out, he told his daughter," she said in a mocking voice. "And of course, Gwendolyn *couldn't resist* telling Herbert." She shook her head. "I still don't understand why it should matter. Everyone knows Herbert Calloway is wealthy, far more than we are—were."

Marcus sprang to his feet, clenched his hands into fists, and delivered the final blow. "Everyone knows wrong. While I was upstairs changing, Arlington called. It seems Herbert Calloway is a charlatan. He duped Miss Grenadier and others into believing him to be a man of unlimited means and worked his way into Boston society in order to find a well-to-do wife!"

Meredith Rose stared at him. For a moment, she didn't move. When she did, she shocked her brother beyond belief. Instead of showing anger or pain, her lips twitched. Her eyes sparkled. Laughter exploded as if from a cannon and filled the quiet library.

Marcus felt his jaw drop. Had she taken leave of her senses? "Are—are you all right?" he stammered when he could find voice enough to speak.

"All right?" Another peal of laughter came, along with a rush of tears that obviously didn't spring from sadness. "It's the joke of the year. Don't you see?" She took a dainty handkerchief from her pocket and dabbed at her eyes. "Gwendolyn Arlington, who shouted to the housetops that I was odd because I didn't want bridesmaids at my wedding, is married to an unscrupulous man who hoodwinked her into an elopement." She went off into more gales of laughter. "Talk about poetic justice; Gwendolyn has it."

Marcus joined her. "Arlington is beside himself," he managed to get out between chuckles. "What's hurting him the worst is that it's his own fault. If he'd kept his mouth shut about business affairs, he wouldn't have Herbert Calloway for a son-in-law."

"So that's what Herbert meant by 'under the circumstances.'" She sobered. "Just how bad is our financial situation, Marcus?"

"It couldn't be worse," he succinctly told her, hating what he had to do, yet relieved by her reaction to Herbert's conniving. "We've lost everything."

She looked around the library. "Even the house?" Her voice quavered.

"Even the house." Marcus squirmed and dropped his head into his hands. "Several months ago, a friend of father's came to me. He had fallen on hard times and desperately needed a large sum of money in order to save his business. I placed a mortgage on the house so I could help him out. I hoped you'd never need to know."

Meredith Rose looked as if she'd been turned to stone. "Can't he pay you back?"

"No. Fire destroyed his business, and he had no insurance. We could have squeaked by if Simpson hadn't stolen our funds. Now there is no way to pay the mortgage. I'm sorry, Merry. So sorry."

She slipped from her chair and knelt by him. One hand stroked his dark hair. "I would rather give up everything than not have you willing to help those in need," she fiercely told him. "I can stand anything as long as we have each other and are together."

Hope flared within Marcus. "Do you really, truly mean that? Even though we've lost our home, our place in society?"

He saw her swallow convulsively before she said in a flippant tone that didn't conceal her sincerity, "Just call me Ruth. 'Whither thou goest' and all that." She pressed her cheek against his hair. "I'll follow you to the ends of the earth, if necessary," she whispered. "I mean," she hastily amended, "to the outskirts of Boston." She wrinkled her nose. "I can't say I'll like it, but at least it's better than being married to a scoundrel!"

Marcus seized both of her hands in his. "Meredith Rose Macrae, you're a brick, and I'm proud of you." He fell silent, dreading the next few minutes. His twin had just survived two devastating blows. God help her be able to come to terms with the final jolt.

"Do you remember the old saying about things, both good and bad, coming in threes?"

Her hands tightened on his until he wondered why she didn't cry out in pain. She raised her chin in the way she had done since childhood when faced with something new and strange.

"Fire away," she ordered. "So far today I've been jilted and informed we're penniless and will be living in a—well—let's call it a less-than-desirable neighborhood. Nothing could be worse." Her eyes widened with fear, and she released his hands. "Unless you're planning to elope, join the Foreign Legion, or you have some life-threatening illness, I should be able to handle it."

"None of those, thank God," Marcus fervently said. "The thing is, we won't be living out near Community Christian Church."

Meredith Rose jumped to her feet. Radiance erased every trace of worry from her lovely face. "You rascal! You saved the best for last. The rainbow *was* a good omen. I don't have to guess what the third happening is. You've been called to a new church. How exciting! When do you start? How long have you known?" She blinked wet lashes. "Why didn't you tell me?"

Marcus's heart thudded. When they were toddlers, he had popped a huge soap bubble his twin had blown with soapsuds and her little clay pipe. A bubble that shone iridescent and beautiful. Now he must do the same thing, only this time Merry was no crying child to be comforted by blowing a new and larger bubble.

Marcus quietly said, "Sit down, please." If his life had depended on it, he couldn't have kept from sounding somber.

Apprehension replaced the joy in her face, and she obediently resumed her seat in the chair opposite his.

"For several months I've felt dissatisfied with where I am serving," Marcus began. "It started when I read stories of how desperately both ministers and doctors are needed in faraway places." He ignored his sister's gasp. "The more I prayed about it, the more I realized God wanted me to go where I am truly needed, where there is no one to replace me should I not be there. I didn't tell you because I felt once you were married, you could accept my leaving and the loss of our money far better."

"But I'm *not* getting married," she protested. "Now you're going to Africa or India or someplace like that. We promised to stay together, Marcus. How can you do this? What will I do? What kind of God would call you somewhere I can't go?"

"He hasn't, old dear," Marcus burst out. He leaped from his chair, pulled her to her feet, and executed a wild dance around the library. "God has called me somewhere you *can* go." Exuberance for what lay ahead spilled like salt from a saltcellar. "It will be an adventure; one unlike any we've ever experienced. My call is to Idaho. A little mountain town called Last Chance."

"*Last Chance*?" She sounded appalled. With a cry of distress, she tore herself free from her brother's arms and raced upstairs, where she flung herself down on her bed and raged, "God, are You some kind of monstrous joker?" The words *you asked me to change your life* flew into her mind, but she fiercely rejected them. No loving God would send anyone—especially her—to a place called Last Chance.

Even though the name perfectly described Meredith Rose Macrae's present situation.

Chapter 4

Last Chance, Idaho—The previous autumn

Briton Farley slid from the saddle of his favorite stallion. He dropped the reins to the ground so the buckskin would stand, and then strode to the edge of the promontory that overlooked the mining town below. He had discovered the lonely spot years earlier and returned again and again, especially when he had a knotty problem to work out.

Brit had seen the spectacular Bitterroot Range that separated Idaho from Montana on the east blanketed with winter snows, etched against fiery sunrises, tranquil beneath cloudless, sapphire skies. Tawny head bared in respect, Brit had quoted Psalm 19:1 countless times: "The heavens declare the glory of God; and the firmament sheweth his handywork."

Today, troubles as abundant as the red, yellow, and golden leaves he trod distracted him from nature's wordless appeal. Brit stared across at the mountain peaks and dolefully whistled "Lone Prairie," then laughed when his horse nudged his shoulder.

"Too bad you can't talk, Nez Percé," he told his horse. "You'd be reminding me there's no problem worth stewing over on a day like this." He yanked off his Stetson, unknotted his colorful kerchief, and mopped his face. Never in the eight years since he had first come to Idaho had he seen a more exquisite Indian summer. It stretched over the land like a blanket of peace.

Brit hunkered down on his boot heels and breathed in the evergreen-scented air. Eight years. He sighed. It didn't seem possible. Thoughts of the decisions shouting to be made faded. So did his present surroundings. He closed his eyes and allowed himself to drift back. Back to life on the Rocking F in Texas. To untroubled days with his father, whose tawny hair, amber eyes, and catlike grace had replicated themselves in Brit. . . .

Michael Farley had become everything in the world to his small son when Brit's mother was stricken with fever and died. "It's just you and me and God now, Brit," he'd said.

"I don't like God. He took my mama," Brit had burst out. If he lived to be older than the Bitterroots, he would remember his father's reply and the pain in his voice.

Strong arms wrapped around him. "We don't always like what God does, but we need to remember this: God loved us so much He sent His Son to die on a cross so all who believe in Him and invite Jesus to live in their hearts can live with Him. Your mama can't come back to us, but someday we'll go to her. She will be waiting for us in a place so beautiful the Bible says we can't even imagine it!"

The child turned it over in his mind. "What if she isn't happy?" His lip quivered. "What if she forgets us?" He buried his face in his father's shirt.

"She won't forget us," Michael assured. His voice softened. "And Son, she could never be unhappy in the presence of God. The wonderful thing is, we can have that presence with us, too.

All we have to do is ask for it."

Brit looked into his father's face, not understanding. Yet the lines of sadness that had etched themselves so deeply when Christine Farley fell ill were miraculously smoothed out. His expression reminded Brit of how the world looked after the sun came up over the low hill to the east and filled the sky with glory. It brought comfort. As long as Daddy looked like that, everything would surely be all right.

Years passed: busy, happy years. Father and son worked as harmoniously as blades on a fine pair of shears. They survived drought and losses and made the most of the good years. They doubled their landholdings and increased their herds. Just after Brit's twenty-first birthday, his father signed the ranch over to him.

"I may live to be a hundred." Michael Farley's weather-beaten face opened into a broad smile. The crinkles at the corners of his expressive eyes deepened. "It doesn't matter. You're ready to take full responsibility." He leaned back in the comfortable, hand-hewn chair that had occupied the same spot in the rustic living room as far back as Brit could remember, then propped his feet on an ancient stool. "Speaking of taking responsibility, when are you going to get married and give me grandchildren? Christine and I were married with you on the way by the time I was your age."

Brit felt himself redden. "I'm too busy for girls," he said gruffly.

His father gave a knowing smile. Golden motes danced in his eyes. "Oh? According to bunkhouse gossip, you could tame and marry just about any pretty little filly for miles around. Is that the problem? Too many to choose from?"

"No." Brit nodded toward the wedding picture of his parents

that graced the mantel over the huge stone fireplace. "I won't marry until I find one like her."

Michael's feet came down with a *thump*. "God willing, somewhere in this world there may be another lass as good and sweet as your mother. Don't pay any attention to my wanting to hear the patter of little feet here in the ranch house. Never marry until you find the woman God intended you to have; then don't let anything stop you."

"Just as you did."

"Yes." Michael stood, crossed to Brit, and dropped a powerful hand to his shoulder. "If she is like Christine, she's well worth waiting for."

They were the last words he ever spoke to his son. That afternoon his galloping horse stumbled and fell, crushing her rider. Michael never regained consciousness. . . .

Nez Percé whinnied.

Brit reached up and stroked the buckskin's black mane, feeling he had just returned from a long journey. Trained to never make decisions in a hurry, he had stuck it out in Texas for a year after his father died. Then Brit knew it was time to move on. Determined to make a fresh start wherever God led him, Brit sold out lock, stock, and barrel. He left most of his money in a trustworthy bank, reasoning it could be obtained when needed by means of a telegram. Scorning railroads, he saddled the sorrel he had withheld from the sale of his stock, mounted, and rode away. He didn't look back. The ranch was no longer his. His parents' wedding picture rested in the bottom of his saddlebags. God went before and beside him. Nothing else mattered.

Curious about the reports of gold, copper, and silver strikes in Idaho, Brit decided to head north and west. The many faces of America captivated him, especially the towering mountains so unlike those in his home state. He missed the companionship of others, so he hired on now and then at ranches along the way. Yet none appealed to him enough to stay in one place a sufficient amount of time to make lasting friends or to satisfy the belief he would know where he belonged when he got there. And—God willing—find a wife.

"What kind of girl would look at a ragamuffin like me?" he ruefully wondered when he reached Boise. To avoid trouble on the trail, he had deliberately made himself as nondescript-looking as possible. "Not that I want one who judges a man by his trail appearance. Or takes up with him for his money." He grinned. No one seeing Briton Farley in his present state would dream he could buy a nice little chunk of Idaho!

He ended up doing just that. After scouting much of the state, he fell in love with the panhandle area southeast of Coeur d'Alene. Forests abundant with game offered food and shelter. Brit stumbled across a down-on-his-luck, half-starved prospector who needed a place to winter. Grizzled and talkative, Charley January agreed to help Brit build a house in return for a grubstake come the next spring.

"Mind if I put up a sign?" the whiskery fellow asked when they finished the snug log house. "I've prospected all over. Made and squandered enough gold an' silver to have kept me 'til I died." He scratched his head. "Don't 'zackly know why, but I feel this may be my last chance to strike it rich."

Touched by the old man's sincerity, Brit agreed. A few days later, a whimsical, tipsy-looking sign appeared in front of the cabin: LAST CHANCE. POPULATION 2. It was all Brit could do to keep from laughing and hurting his new companion's feelings.

When spring came, Charley January asked permission to prospect on Brit's land before moving on. "If I find anythin', you can give me what you think's fair," he said.

"I'm going to run cattle and horses, Charley, but half of the profits from any ore you discover are yours," Brit told him.

"Ya-hoo!" January waved a rusty pick in the air. "Son, we're gonna be rich."

To Brit's amazement, the unlikely prophet's prediction came true. After months of fruitless searching, Charley took shelter one night in a cave on Brit's land. The next day he came tearing into the cabin. He had found silver.

It was the beginning of change. The strike proved rich beyond belief. Tents followed by log cabins sprang up like mushrooms. When the miners saw there was no sign of the ore petering out, they brought their families to Last Chance.

To Brit's dismay, the growing town looked to him for leadership. He was elected president of the school board before Last Chance had either school or teacher. He was also appointed to track down a teacher, a doctor, and a minister. The closest church was Cataldo Mission—Idaho's oldest building—near Kellogg. Built by Indians during the 1850s and 1860s, it was too far away for residents of Last Chance to attend.

Men pitched in, and in short order built a log schoolhouse. The womenfolk prettied up the attached living quarters with cheerful curtains and mail-order rugs for the floor. "In case our teacher has a wife," they said. Brit planned for a church to be constructed if they could find someone willing to do more than take one look at Last Chance and flee as if the devil were after him.

After searching for more than a year, a teacher was found. Unaccustomed to miners and their ways, he left the following spring. Two more followed his example, and complaints poured in about the current teacher. Brit had also been unable to interest a doctor or a minister. He told Charley January in exasperation, "If I'd known I would become the town father, I'd never have let you prospect on my land."

"It ain't so bad." Charley hooked his thumbs beneath his bright red suspenders and smirked. "Fer the first time in my life, folks r'spect me. Besides, since this is *our* town, we kin keep a lid on things, leastwise inside the city limits. Like not lettin' saloons get started." He scowled. "O' course, we ain't got no say who does what out of town. That's why we need a parson right bad." His scowl deepened. "A new teacher, too. T'other day when I was passin' the school, what did I see but that whey-faced feller chasin' two boys around the building, coattails a-flyin'. The rest of the students were chasin' after the teacher. He ain't fit to teach, if you ask me." Charley looked apologetic. "I know you did the best you could, but our younguns need dis-*sip*-line, an' that poor excuse fer a man can't handle it."

Brit sighed, feeling the weight of the world descend on his shoulders. Again. "I know. I thought maybe he'd be better than nothing, but I was wrong. I also kept hoping he might improve. Wrong on that count, too. I'll send out some more notices and see if we can get a nibble. Practically anyone would be better than what we have now." He grabbed a pencil and scrawled, *WANTED. A minister. A doctor. A teacher. If you're any of the above and looking for employment, contact Briton Farley, Last Chance, Idaho.*

What felt like an eternity passed before anyone contacted Brit regarding his advertisement in newspapers across the country. At last a lone letter came. The school board president peered at the return address: Marcus Macrae, Boston, Massachusetts.

"Boston?" Brit snorted. A previous applicant from the East Coast was a misguided store clerk who wanted to come west and hunt buffalo and fight Nez Percé Indians in his spare time! The man was evidently so dumb he didn't know the Nez Percé War had ended in 1877, after Chief Joseph led about eight hundred of his people in a desperate, one-thousand-mile trek toward Canada. Thinking they were safe, they stopped to rest just forty miles from the border and freedom. Chief Joseph's words when he surrendered after a five-day battle became legend: "I will fight no more forever."

Brit hadn't even bothered to answer that application.

He started to toss the Boston letter aside, but curiosity about its writer won. He tore open the envelope. A picture of a smiling young man with a steady gaze fell out. Brit grunted. Marcus Macrae, whoever he was, didn't look like a misguided soul. Or a store clerk bent on killing Indians and buffalo "in his spare time." Brit withdrew the letter and began reading:

> Dear Mr. Farley,
> I wish to apply for the position of minister in your town. I believe God is calling me to Last Chance. I have studied medicine to some extent, so I can be of assistance if your town is still without a doctor.

A list of qualifications and several references followed, then he added, "I will be available in April."

Nez Percé whinnied, bringing Brit out of his reverie. A chill in the air warned day was dying. He'd best do what he came up here to do and get back to Last Chance. Brit bowed his head. "Lord, this Marcus Macrae looks intelligent and sounds honest. He also appears too good to be true. Besides, what other choice do I have?"

A hush fell over the forest—and the feeling Brit had learned to trust and follow all his years of seeking the Master's will. He stood, gathered up the reins, and swung into the saddle.

Tomorrow he would start a one-word message on its way to Boston: *Hired.*

Chapter 5

Every *clackety-clack* of railroad wheels between Massachusetts and Idaho added to Meredith Rose Macrae's misery. Marcus's growing pleasure about the new life on which they were embarking only deepened her depression. She hadn't seen him so excited since he first felt called to the ministry. She stared out the window as the chugging engines pulled her away from everything familiar. To her distressed mind, the train became a monster bent on devouring the shining tracks over which it sped and making it impossible for her to return to her former life.

"Not that I want to," she whispered during a solitary moment when Marcus left to get her a drink of water. Rage sent blood coursing through her body. From the moment staid and proper Boston learned of the Macraes' misfortune, society slammed its doors against them. Not only society. When Meredith Rose told Miss Grenadier she'd be able to finish out the term since she wasn't getting married, the woman looked down her nose and said icily, "Impossible! We have replaced you and Mr. Calloway with more suitable instructors."

"How dare you class me with that charlatan?" Meredith Rose blazed.

"I really don't care to discuss it. Good day, Miss Macrae." Miss Grenadier swept from the room, pulling her voluminous skirts around her as if afraid of contamination. Others did the same. Overnight, the formerly sought-after Macraes became outcasts. Only a few brave souls dared buck the tide of public opinion to come calling. Meredith Rose found it difficult to greet them cordially, and soon even their visits ceased.

"Cheer up, old dear," Marcus told her, with a pat on her shoulder. "No one in Last Chance will give a snap of their fingers for Herbert Calloway or Miss Grenadier and her School for Young Ladies." His eyes twinkled. "We'll follow Jesus' advice to His disciples in Luke 9:5: 'And whosoever will not receive you, when ye go out of that city, shake off the very dust from your feet for a testimony against them.' "

The idea conjured up such a vivid picture in Meredith Rose's mind that she burst into laughter. Yet as the end of life as the Macraes knew it drew to a close, there was neither time nor inclination for laughter. Even Marcus hadn't realized how badly their finances had been damaged. Tight-lipped, he and Merry watched piece after piece of fine china and furniture be sold for what seemed a mere pittance and carted away. The dressmaker greedily allowed Meredith Rose to return her wedding gown since it had never been seen in public but at a greatly reduced price.

The day of departure dawned showery and glum. The twins boarded their train. Neither looked back. Marcus took his sister's gloved hand. "We still have each other," he comforted. "And God."

Meredith Rose wordlessly squeezed his fingers. Yes, they

did have each other. God? She shrugged her shoulders beneath the dark blue broadcloth traveling gown she'd chosen for her plunge into the unknown. Maybe someday she'd recognize the good Marcus said came from hard situations. Not now. Not when the mournful train whistle sounded like a voice crying *a-way, a-way,* as they began their exile.

The trip west was filled with surprises. Rolling hills gave way to farmlands, then terrain so flat it seemed to go on forever. Weary of straining her eyes looking for something to break the monotony, Meredith Rose's first glimpse of the foothills that led up to the majestic Rocky Mountains left her speechless. Interest stirred. Marcus had said Last Chance was in the mountains. Would they be like this?

At last they reached Idaho, but the worst was yet to come. The decrepit excuse for a stagecoach that would carry them on the last lap of their journey little resembled any conveyance fit for human occupation. Meredith Rose felt like howling but gritted her teeth and climbed inside, nearly tripping over two large extended feet.

"Sorry, ma'am." The feet folded back like an accordion. "Ignatius Crane. At your service."

More like Ichabod Crane, Meredith Rose thought. She seated herself in the far corner of the stage opposite the tall, thin, middle-aged man whose graying hair and colorless eyes did nothing to enhance his horse-like face. She didn't dare look at Marcus, who was muffling laughter with a loud cough.

"Who you be?" their traveling companion asked.

"Marcus Macrae. This is my sister."

"Oh. The new parson." Ignatius's down-turned mouth quirked up. "Good. I'm headed for Last Chance myself. This'll give us time to get acquainted." He turned to Meredith Rose. "What's yore front handle?"

She gave him a stare cold enough to freeze Niagara Falls. "I beg your pardon?"

He sighed. "Ain't that just like an East'rn'r. Yore moniker, lady. Yore name."

"*Miss* Macrae." She longed to add, "If it's any business of 'yores,' " but bit her tongue. Uncouth as he was, Ignatius Crane was the first person she and Marcus had met from Last Chance—perhaps one of Marcus's parishioners. A prayer that he didn't represent the general population of their new home winged upward.

Ignatius doubled over in mirth out of all proportion to her reply. "I done heerd tell that folks from Baw-stun had fancy ways. Don't you worry, little lady. I'll see to it folks treat you right." He tucked his chin into his high collar. "What Ignatius Crane says in Last Chance goes." Pride oozed from him like pitch from a pine.

"Are you one of the town fathers?" Marcus asked.

Meredith Rose wanted to pinch him. The last thing she needed in the rocking, jolting coach was a monologue from the only other passenger aboard.

The thin lips changed to a smirk. "You might say that. Me 'n' Brit Farley just about run the town." He stroked his jaw. "School board and all."

For the first time since she left Boston, Meredith Rose experienced a moment of pure enjoyment. If only Miss Grenadier could see Ichabod–Ignatius. She would shrink in horror from this caricature of a man announcing he was the member of a school board!

The amusement didn't last. Long before Last Chance

"hove into sight," as Ignatius inelegantly put it, Meredith Rose's body ached from the jouncing of the stage. She leaned back and closed her eyes, aware of Crane's carping voice going on and on. She did come to attention when Marcus asked, "Have you found a new teacher yet?"

"Nary a one. Yore sister don't happen to be one, does she?"

"She—"

A sharp elbow in her brother's ribs cut off a confession that could do irreparable damage. Meredith Rose leaned forward, forced herself to don her most charming smile, and said, "Mr. Crane, since you are evidently such an important part of Last Chance, do you happen to know where my brother and I will be housed?"

He parted his hair with a bony finger and beamed at her. "Folks take turns offering board and keep, but when I found out the parson was bringing a lady, I just up and says to Brit Farley that it weren't fittin'." He drew himself up pompously. " 'You can't have a real Baw-stun lady shifted from pillar to post,' sez I."

Marcus's eyes brimmed with laughter. "What did Mr. Farley say?"

"Brit? He done agreed with me. Seein' as how we ain't got no teacher right now, you'll stay in the rooms built onto the back of the schoolhouse."

Meredith Rose thought she had heard wrong. "You mean, live in a schoolhouse?"

Ignatius blinked. " 'Course. It's right nice, ma'am. The womenfolk. . ." He rattled on, extolling the virtues of the schoolhouse living quarters. He ended with a triumphant, "If you decide to stay, and I shore hope you will—it ain't every day Last Chance gets quality folks like you—we kin build you a cabin in no time once we get a teacher."

Meredith Rose weakly sank back against the seat, wondering, *What next?*

The opening words of a favorite hymn came to mind. *"My soul in sad exile was out on life's sea. . . ."* She closed her eyes. The last time she'd heard the song was when a highly paid quartet sang it in the church she'd attended since childhood. Her heart had thrilled to the powerful words of the chorus:

> *I've anchored my soul in the Haven of Rest,*
> *I'll sail the wide seas no more;*
> *The tempest may sweep o'er the wild, stormy deep;*
> *In Jesus I'm safe evermore.*

Would there ever be a haven of rest for her again? A place free of tempests where she would feel safe? Certainly not in Last Chance, Idaho. A plan began to take root. She would survive this miserable situation, no matter what it took. Despite his zeal, Marcus would surely grow disheartened if the man opposite them typified those with whom he must work, and he would be willing to go elsewhere. Even now the unpleasant fellow was spouting what was obviously the gospel according to Ignatius Crane. Meredith Rose had never heard such sanctimonious drivel. Her lip curled. She'd met conceited men before, but this scarecrow clearly wanted to be king of the cornfield.

She opened her eyes just enough to observe him through her lashes. Uneasiness filled her. Between his proclamations to Marcus on everything from the way a man should preach to thinly veiled contempt for Brit Farley, Ignatius was sending bold glances her way. The proprietary look in his face sickened her, and she drew her skirts as far away from him as possible.

Just like Miss Grenadier.

Meredith Rose flinched. Her body felt like it was on fire. Where had that odious thought come from? The two situations were farther apart than Idaho and "Baw-stun."

Were they really? She had withdrawn from a fellow human being as surely and as haughtily as Miss Grenadier had done from her. Memory of the humiliation brought shame. Meredith Rose peeked at Ignatius to see if he had noticed her movement, then breathed a quick prayer of thankfulness when he continued to ramble on to her brother. Lout that he was, this man should never have to suffer the way Meredith Rose Macrae had suffered when Miss Grenadier marched out of the room as if fleeing from a contagious disease. Too tired to think, she fell asleep against her twin's shoulder, only to be roused by Marcus's voice.

"Wake up, Merry. We're here."

"So that's what yore name is. Mighty purty." Ignatius Crane's nasal drawl drove sleep away. "We don't hold with Miss-in' and Mister-in' folks out here."

Meredith Rose's temper flared. Parishioner or not, town boss or not, school board member or not, she wasn't going to take this churlish man's guff. "You will either address me as Miss Macrae or refrain from addressing me at all," she spit out.

The admiration she had seen in his eyes changed to an expression that sent a trickle of fear down her spine. Being provoked was no reason to lower herself to this man's level. The way his eyes narrowed brought back a long-ago memory of Marcus saying, "There are some people who are better to have as friends than enemies." Was this the case with Ignatius Crane? If so, what had she done?

Hating the need to retreat, for the second time she forced a smile. "Please don't take it personally," she told the now-belligerent man. "It's just that no one has ever called me

Merry but my brother."

He gave her a suspicious look, but she was saved from having to say more by the stagecoach driver's loud, "Whoa, you miserable critters," and a deep masculine voice calling, "Did you get them, Len?"

"Shore did, and she's a looker." A hearty laugh followed.

Meredith Rose cringed. The stagecoach door jerked open. A strong hand reached in.

"Marcus Macrae? Miss Macrae? Welcome to Last Chance. I'm Briton Farley."

Chapter 6

The respectful way Briton Farley spoke her name did much toward settling Meredith Rose Macrae's qualms about Last Chance. So did the deeply tanned hand that gripped Marcus's. It hinted at strength and security. Whatever else this western man turned out to be, he would be a rock in time of trouble.

Don't be a ninny, she silently chastised herself. *You know nothing about the man except his name.* Yet eagerness to see if Mr. Farley's face lived up to his hands and voice, plus the desire to look well for Last Chance, caused her to straighten her gown and adjust her hat to the proper angle. Fortunately, Marcus had stepped out of the stagecoach, followed by Ignatius. It gave her a moment to collect herself.

Taking a deep breath, Meredith Rose attempted to stand. Unfortunately, she hadn't counted on the toll the long trip had taken on her normally athletic body. Her right foot buckled, and she gave a little moan.

Marcus's head reappeared in the doorway. "What is it, Merry? Are you all right?"

"I'm fine," she retorted, "except my silly foot's asleep." So much for appearing dignified. " 'Pride goeth before a fall,' " she muttered, stamping to restore circulation.

Marcus roared, then Briton Farley's richly amused voice said, "It's actually 'Pride goeth before destruction, and an haughty spirit before a fall.' "

Astonished by the remark, Meredith Rose took her brother's arm and stepped down from the stagecoach. What kind of man not only knew Scripture but wasn't afraid to quote it in front of the driver, Ignatius Crane, and the large crowd behind him? She looked up. And up. Briton Farley topped her brother's six-foot height by more than two inches. Her own five feet seven seemed puny beside him. April sunlight glistened on his bared head and turned his hair to pure gold. The sun was reflected in his laughing amber eyes and enhanced his wide, white smile. Even his worn but spotless work clothes didn't detract from the fact that outside of Marcus, Briton Farley was the finest-looking man she had ever seen.

A vision of Herbert Calloway shimmered in the air between them. The inadequacy of her former fiancé to measure up to this western rancher/miner/president of the school board/town father brought an insane desire to laugh. How outraged Herbert would be to know the woman he'd jilted stood in the dusty street of an Idaho mining town comparing him unfavorably with Briton Farley!

Meredith Rose could feel a smile lifting the corners of her mouth. She impulsively held out her gloved hand. "Thank you for the correction, Mr. Farley," she said demurely.

"Again, welcome to Last Chance." An unreadable expression crept into his eyes. Before she could identify it, Ichabod–Ignatius's nasal tones clanged in her ears like an unwelcome gong. "No need fer that, Brit. I done welcomed her."

Meredith Rose's attention shifted to the scowling man,

who glanced in her direction and added significantly, "Keep this in mind. I seen her first."

"Don't you be pestering Miss Macrae," a buxom woman called from the crowd. She elbowed her way to where the Macraes stood. "I'm Katie Reilly. I own Katie's Kitchen." She nodded across the street at the buildings. Crisp, red-checkered curtains at the shining, many-paned windows made the café attractive. "If Ignatius comes around wanting to court you like he's done every other unmarried girl and woman in town, you let me know. I'll take my rolling pin to him."

A wave of approval and laughter swept through the onlookers. Marcus solemnly shook hands with the restaurant proprietor. "With a protector like you, Mrs. Reilly, my sister should be well cared for." He spun toward Crane amidst a second round of crowd approval. "I believe in turning the other cheek, but there's also a time to smite the enemy. Do we understand each other?"

Ignatius jerked his head in the semblance of a nod but didn't back down. Meredith Rose found herself torn between humiliation, the desire to shriek, and the need to blink back tears at the championship from Marcus and Katie Reilly. "Th–thank you." She turned to Briton Farley and asked, "If Icha–Mr. Crane bothers me, will you smite him or take a rolling pin to him, too?" Her hand flew to her mouth. Had she lost her senses, along with her good intentions to treat Ichabod–Ignatius courteously?

The rancher's smile faded into a grim line. His eyes looked molten gold. "I'll do more than that," he vowed, glaring at the man who had attempted to stake a claim to the new minister's sister, with or without her permission. His rigid stance warned Meredith Rose that although Brit

317

resembled a sleeping mountain lion, when roused, he could be equally dangerous. His voice cracked through the silence like a bullwhip in the hands of a master. "No one, I repeat, *no one* is to force unwelcome attentions on Miss Macrae. Understood?"

Meredith Rose expected Crane to slink away like a whipped puppy. Instead he smirked and demanded, "Does *no one* include *you*, Brit?" He smirked again.

The mood of the crowd changed to an angry rumbling. It expressed more loudly than words the esteem in which the town of Last Chance held Brit Farley. The big man clenched his hands into fists and crouched as if preparing to spring. Primitive feelings Meredith Rose hadn't known she possessed rose within her. Her fingernails bit into the palms of her hands. For one mad moment she hoped Brit would pound the repulsive Crane until he cried for mercy.

Her defender slowly relaxed. One tawny eyebrow raised. "As a member of the school board, I'm sure you understand the meaning of *no one*," he quietly said. He offered his arm to Meredith Rose. "Now if you folks will come with me, I'll show you where you'll be living." He smiled at the crowd. "Pastor Macrae and his sister have had a long, tiring trip. There will be plenty of time for everyone to greet them later."

Katie Reilly sniffed. "*If* they stay, after what Ignatius just did."

Crane cast a malevolent glance in her direction, then stared at Meredith Rose. It took all her self-control to remain calm beneath his scorching gaze. Denied of the chance to "court" her, would he become her enemy—and Marcus's? Could he stir up trouble against them?

Marcus patted Katie Reilly's shoulder. "Let's just forget

what happened. It takes all kinds of people to make a town." He offered the grin his twin believed could get him almost anything he wanted, and addressed the crowd. "There will be church this coming Sunday. I hope you'll all be there." He even gave Ignatius a friendly smile.

"We'll be there, Parson," a loud voice called. "Any man who stands up for his womenfolk should be able to tell us something worth hearing!" A hum of appreciation followed. It warmed Meredith Rose's cold heart, but not as much as the strong hand that gently rested on hers for a moment before Briton Farley said, "Don't let Crane disturb you, Miss Macrae. He's actually harmless. Most of the folks here are good people, rougher than you're used to, but kindhearted and real."

"I'm surprised at the amount of brick and frame businesses," Marcus confessed. He gestured down the street that stretched before them. Meredith Rose's gaze followed his pointing fingers, then traveled to the wooded slopes surrounding the town. All the way from Boston, she had tried to form a picture of where she and Marcus would be living. So far, there seemed to be nothing to dread. The town nestled between the mountains like a baby in the folds of a blanket. She could hear the distant rumble of machinery that must belong to the mines, but it wasn't close enough to town to be more than a reminder of why Last Chance existed.

"We are making a real town here." Brit grinned. "It's a far cry from the day my old prospector friend Charley January put up a sign in front of the log house he helped me build. It read: LAST CHANCE. POPULATION 2." He hesitated. "After you settle in, I want you to come out to my ranch." Again the unreadable expression Meredith Rose had seen when they first met came into his eyes. After a moment, he said, "Please forgive me if I stare, Miss Macrae. You remind me of someone who once meant everything to me." Sadness darkened his gaze.

Meredith Rose's spirits had been rising at finding out Last Chance wasn't as bad as she'd expected. Now they plummeted. Had the woman been his wife? He had obviously never gotten over his loss. *Why should you care?* she fiercely demanded. *He is nothing to you except the tool that brought you to Last Chance. The sooner you convince Marcus that God really isn't calling him to work here, the better. What are you, a silly schoolgirl to be attracted by a sunny smile and a man who springs to the aid of maidens in distress? A modern Sir Galahad, riding on a white horse?*

For the second time that day, she blurted out words best left unspoken. "What kind of horse do you ride?"

Brit blinked. "My favorite is my buckskin stallion Nez Percé."

"What color is he?"

"Golden tan with a black mane and tail. Why?"

"I just wondered."

So much for fairy tales. Sir Galahad wouldn't have been caught dead on a buckskin horse, even if there had been such mounts in the days of King Arthur. She fell silent, lengthening her stride to keep up with Brit's long steps. Was she the same Meredith Rose Macrae she had been for the first twenty-seven years of her life? So far today she had endured a boor, found at least two new advocates, longed to see Ichabod–Ignatius pounded, and felt disappointed to discover a stranger's heart was held captive by a lost love. Yet she felt more alive than she had in years.

Perhaps it was the friendliness of the crowd who supported her against one of their own. Or the blue, blue sky and smiling sun. Whatever the reason, she felt ready to face whatever came next, even living in a schoolhouse!

When they reached the log schoolhouse sitting on a knoll and encircled by trees and wildflowers, Meredith Rose could scarcely conceal her curiosity. What would it be like inside? She didn't have long to wait. Brit flung open the door. The familiar smell of chalk mingling with the unfamiliar tang of forest sweeping through the open windows made her homesick. In spite of what had happened, she had enjoyed teaching at Miss Grenadier's School for Young Ladies.

She noted the carefully crafted wooden desks, so in contrast with pictures of early schoolrooms she had seen in magazines depicting backwoods schools. Open cupboards held a goodly amount of supplies. An American flag proudly stood at one side of the room; a large black wood-burning stove at the other. Meredith Rose's gaze turned to the teacher's desk. An open Bible rested on its polished surface.

"What a well-equipped school," Marcus burst out. "Merry, you could do wonders here!" Remorse killed his enthusiasm but too late. The cat was not only out of the bag, it perched on the teacher's desk and smirked at Meredith Rose.

Brit looked delighted. "Miss Macrae, don't tell me you're a teacher!" Words tumbled out like a mountain stream rushing to the sea. "Thank God!" He grabbed her hand and squeezed it. "You are truly an answer to prayer."

It took great effort, but she ignored his heartfelt exclamation and said, "I? Teach here? Preposterous! I'm sorry, Mr. Farley, but I'm afraid you will need to keep praying."

"How do you know God didn't send you unless you try?"

The question caught her unawares. She freed her hand and fumbled with her gloves. Putting all the chill she could summon into her voice she told him, "For one thing, I only taught such subjects as deportment, drama, music, and art."

"Fine." He beamed. "Our youngsters will be all the better for knowing those things as well as their ABCs. It won't be hard. There are only a few weeks left this term, and you'll have this summer to get ready for fall."

If anything in the world could have changed Meredith Rose's mind, it would have been Brit's golden smile, his absolute confidence in her ability, and his belief that God had sent her to Last Chance. She felt herself wavering. Should she consent to teach the short session with the understanding they must replace her in the fall?

His next words came like a deluge of ice water. They steadied her determination not to be swayed by this appealing westerner. "It isn't like you have to teach all forty-eight classes," he assured her. "The older students help by listening to the younger children's lessons."

Meredith Rose gasped. "Forty-eight classes?"

Brit looked surprised. "Of course. Six subjects times eight grades equals forty-eight." He ticked them off on his strong fingers. "Reading, writing, and arithmetic; spelling, history, and geography. Of course, if you add art and music and drama it *will* make a mite more work."

Meredith Rose weakly sank into a chair, wondering if the sound in her head could be God laughing. Eight grades in a one-room schoolhouse? Six subjects for each grade? A 'mite more work' if she added art and music and drama? From wedding bells to school bells in a few short weeks. It was enough to make her want to tear her hair and catch the first stage out of town.

Chapter 7

How do you know God didn't send you?" Brit Farley's challenging words beat in Meredith Rose Macrae's mind. Marcus didn't help. "Give it a try, old dear," he said. "Children here have the right to learn. You can teach. It's as simple as that." His eyes darkened to the color of the Idaho night sky. "Besides, we can use the money."

Meredith Rose gasped. "Are we that hard up?"

"We're all right so far, but my salary is partially dependent on the offerings. Teaching would also keep you from being bored." He waved one hand around their living quarters. Although rough compared with Boston, the small living-room and kitchen combination and the two minuscule bedrooms were comfortable. The cheap but cheerful curtains, rag rugs, hand-hewn furniture, and blazing fire in the small fireplace gave a warm and cozy feel. "You certainly won't be spending much time doing housework!"

Meredith Rose opened her mouth to indignantly deny any intention of teaching in Last Chance, then quickly snapped it shut. If she were to persuade Marcus to leave, they would need money until he could find a church elsewhere. Even the small amount she would earn in the few weeks remaining in the spring term would help. "I—I'll think about it," she promised, even though her soul revolted at the idea.

A thunderous knock sounded at the door leading outside of their quarters. Meredith Rose burned with resentment. Were she and Marcus to have no privacy?

"It's Katie Reilly," a voice called. "Preacher, we need your help."

Marcus flung the door open. Katie stumbled inside and held out the small boy she carried. Blood oozed between her fingers from the child's flannel-clad shoulder. "It's Sammy, my youngest. I told him and told him to stay out of the street." She gulped. "He didn't—and a horse kicked him."

"It weren't my fault, Katie. Honest." The grizzled old man who had followed Katie inside looked ready to burst into tears. "He tore out of the café and fell right in front of us. My horse tried to jump over him, but his hoof hit Sammy."

"Aw, Ma, I ain't gonna die," the red-haired urchin protested. He squirmed and stared at Marcus. "Brit Farley says you know how to fix folks." Meredith Rose marveled at the total trust and hero worship in Sammy's eyes.

"Let's see what we can do." Marcus pried Katie's fingers free from her son's shoulder and set the boy on the kitchen table. "Bring my medical bag," he told his sister, sliding the blood-soaked shirt off Sammy's skinny body. "Not too bad, Mrs. Reilly. See?" He showed her the shallow groove. "This is going to sting, Sammy." Marcus swabbed the cut with antiseptic.

Sammy screwed his face into an awful scowl, but not one tear escaped. He gave Marcus an anxious, gap-toothed grin. "You'll tell folks I didn't cry, right? Men don't cry when they get to be six."

Meredith Rose was torn between wanting to laugh and wanting to scoop the child in her arms and hug him. She bit her lip and was glad that Marcus solemnly promised to make sure everyone knew how brave Sammy had been. He finished his task, put a soft bandage over the wound, and tied it off in a jaunty knot. "All done."

"Thanks." Sammy slid off the table and looked at Meredith Rose. "Hey, you're purty. Are you my new teacher? I heard Brit Farley tell Ma he was gonna—"

A strong hand covered the child's mouth. "Men don't snoop on other folks's conversations, and if they do, they don't repeat what they hear," his mother warned.

Of all the times for Katie Reilly to give Sammy a lesson in manners, why did it have to be now? Meredith Rose wondered. She would love to hear just what Brit Farley was "gonna" do about convincing her to teach school in the town he controlled!

"How much do I owe you?" Katie asked Marcus.

"Nothing. I'm not a real doctor."

Katie sniffed. "Maybe so, but we're right glad to have you." She led Sammy out.

"That goes for all of us." The old man held out a toil-worn hand. "I'm Charley January. Welcome to Last Chance."

Now that the crisis was over, Meredith Rose had time to observe him. Rough but clean clothes. Kindly eyes in a whiskered face. "Are you a prospector?" she asked.

"I was 'til I up and found silver on Brit Farley's land." Charley swelled with pride. "Me 'n' him went fifty–fifty. That's the kinda feller he is. Grateful fer me helpin' him build his log house. You gotta come visit us." He pumped Marcus's hand up and down.

Meredith Rose saw her brother surreptitiously flex his fingers when Charley finally released his grip. Evidently age and hard work hadn't diminished the strength in Charley January's gnarled hands. Or the steady look in his eyes. On impulse she said, "Would you like a cup of coffee, Mr. January?"

He brightened up. "I'm just plain Charley, an' I'd love one."

Two hours and countless tall tales later—most featuring Briton Farley as the all-conquering, bigger-than-life-and-twice-as-natural hero—Charley left, although obviously reluctant to do so. Meredith Rose stared at Marcus. "So this is Last Chance, where anything can, and apparently does, happen!"

"We knew it would be different."

"Different?" Laughter swelled and burst into the quiet room. "I never knew the meaning of the word until now!" Yet long after she lay in bed watching the brilliant stars in the cold night sky, Meredith Rose couldn't help wondering what it was about Briton Farley that inspired such trust in an old prospector and a child as young as the adoring Sammy; Sammy, whose innocent, "Are you my new teacher?" had touched a chord in her heart silenced by her former fiancé's defection. Maybe teaching for a few weeks wouldn't be so bad after all.

The next day Meredith Rose sent word to Brit that she would take over the school. The look of profound gratitude in his amber eyes when he appeared at her door to thank her sent a thrill through her unlike any she'd ever felt for Herbert Calloway.

"You'll never know what this means," he told her. "I thank God. By the way, I'll be there come Monday morning to introduce you." A lazy grin and raised eyebrow did little to detract from the candle lit in Meredith Rose's heart.

She spent all day Saturday frantically reviewing the material in the schoolbooks Brit brought to her. He had consulted with Sadie Reilly, the only eighth-grade girl that term, and painstakingly provided a list of the fifteen students and where each was in his or her studies. It helped immensely.

"Now if I can only keep one step ahead of them," Meredith Rose told Marcus.

"You can, Merry." Her brother rumpled her hair and frowned. "Now if *I* can only keep one step ahead of my congregation! From what I hear, they know their Bibles upside down and backwards, especially Brit Farley." He went back to studying.

Meredith Rose muttered, "So that's his secret!" but not loudly enough for her twin to hear. She did *not* need Marcus teasing her about undue interest in the town boss. Her own unruly heart was already accusing her of it.

🍇

Marcus Macrae need not have worried about his first sermon in Last Chance. After much prayer, he chose Matthew 13:44 for his text: " 'Again, the kingdom of heaven is like unto treasure hid in a field; the which when a man hath found, he hideth, and for joy thereof goeth and selleth all that he hath, and buyeth that field.' "

A ripple of surprise ran through the packed schoolhouse-turned-church. Heads nodded. This they could understand! They were dependent on finding treasure. Working mines fed families, supported local businesses, and provided shelter and clothing.

For almost an hour, Marcus held the attention of men, women, and children who had been taught church was a place to listen and not just be entertained. He closed with Luke 12:34: " 'For where your treasure is, there will your heart be also.' "

After a moment of silence he quietly asked, "Where is your treasure? Your heart? If it is not with our heavenly Father, all the silver and gold in the world are worthless." He bowed his head. "Lord, we thank Thee for Thy love and for the gift of Thy Son. In Jesus' name, amen."

The congregation's *amen*s resounded through the room and bounced off the rafters. Then Brit Farley stood. "Preacher Marcus insists that no offerings be taken during services." He shook his head. "Sounds mighty peculiar to me, but he says the Bible tells us to do our giving in secret." He held up a flour sack. "For those who can and choose to give tithes and offerings, this will be at the back of the room on Sundays. No one, not even our preacher or the deacons, will know who gives what." He strode down the aisle and hung the sack on a nail.

Meredith Rose heard a grunt of disapproval from Ignatius Crane. He had placed himself directly behind her and she had felt his gaze boring between her shoulder blades throughout the service. Evidently the new regime didn't meet with his approval. If she were a betting person, she'd wager the highlight of Ichabod–Ignatius's week was ostentatiously placing his offering in the plate for all to see!

People began collecting their belongings, then Brit said, "School will begin at eight o'clock tomorrow morning. Miss Macrae will be our new teacher."

Hearty applause followed. "Miss Macrae" wished the floor would open and swallow her. She'd hoped to begin teaching without fanfare. So much for her hopes. "I'll be there to observe you for a few days," an unwelcome voice said in her ear.

Meredith Rose whirled. "That will not be necessary, Mr. Crane," she said in her iciest voice. "I am sure I can teach without your interfer—without your help."

He smirked. "Nevertheless, I'll be there. We've had bad luck with our teachers. As a member of the board of directors,

I'll make sure our younguns are taught proper."

She cast an imploring look at Brit, handsomer than ever in his Sunday suit.

"Once Miss Macrae has time to settle in, I'm sure she will be happy to invite the school board members to visit," he said easily. He smiled, but again Meredith Rose sensed a readiness to pounce if necessary. "Tomorrow morning I will introduce her, then make myself scarce. She needs to *and will be* left on her own. By the way, I've been meaning to talk with you about. . ." His voice trailed off as he firmly edged Ignatius away, leaving the new teacher filled with gratitude.

From the time Meredith Rose rang the school bell the next morning, then took her place behind the hand-hewn teacher's desk, she became the object of adoration from even the most unruly students. She attributed it to Brit Farley's warning that if they made trouble for the new teacher, they would answer to him. And to Sammy Reilly's loud praises about how Preacher Doc "fixed" his shoulder. In any event, long before the spring term ended, the young woman found herself actually anticipating each new day and searching for ways to keep her students interested.

She also discovered the heart she had vowed to never again give away pounded like a war drum each time Brit Farley stepped inside her classroom. She found it amusing to note the number of flimsy excuses he used to ride up on Nez Percé just as school was letting out. Sometimes it was to make sure she had enough school supplies. At other times, he wanted to know what progress this or that student was making. Meredith Rose came to look forward to his brief visits.

When the term ended and summer came, Brit was busier

than ever with his ranch and mines. She seldom saw him except on Sunday at church and sometimes not even then. Rumors of trouble in other areas reached Last Chance: stories of miners' strikes that turned ugly. Wallace, Idaho, had faced such troubles a few years earlier. Tension mounted during a mining labor strike. Soldiers pitched their tents in a vacant lot close to brick and frame businesses in order to keep the peace.

"God forbid such a thing will come to Last Chance," Marcus told his twin.

Fear clawed at her. If it did, would Brit be in danger? In the space of a single heartbeat, realization came. She cared far more for Briton Farley than she had been willing to admit, even to herself. In the privacy of her room, she chastised herself severely. "What have you, a Boston lady, to do with a man of the West? A gulf lies between you; a chasm wider than the miles stretching between Massachusetts and Idaho. He could never be part of your world."

You could be part of his, a little voice whispered.

Meredith Rose laughed scornfully. She, settle down in Last Chance, the wife of a rancher and mine owner? Never! Brit Farley had installed every convenience possible in his log home, including running water from a nearby stream. Yet it was still a primitive house in a wilderness that both drew her by its beauty and repelled her by the lack of amenities she had been accustomed to all her life.

That home could be glorified by love, the voice persisted. *Think of Brit Farley coming home to you at day's end. Think of meeting him at the door and lifting your face for his kiss. Think of him catching you up in his strong arms and keeping you safe from the storms of life. Think of bearing Brit's children: a tawny-haired boy with his father's amber eyes; a dark-haired daughter who looks*

like you and Marcus. Of raising them in God's Word to be His chil-
dren. Marcus loves it here, and the people are generously supporting
him. Why fight it, Meredith Rose?

"Even if I could overcome my feelings about Last Chance,
I'd never be anything more than second choice, chosen because
I remind Brit of the woman who 'once meant everything to
him,' " she protested, remembering the sadness in his eyes
when he told her why he stared at her. Torn by the conflicting
images that knocked at the door of her heart and threatened to
undo her, Meredith Rose cried herself to sleep for what might
have been, if Brit hadn't made clear his heart still belonged to
his first love.

Chapter 8

The little voice that had whispered to Meredith Rose was right. Marcus had fallen in love with Idaho. He exulted in the long hours he put in visiting townspeople and witnessing of his Lord, helping those who were sick or afflicted with ailments and injuries within the scope of his medical knowledge. Last Chance had become his home.

When Zeb Perry and his wife moved to Last Chance with their daughter, Alice, Marcus's joy increased. Alice, a modest young woman whose fair face shone with the goodness that comes from within, attracted Marcus as no woman had ever done. He wisely bided his time but felt that God had directed his and the Perrys' footsteps to the isolated mining town for a reason. If the look in the blue eyes gazing up at him from beneath Alice's simple bonnet were to be believed, she cared for him, as well.

Yet Marcus's growing love was bittersweet. How would Merry react when he told her he wanted nothing more than to marry sweet Alice and spend the rest of his days serving in a place his twin hated? Would it mean separation? The thought left him miserable. Why must he be a wishbone, pulled between the girl he hoped to make his wife and Merry, his other half—the half who had promised they would never part. In spite of her being a good sport about the teaching, Marcus sensed Merry was also biding her time—waiting until she could convince him to leave Last Chance.

One evening when they strolled to a wooded knoll at the edge of town and watched the setting sun slide behind a high green hill, Meredith Rose spoke. "You're in love with Alice. Are you going to marry her?"

Marcus didn't quibble. "Yes, God willing."

The rosy afterglow filling the sky and reflecting on her face didn't hide the desolation in her eyes, but she quietly said, "I am happy for you."

"What about you, Merry? Will you stay? Our school still needs a teacher." He didn't dare add that a certain rancher-miner also needed her. Neither Brit nor Merry had been able to hide from him their growing feelings. They had started with a spark of attraction when she first stepped down from the stage. Brit would be good for his twin. Strong enough to curb her haughty spirit—as evidenced by the way he had coaxed her into teaching—he was also gentle enough to appreciate and cherish her.

Her shoulders drooped. "I know. The board of directors asked me to stay."

"I hope you will." Marcus took a deep breath, then delivered a blow he knew would shatter her dreams. "Merry, even if you leave, I can't. This is where I belong."

"You'll marry Alice, and there will be no place for me." She held up her hand to still his protest. "The town will build you a home. Unless I continue teaching, I can't live at the schoolhouse." Her blue eyes flashed. "Marcus, even if it means never

333

seeing you again, I won't live with you and Alice. I won't be the spinster sister people laugh at behind her back!" She turned in a whirl of pink muslin skirts and ran, leaving her twin sick at heart and knowing only God could help him and Merry.

❦

For two wretched days, Marcus and Meredith Rose avoided the subject ever on their minds. "Lord, is it wrong to pray she will change her mind?" he asked again and again. "I can't bear to think we will be separated." Mark 10:7 came to mind: "For this cause shall a man leave his father and mother, and cleave to his wife."

"I know, Lord," Marcus brokenly said. "But the thought of watching Merry board the stage and ride out of my life is more than I can bear."

Before anything was settled, the arrival of two slick strangers overshadowed the twins' personal problems. The strangers came with the sole intention of inciting the miners to strike against the Last Chance mine owners, Brit Farley and Charley January. Brit learned of their secret meeting from Katie Reilly. Sammy had been scrunched down under a table at Katie's Kitchen hoping someone might have dropped some change.

"They didn't see me," he told his mother. "They said they were gonna get the miners to strike an' show Brit Farley who's boss of this town." He clenched his grubby hands into small fists. "Just let 'em try!"

Brit and Charley echoed Sammy's inelegant response when Katie sent word. They burst into the meeting held in a stand of trees at the edge of town and confronted the troublemakers. "We deal with *our men*—not with the likes of you," Brit barked.

"We done told 'em that," a loyal miner called. A growl of agreement ran through the crowd. "We only came tonight because we wanted to hear what they had to say. You've always treated us fair an' square. That's good enough for us."

Charley wasn't to be outdone. He cackled and pointed to the road out of town. "Git." A grin spread across his grizzled face. "Y'might say this is yore Last Chance."

The troublemakers hightailed it away as if it really were their last chance, followed by a chorus of loud *haw-haws* from those they had considered easy marks.

When Meredith Rose heard about the incident, she marveled at the miners' allegiance. For a fleeting moment she pictured Herbert Calloway inspiring such loyalty. The idea was so far-fetched she laughed until she cried. Thankfulness that she hadn't married the dancing master filled her. At times it was hard to remember what he looked like. Boston and her former existence seemed long ago and far away. Life in Last Chance might be crude but never by any stretch of imagination could it be called dull.

The little town went all out for Independence Day. On July 1, Sammy Reilly stopped his teacher in the middle of the street and asked, "Didja hear about the Fourth of July? Every year, there's a pick-a-nick out by the mine." His red hair waved in the warm afternoon breeze. "You never seen such food!" He rolled his eyes and licked his lips. "Chicken 'n' cake 'n' pie 'n' lemonade 'n' all kindsa stuff. We play games, too, an' at night the sky gets all lit up from fireworks." He danced around her in anticipation. "I can't wait!"

"I guess we'll have to," Meredith Rose told him.

He sidled up to her and looked into her face. "Are you gonna be my teacher again? Ma says she shore hopes so an' that if Brit Farley lets you get away, he's plumb loco. He ain't, is he?"

The pleading in the child's face prodded Meredith Rose into announcing a decision she had slowly been moving toward for several days. She couldn't leave Last Chance. It wasn't right to ask her twin for money the congregation had contributed for his upkeep. What little she had earned wouldn't get her far. If she stayed for the full autumn term and hoarded everything she made, she'd have a nest egg. "No, Sammy. Mr. Farley isn't loco. I'm going to be your teacher."

His skinny hand grabbed hers and squeezed. Then he let out a war whoop and sped away. "Hey, Ma, Teacher says Brit ain't loco an' she'll stay!" His voice echoed up and down the dusty street.

Katie Reilly appeared at the door of her café. "Well, that's mighty good news. Right, Brit?"

To Meredith Rose's chagrin, the tall, familiar frame of the town boss followed Katie out of the café. "Which? That I'm not loco, or that Miss Macrae is staying?"

"Both, you big galoot," Katie retorted. She sniffed. "Land sakes, my biscuits are burning." She shoved past Brit and ran back inside.

Unable to escape the man who purposefully headed toward her, Meredith Rose knew she had to brazen it out, but why did Brit have to learn she was staying like this? Before she could think of a casual remark, he halted in front of her, just long enough for a wide smile to creep across his tanned face. The next instant his powerful arms caught her by the elbows. He lifted her off her feet, then swung her in a circle. Her thin white gown ballooned about her. "That's the best news this town has heard in a month of Sundays," Brit rejoiced. "Miss Meredith Rose Macrae, I just plain love you!"

Her heart soared. Did he mean it? Really mean it? *Don't be*

336

stupid, she told herself. *He's just glad to have a teacher for his precious town.* Yet all the rationalizing in the world couldn't crush the warm feeling his strong arms produced.

"So that's what's been going on," an accusing voice said. "No wonder you claim-jumped me when I said I seen her first."

Brit set Meredith Rose down but kept one hand protectively on her arm. She turned and gasped in horror, knowing who she would see. Ignatius Crane had a talent for popping up at all the wrong times, like some evil jack-in-the-box. She felt Brit tense and was astonished at his self-control when he said, "Just celebrating the fact we now have a teacher for next fall, Ignatius."

The man's colorless eyes gleamed with unholy glee and satisfaction. He self-righteously drew himself up into a symbol of smugness. "I doubt that. I intend to see that the board of directors and the parents of our younguns are aware of this shocking public display." He tucked his chin under until he looked like a plucked chicken. "Like teacher, like pupils, I alwuz say."

Brit released Meredith Rose so suddenly she stumbled and nearly fell. In all the weeks she'd known him, never had she seen him like this. Woe to Ichabod–Ignatius! He had awakened a sleeping mountain lion.

Brit grabbed the vindictive man by his collar and lifted him off the ground. He shook him as a dog shakes a rat, then flung him down. "If you ever again say one word against Miss Macrae, I will personally see to it you leave town in a manner you will never forget. Now pick yourself up and get out of my sight before I lose my temper."

The words *before I lose my temper* were Meredith Rose's undoing. She laughed until she cried. Knowing it would make

Ichabod—Ignatius hate her more than ever couldn't stop her. It was just too funny. So was the way her former would-be suitor scuttled away after a baleful glance at the cheering crowd on both sides of the street.

"May I see you home, Miss Macrae?" Brit dusted off his hands and grinned. Every trace of anger had fled, and his amber eyes sparkled.

"Thank you." She took the arm he offered, realizing the encounter had shattered her perspective. Was Brit seeing her for herself and not as a mere reflection of the woman he had loved and lost? *Please God, let it be so,* her hopeful heart pleaded.

Chapter 9

Briton Farley slid from the saddle and patted Nez Percé. He strode to the edge of his favorite promontory and hunkered down on a huge rock. "Now you've gone and done it," he rebuked himself. "What got into you? Grabbing Merry Macrae in the middle of town and blurting out that you loved her?"

Nez Percé nudged him. Brit stroked the buckskin's soft nose. "Learning she's going to stay isn't an excuse," mumbled. "It's a wonder she didn't run screaming her head off and thinking I'm worse than Ignatius Crane!" His face scorched with shame. "I've never even dared call her anything to her face except Miss Macrae." He pictured the rich black hair, the lake-blue eyes. "Merry. A lovely name for a lovely person. Will she ever give me the right to use it?" He sighed. "Her uncanny resemblance to my mother had me roped, tied, and branded the minute she stepped out of that creaking old stage."

Memory of a long-ago conversation with his father came to mind. *"God willing, there may be another lass as good and sweet as your mother. . . . Never marry until you find the woman God intended you to have; then don't let anything stop you."*

Brit groaned. He had found her, but even if Meredith Rose Macrae someday learned to care for him, would her love be strong enough to overcome her distaste for Last Chance? Brit bowed his head. "Thy will be done, Lord." It was one of the hardest prayers he'd ever offered.

A slight breeze crept across the promontory. It cooled the silent man's heated face and stilled the tumult in his heart. If nothing but friendship ever grew between him and Meredith Rose, he would still defend her against the Ignatius Cranes of the world. He rose, vaulted into the saddle, and turned Nez Percé homeward.

❦

Independence Day dawned bright and beautiful. Last Chance was in an uproar. It seemed everyone in town either rode horseback or were transported by wagon to what Sammy called "the pick-a-nick place." A gap-toothed smile showed his joy was complete as he plopped down between his teacher and "Preacher Doc" in the Reilly family wagon. Marcus looked equally happy when Alice Perry climbed in and sat down beside him.

Glad she'd been wise enough to wear a riding habit and could clamber in and out of the horse-drawn, straw-filled conveyance without a loss of dignity, Meredith Rose smiled down at Sammy.

"This is a new experience for us," she told a beaming Katie Reilly. "Marcus and I have never been on a hayride."

"It should be a straw ride," Sammy piped up. "Hay gets saved for the horses. This is straw." He hollered at the tall man riding beside them. "Ain't that right, Brit?"

"Right, Sammy." Brit Farley chuckled. "You're pretty smart."

"I oughta be." Sammy looked indignant. "I'm almost seven

an' Teacher says—" He broke off and disgustedly added, "Aw, why'd *he* have to come?"

Meredith Rose glanced in the direction of the stubby, pointing finger. Her anticipation seeped away. Ignatius Crane had urged a horse as sorry-looking as its owner into an awkward gait and was in danger of overtaking the wagon.

Katie made a dismayed sound but quickly said, "Now, Sammy, it's right and proper for everyone to celebrate the Fourth of July."

Sammy scowled. "He never did before. He prob'ly thinks he can court Teacher. He can't." The child squared his skinny shoulders. "Me 'n' Brit'll see to that. Right, Brit?"

The steady look in Briton Farley's eyes made Meredith Rose's heart flutter. So did his quiet, "We sure will, if she says it's all right."

"All right?" Sammy scrambled to his feet and glared. " 'Course it's all right! Teacher don't want that long, tall drink o' water hangin' around her."

Marcus Macrae burst into laughter and pulled Sammy back down. "Whoa, there. You don't want to fall on your head." His eyes twinkled. "Know what? I'm pretty sure my sister is glad to have such good protectors. Right, Merry?" he parroted.

Meredith Rose felt herself grow scarlet. She kept her attention on Sammy and agreed, "Right," but Brit let out a "yippee-ki-ay" that set Nez Percé prancing. The look in Brit's eyes brought a flood of happiness. She turned toward her twin, knowing he understood. For the first time since the harsh words she had spoken had created a wall between them, she and Marcus were again part of a whole. Meredith Rose silently resolved they must never again be separated by anger or disappointment.

The ride to the chosen site sped by much faster than the pace of the plodding horses warranted. The world around her became more beautiful to Meredith Rose than anything she had ever seen. The air sparkled with sunlight. Birds sang praises to their Creator. Squirrels scampered, and rabbits nibbled on wild clover.

Lord, she prayed, *I never noticed before how wonderful it is. Do I feel this way because of Briton Farley? Suddenly all the obstacles between us no longer seem to matter. Was this Your plan, long before I asked You to change my life? I could be content here forever—if Brit loves me. Did he mean what he said that day in the street? Maybe he doesn't just want me to stay because the children need a teacher.*

She stared at the wild roses beside the road. All the costly bouquets she had received were no lovelier than the simple posies blooming where God had placed them.

The deepest peace she had ever known stole into her heart. If it were according to God's will, a rose would one day bloom on Briton Farley's ranch. A Meredith Rose.

A small hand tugged at her arm. "We're here, Teacher." Sammy grinned. "C'mon. I'm holler as a log, an' Ma brung fried chicken."

Meredith Rose didn't have the heart to correct his grammar. There would be time enough for that come September and the beginning of fall term.

Hungry people made a shambles of the carefully prepared picnic. Meredith Rose groaned. "I haven't eaten this much in years."

"You'll work it off," Brit promised. "It's almost time for games." He raised his voice. "If any of you want to see the mine, I'll take you now."

"We do." Marcus leaped to his feet and helped Alice Perry up. "Who else?"

"We're coming." Jovial Mr. Perry and his wife chorused.

"You all go ahead." Katie Reilly waved them off. "I'll pass. I've been in the mine." Several others murmured agreement, reducing the exploring party to less than a dozen. Ignatius Crane wore a long-suffering look but mumbled it was his duty to go. When they reached the mine shaft, Brit lighted a lantern and warned them to stay together; then he led the way inside.

To Meredith Rose's annoyance, Crane trod so closely behind her she thought he'd step on her boots. She determined to rid herself of the leech-like man, so she allowed the others to pass her and Sammy and round a bend. The light from Brit's lantern grew dimmer, casting feeble, flickering shadows on the craggy, timber-shored walls.

Anxious to rejoin the party, she turned to Ichabod–Ignatius and said in a tone so haughty both of her companions gaped, "Mr. Crane, if you don't stop following me, I am going to bring charges against you." What those charges were, she had no idea, but it sounded good. "You have pursued me from the moment we met. You will cease doing this immediately or take the consequences!"

Crane's mouth opened and closed like a fish out of water before he threatened, "I can make you sorry fer this. I'm a just man, but I've stood about as much from you as I'll take." He laid a clammy hand on her arm, and his eyes gleamed in the semidarkness. "You think you're gonna be our schoolmarm come September. Well, you ain't. Not when I tell the parents and board of directors how you've been breakin' the commandments God give us to live by."

Sammy snatched the man's hand off his teacher's arm

and blazed, "You're loco. Teacher made us learn the Ten Commandments, and she ain't never broke 'em."

Crane smirked. "The second commandment tells folks plain as day we ain't to make no graven images or likenesses of anything in heaven or earth or water under the earth." He cackled, then sanctimoniously folded his arms. "I peeked in the winder of the schoolhouse and seen her a-drawin' pitchers of what she said the disciples mighta looked like. We don't want no one corruptin' the minds of our younguns. O' course, if you were a mite friendlier, I wouldn't tattle on you."

Meredith Rose did the worst possible thing. She giggled. If only Miss Grenadier could know her former art instructor was being charged with corrupting the children of Last Chance. Her high spirits crashed at Crane's expression. Blind, unreasoning terror attacked. She grabbed Sammy's hand and fled in the direction the others had gone. They rounded the bend. Instead of welcome lantern-light, only a faint glow brightened the way. Fear lent wings to Meredith Rose's feet but the *thud-thud* of heavy boots warned they could never outrun their pursuer.

Sammy tugged her to a stop. "This way." He pulled her into a dark passageway at the left. "We can hide 'til he goes past."

Meredith Rose stumbled after him, hoping Crane hadn't heard them turn.

He evidently had, for he called, "Don't go in there. You'll get lost."

"Aw, he's just talking so's we'll stop," Sammy whispered. "C'mon, Teacher."

With a prayer that Sammy knew what he was doing, Meredith Rose followed. Nothing that lay ahead could be worse than having Ichabod–Ignatius touch her again.

Chapter 10

Sure-footed as a mountain goat, Sammy Reilly led Meredith Rose Macrae away from Ignatius Crane and into the silver mine. "Don't be scairt 'cause it's dark," he told her. "I'll take care o' you."

"I'm sure you will." She strained her ears. The sound of Crane's footsteps had ceased. Never had she heard such silence than what prevailed in this velvet-black place. "Uh, Sammy." She cleared her throat. "How will we get back?"

His skinny hand patted hers reassuringly. "Easy. Brit says al-wus remember the way out. We'll make two left turns and two right." He sounded so confident that some of Meredith Rose's rising fear dwindled.

"How will we know when Icha—Mr. Crane is gone?"

Sammy snorted. "Huh! You won't catch him in here. I bet he's already sneaked out so's folks won't know he scared us. It won't do any good. I'm gonna tell Brit." He paused. "I told you him 'n' me'd take care of you."

She wanted to hug him but refrained, sensing his young manliness might be offended. "I do appreciate it," she solemnly told him.

After what felt like a century but couldn't have been more than fifteen minutes, Sammy announced, "We c'n go now." He took her hand and confidently led her back the way they had come. Before they arrived at the main passage, the welcome sound of Brit and Marcus's voices calling their names reached them.

"We're here, Brit," Sammy shrilled, stepping into the open with his teacher.

The lantern in Brit's hand shook as he held it high. "Sammy Reilly, what in thunder possessed you to take Miss Merry off like this?"

All the small boy's bravado crumpled. "I–I. . ."

Meredith Rose knew men often yelled when worried, but Sammy's woebegone face roused her ire. "Briton Farley, you should be thanking Sammy, not bellowing at him!" She ignored a sob rising in her throat, marched over, planted herself in front of Brit, and glared into his face. "Ignatius Crane frightened me, and Sammy helped me get away." The last word came out as a squeak, for Brit put both arms around her and kissed her like she'd never been kissed before. Thoroughly. Tenderly. Reverently.

"It's the last time he or anyone else will frighten you if I have anything to say about it! Meredith Rose Macrae, I love you as I have never loved any other woman. Will you marry me?" Without waiting for an answer, he kissed her again.

She felt she had at last come home. A loud *haw-haw* from Marcus, and Sammy's ecstatic, "Oh, boy, wait'll I tell Ma!" brought her to her senses and out of Brit's arms.

"Hold it, Pard. She hasn't said yes yet," Brit reminded Sammy. "Women have been known to say no. Or even change their minds."

Sickening reality shattered Meredith Rose's bliss. She stepped back, knowing her face was whiter than falling snow. "Is that what happened with the woman I remind you of? The one who m—meant e—everything to you?" How maddening that her voice broke on the last words!

A poignant light gleamed in the amber eyes. "Merry, that woman was my mother. She died when I was just a few years old."

Silence fell over the group but not for long. Marcus, the irrepressible, drawled, "'Wal, I reckon that'll be aboot all,' as the cowboys say." He glanced down at Alice Perry, whose blue eyes looked enormous in the dim light. "At least for now." Even the dim light couldn't hide the pretty blush that rose from the collar of her hand-sewn dress.

Sammy anxiously reminded his teacher, "You ain't said yes."

"So I haven't." She smiled down at him, then looked straight into Brit's clear eyes. What she saw there more than repaid all the heartache she had experienced over the last long months. "Yes, Brit, I will marry you. On one condition."

He straightened as if burned with a branding iron. "Which is?"

With a flash of clarity, she knew Brit thought she'd ask him to leave the town he loved and had founded to take her back to Boston. Boston? Twenty-seven hundred miles and a lifetime away. Heedless of their audience, she placed her hands on his shoulders. "It's just that I'd like for the school bell to ring on our wedding day."

"Is that all? I thought—"

"I know." She stood on tiptoe and kissed him. "I'd also like a Christmas wedding."

Brit tilted his head to one side. A delighted smile appeared. "Sounds good to me. Fall roundup will be over, which means time for a honeymoon."

It was enough for Sammy. "Ya-hoo," he screeched, racing

out of the mine like a speeding bullet. The announcement of the brand-new engagement floated back. "Ma, ever'body, Brit 'n' Teacher's gettin' hitched come Christmas!"

Mischief shone in Brit's eyes and he glanced at Marcus. "Now all we have to do is run Ignatius Crane out of town and wait until December!"

"Amen to that!" Marcus heartily agreed, but they were deprived of the satisfaction of ridding the range of the unpleasant man. Ichabod–Ignatius, as Meredith Rose would always call him, had shaken the dust of Last Chance off his boots and departed for parts unknown long before the picnickers returned to town.

On Christmas Eve Day, sunlight burst through the December clouds and streamed through the windows of the living quarters behind the one-room schoolhouse in Last Chance. It rested on Meredith Rose Macrae in her simple white gown and veil.

The sound of those entering the classroom and taking their places for "Teacher and Brit's" wedding was music to the bride's ears. So was the joyous tolling of the school bell that summoned students to their studies and worshipers to church.

Marcus Macrae stood at the window, looking across the street to the close-to-completion home where he and his Alice would live after their wedding in the new year. A dedicated teacher and his family would occupy the schoolhouse quarters, and a church would be built in the spring. Marcus smiled. "Well, old dear," he said, "this is it."

Merry turned her radiant face to him. "If you had told me last March all this would happen, I wouldn't have believed it. I railed against God, Marcus, thinking He had ruined my life. All the time He knew where I—where we—belonged." She gave him a tender smile.

"I know, and I thank Him." A rush of love for his twin threatened to overwhelm Marcus. To cover the emotion-filled moment, he resorted to humor. "I could give you all kinds of brotherly advice," he began, "but I won't. Instead, I'll just say this. If you ever write the story of your life, you can call it *School Bells and Wedding Bells*. After all, you *are* a schoolhouse bride!"

The door flung open. Charley January, who would walk Merry down the aisle, and Sammy Reilly, Brit's best man, came in. "Time to get this shindig started," Charley gruffly said. He turned bright pink when Meredith Rose kissed his freshly shaven cheek. Sammy chortled, then went with Marcus to find Brit.

Meredith Rose picked up her bouquet of Christmas roses. Brit had smiled when she asked how he had managed to get them; then he quietly said, "I have ways."

She took Charley's arm and stepped into the schoolroom that held so many good memories. She stopped short. Fragrant cedar boughs tied with red ribbon framed every window. Fat white candles glowed with a lovely light—but it could not compare with the light in the eyes of the man who held her future in his strong but gentle hands. What cared she for satin gowns, priceless lilies, jewels, and fine houses? Her home would be a spacious log house that kept out the storms of life. She and Brit needed no "charm from the sky," to hallow that home. God had directed them to Last Chance to give them a new beginning.

And from his place at the front of the schoolroom, Brit waited for his bride. His heart swelled with love for the white-clad figure coming toward him. Surely no man had ever been more blessed. The God who had given His Son to the world had granted the desire of Briton Farley's heart by bestowing on him a "Merry" Christmas.

COLLEEN L. REECE

Colleen, born in a small, western Washington logging town, describes herself as "an ordinary person with an extraordinary God." As a child learning to read beneath the rays of a kerosene lamp, she dreamed of someday making a difference with her writing. Yet she never dreamed she would one day see 135 of her "Books You Can Trust" (motto) in print with more than three million copies sold.

Several of Colleen's earlier inspirational titles have been reissued in Large Print Library Editions. She is deeply grateful for the many new readers who will be exposed to the message of God's love woven into her stories. In addition to writing, Colleen teaches and encourages at conferences and through mentoring friendships. She loves to travel and is always on the lookout for fresh, new story settings, but she continues to live just a few hours' drive from her beloved hometown.

A Letter to Our Readers

Dear Readers:

In order that we might better contribute to your reading enjoyment, we would appreciate your taking a few minutes to respond to the following questions. When completed, please return to the following: Fiction Editor, Barbour Publishing, Inc., P.O. Box 719, Uhrichsville, OH 44683.

1. Did you enjoy reading *Schoolhouse Brides*?
   ❑ Very much—I would like to see more books like this.
   ❑ Moderately—I would have enjoyed it more if _____
   _____
   _____

2. What influenced your decision to purchase this book?
   (Check those that apply.)
   ❑ Cover   ❑ Back cover copy   ❑ Title   ❑ Price
   ❑ Friends   ❑ Publicity   ❑ Other

3. Which story was your favorite?
   ❑ *Dear Teacher*   ❑ *The Reluctant Schoolmarm*
   ❑ *Prairie Schoolmarm*   ❑ *School Bells and Wedding Bells*

4. Please check your age range:
   ❑ Under 18   ❑ 18–24   ❑ 25–34
   ❑ 35–45   ❑ 46–55   ❑ Over 55

5. How many hours per week do you read? _____

Name _____

Occupation _____

Address _____

City_____ State _____ Zip_____

E-mail_____

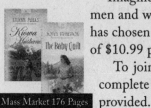